PRAISE FOR ROD DUNCAN

"It's all steampunk and circus wonder as we follow the adventures of Elizabeth Barnabas. The double crosses along the way keep the plot tight and fun, and the conclusion sets us up nicely for book two."
The Washington Post, Best New Science Fiction and Steampunk

"Steeped in illusion and grounded in an alternative history of the Luddite Rebellion, Duncan's strong supernatural mystery serves ably as both a standalone adventure and the start to a series… Strategically placed steampunk tropes inform but do not overwhelm Elizabeth's headlong quest to find a missing aristocrat sought by the Patent Office, which is fixated on both achieving perfection and eliminating 'unseemly science'."
Publishers Weekly

"If I had a bowler hat, I'd take it off to the author of this beautifully crafted steampunk novel."
Chris D'Lacey, author of The Last Dragon Chronicles

"Duncan is an accomplished crime writer, and this detective story with fantastical elements shows his chops to great effect, and the steampunk elements don't overtake the story; instead, they add just enough to make it more interesting."
My Bookish Ways

"A magic box pulsating with energy. Compulsive reading from the get-go, the blend of steampunk alternate history wrapped in the enigma of a chase makes for first-rate entertainment in this finely crafted novel."
*Graham Joyce, author of Y*ear of the Ladybird

The Bullet-Catcher's Daughter

ROD DUNCAN

Unseemly Science

BEING VOLUME TWO OF
THE FALL OF THE GAS-LIT EMPIRE

ANGRY
ROBOT

ANGRY ROBOT
An imprint of Watkins Media ltd

Lace Market House,
54-56 High Pavement,
Nottingham
NG1 1HW
UK

angryrobotbooks.com
twitter.com/angryrobotbooks.com
It's all research, my dear

An Angry Robot paperback original 2015

Cover by Will Staehle
Set in Meridien by Epub Services

Distributed in the United States by Random House, Inc., New York.

ISBN 978 0 85766 427 3
Ebook ISBN 978 0 85766 428 0

Printed in the United States of America

9 8 7 6 5 4 3 2 1

CHAPTER 1

Revolution was never sparked by political philosophy. It has ever been the price of bread that shakes the pillars of the world. Yet they lock up thinkers and leave the bakers free.

FROM REVOLUTION

There was never a public hanging without a mob. And of those concerned citizens who crushed together at the foot of the gallows, no less than half belonged to the gentle sex. Lewd heckles were as likely to be called out in women's voices as in men's, and a sea of hat feathers quivered above the heads of every such expectant crowd. Thus, it was not to hide my sex that I stepped out that day disguised as a man. Rather it was to hide my identity.

But disguise is merely an outer layer. There was something in the bewhiskered face staring back at me from the hand glass that always triggered a deeper transformation. By the time I crept from the houseboat and closed the hatch behind me, my movements had changed to that of a man. Striding off along the canal, I found myself planting my heels rather than my toes and letting my shoulders roll as I walked. It was a gait that might seem unnatural. But from years of practice it was my second nature.

Had anyone been awake and watching, they would have assumed they saw my brother, the private intelligence gatherer, off on another of his nocturnal adventures. Thus I climbed the embankment without fear of discovery and set off along the track towards the road.

There is a time between the revelries of night and the necessity of morning when the comfortable classes do not venture from the warmth of their beds. This was such a time. No lights shone in the scatter of houses between the canal and the road. The smell of dew hung in the air and the crackle of gravel under my boots seemed loud. I turned but saw no one following, though for a moment I had felt a tingle on the back of my neck.

Having waited on the roadside only a few minutes, I heard iron-shod hooves of the five o'clock omnibus approaching, then saw its lamps shining through the thin mist.

Everyone stared as I climbed aboard. The driver and conductor were uniformed in company blue. Everyone else wore the clothes of the working masses – coarsely woven wool in drab greys and washed out browns, flat caps and simple bonnets. My top hat and taupe jacket did not blend in.

I edged along the aisle towards the back with every face turning to track my progress. All the benches were taken. But as I reached up to grip the leather strap, a weather beaten woman struggled to her feet.

She must have been twenty years my senior.

"Here you go, sir," she said.

I hesitated. But to refuse would have been to attract yet further attention. Swallowing a pang of guilt, I nodded my appreciation and sat. The driver called, "Walk on." He flicked his whip and the horses set us rattling along the road.

With a waft of body odour and tobacco smoke, the man next to me leaned closer. "You'll be going to the hanging then," he said.

"Not at all."

"It's alright. There's most on this bus would go if they'd money for the crossing. The works foreman's going. Taking the wife and kids. Better than a holiday, he says. And cheaper."

Those close enough to be listening nodded sagely. That turned out to be most of the omnibus. I stared directly ahead, trying not to meet anyone else's gaze.

If all the passengers would have liked to attend, I wondered how many there would be in the crowd at the hanging. The newspapers had been following the story for many months. The public's hunger for salacious detail had been fed with a mixture of fact, speculation and bizarre statements from unnamed sources. Even respectable titles had joined the discussion.

I alighted at St Margaret's coach station, grateful to put the stuffy confinement of the carriage behind me. The gas lights had been extinguished already, so I had to pick my way over the uneven cobbles with care. The sky was showing the first grey of dawn but that only seemed to deepen the shadows.

I was not the only one making my way up Churchgate

in the direction of the border. Two gentlemen and a lady walked on ahead of me and I spotted another man behind. By the time I reached the clock tower, that thin scatter had turned into a trickle. The official border crossing was naturally closed. Not that anyone would have thought of using it. Two Republic guards in blue uniforms sat slouched in the kiosk nearest me, perfectly mirroring two Kingdom guards in red uniforms in the kiosk on the other side. It was the eternal symmetry of the divided city.

Approaching Cheapside, the trickle had grown to a stream so that by the time I reached the Odeon Crossing I had to queue, taking my turn to pass payment to the owner. Then I was feeling my way through a dank passageway below overhanging eaves, emerging a few moments later on a street the far side of the border.

In the Kingdom I was wanted by the law. Even in disguise, I would not normally have risked the crossing. But today the crowd would protect me. I would be one face among thousands. Tens of thousands if that many could fit around the gallows.

The Eastern sky had turned from grey to red. Streams of people threaded between empty market stalls, converging as they progressed. Tens became hundreds. I found myself jostled as we funnelled into the narrow confines of Angel Gateway.

Though I could see no individual who was talking, a low shuffling hum issued from the crowd. The sound put my skin on edge. There was a grim energy to it. Like a swarm of insects, stirred up and ready for some terrible event.

Then, suddenly, we were through the passageway and stepping out onto the wide plaza of Gallowtree Gate, already crowded. And there I saw it – a sturdy platform of squared-off timbers standing clear of the heads of the crowd. Above it ran the single beam from which dangled three short chains, each ending in a hook. A casket and a barrel rested on the right hand side.

The pressure of new arrivals was pushing the crowd forwards. We were being crushed together – children and the old, highborn and commoners.

I had never been to an execution before, though I had read reports. They spoke of a party atmosphere, of jeering and gossip and the throwing of rotten fruit. But this crowd whispered. This crowd seemed more like an army on the dawn of battle.

Raising myself onto my toes I could just see a line of red uniforms – men at arms standing in front of the gallows platform. Their shouldered muskets looked like a thin stockade. Too flimsy, I thought.

I felt the approach of the condemned woman before I heard the cart. A shiver of tension passed through the crowd. The low drone dropped away to almost nothing. And then she was there – a slight figure in the distance, just visible above a sea of heads, as if she was wading. And like a sea, the crowd surged. Bodies pressed and I found myself shuffling forwards. How they made room for the cart, I do not know. Yet soon she was behind the scaffold.

First to climb the wooden stairs was the rotund figure of the executioner, Clarence Hobb, masked yet a celebrity known to all. Over his shoulder rested a length of rope, one end tied in a noose. Next up was a red coated marshal carrying a roll of parchment. Then the condemned woman began to climb. A sound like a breeze moving through dry grass whispered around me as all drew in breath.

When I first met her she had been wearing fine clothes. Now they had dressed her in a coarse shift, bone-white and shapeless. Her blonde hair had been tied back in a tight ponytail. Her arms were held awkwardly behind her. I could not see her feet but somehow knew they would have taken her shoes.

She did it for love, the newspapers had proclaimed. All she had wanted was reunion. But she had fallen hopelessly, madly in love with a man separated by a gulf of class that could never be crossed. The aristocrats tutted their disapproval. And now they would have their revenge.

But I had seen the story first hand. If there had been a crime, then I was its chief victim. She had promised me much and I believed her good for it, fooled by a sateen blouse.

Draped in calico, she stood before the huge expanse of the crowd. If any had come to see some noble moment, a gesture of defiance against the aristocrats, they would be disappointed. She was a girl, scared and alone. There would be no final speech.

Clarence Hobb had been testing the middle of the three chains, gripping the hook and lifting his feet so that his considerable weight hung from the beam. Now he made fast the rope. I watched as he placed a sack over her head and pulled a drawstring to gather in the hem of the shift around her ankles.

The last men to climb onto the platform were two red-coated guards, muskets shouldered. They positioned themselves on either side of the executioner and stood to attention.

I would have given anything to be somewhere else. But I could not leave. Though she had done me a terrible wrong, the woman on the scaffold felt like a sister to me. Both of us had been raised in the world of the travelling show. Both had suffered at the hands of the aristocrats. It was merely chance that she now stood with Clarence Hobb arranging the noose around her neck whilst I watched, hidden in the crowd.

She had sent me a gift as she awaited trial – an old copy of the *Bullet-Catcher's Handbook*. She had hinted at a mystery within its pages. But if it held anything of value, I had not found it. I resolved to burn the book when I returned home and forget that any of this had happened.

The marshal unrolled his parchment and began to speak. "Through the power invested in me by his Majesty the King, I hereby announce and proclaim before you all standing witness that Florence May has been convicted of the following crimes: the theft of seventy-five golden guineas from an aristocrat of the Kingdom, the theft of clothing and writing paper from the same household, interception of the avian post, fraud by false signature and…" Here he paused to survey the faces of the crowd, as if to make sure all were listening. "…impersonating one beyond her station."

The marshal waited for a moment as if expecting cries or jeers. There were none.

"The aforementioned Florence May, having been found guilty of these crimes, has been sentenced to be hanged by the neck until dead on this day, 4th March 2009."

He re-rolled the parchment and nodded to the executioner. For a moment everything was still and symmetrical. She seemed very small between the men at arms. I thought I saw her body shiver. Then Clarence Hobb pulled the lever. The trap opened with the sound of a slamming door. She dropped. I heard the rope twang as it went tight.

Her body jerked. Her legs and shoulders twitched. One second, two seconds, three seconds. Then the spasms were over. Her body dangled, swaying slightly. A man standing next to me looked away but I could not.

The men at arms and Clarence Hobb hauled her back up onto the platform and laid her in the casket. She seemed of little weight in death. I watched as Hobb began covering her with broken ice from the barrel. Each shovel-full shone for a moment, brilliant white in the morning sun.

The hum of the crowd had grown louder. Its pitch was higher. Somehow unwholesome. The King's marshal seemed unsure of himself.

"You can all go home now," he announced.

But nobody did.

It was dusk by the time I returned to my houseboat. I stripped off the disguise and scrubbed away the makeup until my face felt raw. Then, kneeling before the stove in only my chemise, I kindled a fire of sticks and placed the *Bullet-Catcher's Handbook* in the middle of the flames. I watched as the wrinkled leather binding darkened. The corner smoked then caught. In a few moments my last connection to Florence May would be gone and I would be able to forget.

I burned my hand taking it out again.

CHAPTER 2

Dress your barker in the finest clothes. For to sell an illusion your audience has not yet seen is the greatest trick of all.

THE BULLET-CATCHER'S HANDBOOK

Sunday morning by the canal, one mile north of the city – there was no better place to watch the middle classes at rest. They strolled, taking the air, pushing perambulators and gawping into the boats. For the small community moored on the North Leicester Wharf, and after five years I counted myself as one of them, it was a time to pull curtains across portholes and endure.

My own craft, *Bessie*, attracted more attention than most. Among the working boats it was a rarity to see one kitted out solely as a home. Her side-paddles, though rusted into immobility, presented an elegant aspect.

It had been almost two weeks since the hanging. My hand had mostly healed and I had started sleeping again. Pushing open a canal-side porthole, I breathed the fresh air, as if trying to inhale the countryside

14

itself. Morning sunshine had already lifted the scent of spring flowers and the day promised warm. I smoothed my skirt under me and sat, watching a watery reflection dancing on the ceiling.

I had been sitting that way for some time, when I was jarred from my thoughts by a loud chatter of voices on the towpath and a tilting of my boat. I sighed. They would blush at the thought of stepping onto a neighbour's lawn without permission but as a boat dweller, I had placed myself beyond the restriction of social norms.

"One hand on the steering thing, Maria. Just so! And one on the roof." It was a man's voice, young and enthusiastic. "Now hold still. I'm going to remove the lens cap. One flintlock. Two flintlock. Three flintlock. And you can breathe."

I felt the urge to confront him. How satisfying it would be to embarrass the man into getting off the boat. Nothing mortifies a good Republican more than embarrassment. But a gorilla in the zoo asking visitors to move along would have had more chance of success.

"Your turn now, mother. Stand just where Maria did. I'll change the plate."

I shouldn't even have been listening. It was a beautiful day. Two ducks were swimming past under the porthole. But all my senses were focussed on the intruders.

"I'm going to remove the lens cap. Stop smiling now. Perfect. One flintlock. Two flintlock..."

A pause followed. The boat shifted again. Then the young man was speaking, his voice higher in pitch: "Perhaps you didn't realise, but I was making a photograph. You've quite ruined the plate."

Hearing the sounds of a tussle, I sat straighter.

"Let me through!" It was the voice of my student, Julia Swain.

"You should really take more care," said the man. "You only had to wait a second more."

I sprang across to let her in. There was a flurry of navy skirts and ivory trim as she flounced down the steps into the galley. I caught a glimpse of "mother" on the deck, rigid with agitation, fanning herself at speed, as if social awkwardness is a thing that might be wafted away. Then I had the hatch closed.

"Julia, I do believe you've ruined the gentleman's photograph."

I found myself smiling for the first time in days.

At eighteen, she was only two years my junior. But our different lives and roles made it seem more.

"How do you manage?" Julia exclaimed. "They're so rude!" Her cheeks were flushed. She pulled off a straw hat, letting her blonde hair fall.

"If life were easy, we'd never grow beyond childhood," I said.

She gave me a look. "Are you such a saint, Elizabeth?"

"You know I'm not."

"Then please fetch a pistol and shoot that horrible man! Flintlock indeed!"

"There's scope for us all between saint and murderer," I said, easing the hat from her hands before she worked its rim to shreds. "Sit. Watch the ducks. I'll make a pot of tea."

She did not sit, but paced up the narrow galley and

down again. Out of the corner of my eye, I watched as she picked up a saucer and ran her thumbnail over a chip in the rim. She could sniff out flawed logic faster than anyone I knew, but didn't always realise the transparency of her emotions.

Using a cloth to protect my hand, I lifted the kettle from the stove. Steam rose from the pot as I poured.

"How's your mother today?" I asked.

Julia's expression hovered between surprise and annoyance. "Did she tell you?"

"She never tells me anything. But you're wound tight as a spring. That usually means you've been... discussing something."

I occupied myself with setting out the tea things on the small table. Julia dropped herself onto the bench. "Why is mother so difficult? She knows I want to read the law. I've been sure of it ever since our trip to London."

"She loves you. That's all. No parent wants to see a child leave. The Kingdom may be close, but from here it's a world away."

"If she's set on keeping me, why introduce so many eligible men?"

"But if you go to university..."

"I will go!"

"When – if. Either way they'll miss you."

"And married? How often do they think my husband would let me return?"

It was not the first time we had navigated this topic. But the intensity of Julia's feelings seemed to be increasing. That couldn't make for harmony in the Swain household.

"What of your father?" I asked.

"He scurries away to his workshop whenever I raise the subject. As if engines and gears were more important than my future."

And what of myself, I thought. What would I do if Julia left for a university in the Kingdom? She was the only one who knew that I earned my living gathering intelligence for private clients. All my other neighbours had swallowed the illusion and believed I was kept by a brother. But to carry a great secret is to be alone. And if Julia were to cross the border, that is exactly what I would be.

"If your mother won't relent, she won't relent," I said, trying to move the conversation on. But then I saw Julia glance furtively over her teacup and knew there was more to come.

"Elizabeth, have you heard of Mrs Raike's girls?" she asked.

"Should I have?"

"If you read the newspapers you would. Mrs Raike is the subject of much discussion. She marshals young women from good families in and around Derby. They do charitable works – educate the children of miners, ironworkers and the like. They bring learning into prisons."

I frowned, unable to imagine Mrs Swain allowing her daughter to enter a prison. Even a Republican one.

"They also bring advice to those in need," she continued. "Among which is advice on the law. There is a case they're working on presently – on behalf of the beleaguered ice farmers of Derbyshire. And *that* is what I'll be helping with."

"Will be? Surely your mother won't agree?"

Julia blushed. "I told her that working with Mrs Raike, I would have need to associate with the lawyers who make themselves available *pro bono publico*. And from among them it might be that I could find myself..." She tailed off.

"A husband?"

"It was the only thing I could think of."

I put my knuckle to my mouth and bit, trying not to let my laughter burst.

"It's not funny!"

"What about your lawyer friend in London?" I asked, unable to suppress a giggle. "Have you been entirely frank with your mother?"

"I'll be true to my word," Julia said. "If I find a Republican lawyer to be his equal, I'll make myself available."

"*Pro bono publico*?" I asked.

I was about to point out that since her view of the lawyer in London with whom she exchanged letters was so high, it seemed improbable that she'd find his match anywhere in the Gas-Lit Empire, let alone in Derby. But as I opened my mouth to speak, the boat tilted once more. We both looked towards the aft hatch. Feet scuffed on the deck.

"They're so rude!" said Julia.

"Normal rules don't apply when you live on a boat," I said. "Socially, I'm beyond the pale."

"You're surely not!"

"Well, let's put it this way – such proposals as I've received haven't been for marriage."

I was enjoying Julia's scandalised expression when

the scuffing feet moved closer and whoever it was that stood outside rapped briskly on the roof.

Readying myself to discharge a volley of hard words, I opened the hatch. But the sight of a pair of pointed shoes and moss-green corduroy trousers made me close my mouth. A burgundy and purple paisley waistcoat covered the man's round stomach. On either side of his round face, a thin moustache had been waxed to upward curving points. Removing his hat, he bowed.

"Am I addressing the lady of the house... or boat?"

"What do you want?"

He made to climb down into the galley, but I stood my ground and he came to a halt on the second step.

"I have business to discuss," he said. "An offer. Not to be missed."

"What is it you're selling? Window glass? Linen? Insurance?"

"I would never discuss your business in the open. But yes, insurance of a kind. You are Elizabeth Barnabus?"

His clothing, unmistakably Royalist, had raised my curiosity and kept me from slamming the hatch. But it was hearing him speak my name that caused me to step aside. He clambered down into the galley – much to Julia's alarm.

"Ladies. Thank you." Holding his hat over his belly he stepped past us and surveyed the interior. "Very nice. Very... unorthodox. But then, I know you were a member of a travelling show before you fled to the Republic. Driven by a family debt, I understand. A life of indentured servitude awaiting – should you place a foot back in the Kingdom."

"You have me at a disadvantage," I said.

"I have indeed. That is my skill. My profession. And if you will permit, it is your evil-wishers that I would disadvantage." Dipping his fingers into a waistcoat pocket, he flourished a visiting card, which I accepted. His fingernails were shiny, as if varnished.

I read aloud: "Yan Romero. Solicitor. Making the Law your servant."

Thick card and gold lettering gave the impression of substance, as did the Chelsea address, though it could have been the address of a brick privy for all I knew.

"Mr Romero," I said. "I don't need a solicitor."

"When you think you don't need one – that's precisely when you're in danger."

"I really don't."

"There you go!" He brushed his hands against each other as if the point were proven.

"You expect me to guess the danger? Is that it? Has someone dropped a grand piano from an airship overhead? Pay up and you'll tell me which way to jump?"

"A grand piano," he said. "Very good. Yes. Even now it hurtles towards you. But I am here in the nick of time, so to speak. Retain my services and I will take your hand and lead you safe."

"Your price?"

"Five guineas a month. Plus expenses. Two months payable in advance. And court costs should it come to that. A snip. A pinch of snuff. And in return – your life."

"Ten guineas!" Julia spluttered.

"You've travelled a long way to go home empty-handed," I said.

"Then perhaps you would be so kind as to pour me a cup of tea?"

I folded my arms. "Or perhaps not."

"How long has it been?" he asked. "You fled the Kingdom five years ago. Or is it six? The records are vague as to the date of your crossing the border. Strange that none of that famous Republican servility has rubbed off on you."

I should have liked him to scowl or swear. Instead a slow smile formed on his face. He bowed with no detectable sincerity, swivelled and climbed back out to the deck. Julia made to slam the hatch closed. But I put out a hand to stop her.

"The man's a charlatan!" she cried, loud enough for Romero to hear.

He stepped off the boat forcefully leaving it swaying under our feet. I poked my head above the deck and watched him mincing away. Nothing of his visit made sense. A man of expensive tastes does not cross the border merely to offer legal advice to a poor exile living in a houseboat. Ten guineas might be a small fortune to me, but I doubted it would purchase many pairs of those shoes. Italian leather they'd seemed.

Julia must have caught my frown. "Please don't say you're taking him seriously."

"Watch him," I said. Then I ran back to my cabin, scooped my hair under a straw sun hat and was back at the hatch before Romero was out of sight.

"You can't mean to follow?"

"Better that than pay ten guineas." I snatched my

purse and a cornflower shawl and was on the deck before Julia could object further.

Instead of climbing the bank and heading off towards the road, Yan Romero had set out along the towpath. He was one hundred yards ahead of me – a good distance from which to follow. For once I found myself glad of the Sunday tourists. With my hat brim angled down and the shawl over my shoulders, I felt secure. Dressed in muted shades, all Republicans would look alike to him. And after five years, I had learned to blend in.

He did not strike me as a man who would choose to take the air as recreation. Nor was he poor enough to need to walk. I glanced at the surface of the path. This could not have been the way he came. I would have seen the mud on those ridiculously pointed and polished shoes.

With these thoughts tumbling, my concentration must have slipped. Too late, I saw that Romero had stopped. A pair of ladies had stopped also and the three were standing in conversation. I slowed as much as I could without drawing attention to myself.

Only sixty yards separated us now. One of the ladies was pointing across the canal. The lawyer nodded. It should not have taken him so long to get directions, if that was what he was doing. In my mind I shouted at him to finish. But the ladies seemed to be asking him about his waistcoat – attention he was sure to enjoy.

Forty yards.

I could hear the voice of one of the ladies now: "… don't know where one might find such fabric. Not in the Republic. Unless one were to source it from a factory. Do you think?"

"But I can't imagine our factories would produce it," said the other. "Unless for export."

Twenty yards.

My foot caught a piece of gravel and sent it skittering into the water. Romero looked in my direction. Tilting my head forward to drop my hat brim further, I quickened my step. One of the ladies stepped aside to make room.

"Good day," said the lawyer, as I passed.

I made no answer.

Romero's voice was behind me now. "Republican manners confuse me," he said.

The ladies giggled. "Without a chaperone she couldn't speak to a strange man."

"You think me strange? Now I'm offended."

More giggles. Then they were beyond my hearing.

If they had been directing him, he would soon set out to cross the canal, for that was where the lady was pointing.

I did not risk a backward glance until I was climbing the brick steps of the bridge. By then he was well behind, seeming in no hurry. I crossed the water and headed up the road into the small town of Syston. If he intended some other destination, I had lost him already.

It being Sunday, the streets were quiet. Finding a small park next to the road I sat myself on a bench in the sunshine. My thinking was this: a man of expensive tastes does not cross the border for the possibility of a single client. And if Romero had found some danger threatening several people, I did not see why we should all pay for the same information.

There was a deal to be done if I could locate another of his targets.

So I waited.

The shadows of the trees shifted across the road. A man on a penny-farthing lifted his homburg to me as he rattled past. I could hear children playing in the distance. But of Yan Romero there was no sign.

At last I got up and started to make my way back towards the canal. For every tingle of risk-taking excitement, there is a corresponding weight of despondency that follows when nothing has come of the adventure. I wondered whether Julia would still be on my boat. I expected that I would find her gone and the key hidden under the pot of geraniums on the roof.

I was trudging back along the lane between hawthorn and crab apple and had just passed the final cottage, when a man coughed behind me.

"Excuse me," he said. "We passed earlier on the canal path."

All the excitement that had left me, now rushed back. No need to turn, for I recognised Yan Romero's London accent.

"Excuse me?" he said again.

But I was hurrying away, back across the bridge, gripping and lifting my skirts to run, not caring that I was being stared at. For the first time in two weeks the darkness had been washed from my mind. The lawyer could only have come from one place to emerge behind me. He had been visiting the last cottage in Syston.

CHAPTER 3

Legal jurisdictions are like sturdy beams. It is the joints between them that are weak. In such places all manner of dirt will gather.

From Revolution

It was late afternoon when I returned. I lifted the geraniums on *Bessie*'s roof and found the key. The tourists were long gone, but as I unlocked the hatch, I thought I heard someone move behind me. Glancing back I found the towpath empty. The experience unsettled me.

A note in Julia's hand lay on the galley table. A page torn from her copybook, I thought.

I shut up the stove. I hope this is right. Next time, I want to go too. I worry. You know I do.

The words made her sound like her mother – an observation that dampened my mood. I did not like to think of what she would become if forced into a life of middle class domesticity. All that uncompromising drive would surely turn to bitterness.

Though I had not previously allowed Julia to accompany me in my work, little risk seemed to be posed by this investigation. I resolved to take her with me when I returned to Syston to seek out Yan Romero's other client.

But the following day, being Monday, Julia was obliged to help the maid with the laundry. A fire had to be built, the copper heated and linen pounded in the tub. Her parents had instituted this new regime in order, Julia believed, that she might be put off from any idea of making her own way in the world. And whilst she did not like it, she seemed to take perverse satisfaction in banking her sufferings as tokens of resolve.

I had seen the blisters on her hands. "From the mangle," she had said, a glint of triumph in her eyes.

On Tuesday morning, I wiped condensation from the porthole glass and looked out on a world heavy with dew. Having selected an indigo shawl to drape over my shoulders, I locked up the boat and joined Julia on the towpath. Then together we set out towards Syston.

"Thank you, thank you, thank you," she said.

Yan Romero had emerged from the last house on the lane. It was the kind of cottage a farm labourer might occupy. A strange destination for an expensive lawyer. A strange destination for an intelligence gatherer, come to that. But if something was threatening my life, as he had suggested, this was my chance to find out more.

I glanced at Julia, walking beside me. "Can you stop doing that," I said.

"Stop what?"

"Bouncing."

"I'm not!"

"You surely are! You're on your toes with every step. You're supposed to make my visit seem more respectable not less so."

"Our visit," she corrected.

"You must keep quiet and let me talk. Even if you think I'm doing it wrong."

"I promise. But this is so exciting. You're taking me on an investigation!"

"Then repay me by not saying it out loud."

Whereas Sunday had been bustling with tourists, Tuesday's only sounds were the slow chug of cargo boats, the lapping of wash on the canal bank and the call of birds from bushes and alder trees.

I had not been idle since Sunday. No one around the wharf had been able to tell me who lived in the cottage. But the boy who worked for the dairy had seen a man there and taken payment for a delivery of cheese. "Smooth hands," the boy had reported. "And clean nails." All said as though these were signs of some terrible wrongdoing.

We had reached the bridge over the canal and I slowed to let Julia go first. But instead she folded her arms and looked at me.

"What's wrong?" she asked. Then, when I made no immediate answer, she added: "You've been frowning all the way."

"Oh," I said. "I'm sorry."

"What's your worry?"

"A gap," I said. "That's all. A gap that needs filling."

She would have asked more but I started climbing

the brick steps and, there being no room for the two of us to walk abreast, she could do nothing but follow. Once we were across and heading down the lane, the sight of the cottage distracted her.

"You're bouncing again," I said.

From a distance it seemed a pleasant enough building, though its roof sagged in the middle. But the closer we came, the more obvious its decrepitude. A few green daffodil stems poked through the weeds of the front garden. Paint was peeling from the frames of two deep-set windows. One pane of glass had been replaced by a board.

I knocked on the door then stood back, glancing up to the chimney. There was no fire inside, but I could smell smoke. Burning paper, I thought. We waited in silence. I knocked again. Then, hearing no movement, I picked my way around the side of the house.

A clothes line had been strung between two trees at the back. A bed sheet hung limp in the still air. I stopped and stared, feeling my pulse accelerate. The linen was not white, but pale yellow.

"What is it?" whispered Julia, close behind me.

I put my finger to my lips and she fell silent.

A heap of ash smoked among the weeds of what should have been a garden. The embers were still glowing. I glanced at the cottage. The back door was open, though it was too dark to see inside. The papers around the edge of the fire hadn't burned completely. I stepped closer, angling my head to read the charred corner of a document. In a fine copperplate hand it listed goods – sacks of coffee and nutmeg, their weight, number and grade.

Lifting my skirts an inch, I poked at the paper with the toe of my boot, trying to turn it. It crumbled. I began searching for other readable fragments, but Julia tugged urgently at the puffed sleeve of my blouse. My eyes snapped up to the doorway where a man stood watching us.

"It's dangerous," I said, blurting the first words that came to my tongue. "The fire I mean. You shouldn't leave it unattended."

He stepped out from the shadow of the doorway, gripping an iron poker, giving the impression of one who had used such an implement before. And not just for stoking.

"What are you doing?" he demanded.

Julia took half a step back.

"I came to see you," I said.

He was dressed to fit the cottage – a poor man's jacket, patched at the elbow, slate grey trousers thinning to thread at the knee. He edged around the fire. I followed his glance down to the papers I'd been trying to read.

"Come inside," he said.

My eyes flicked to the poker and then to the narrow doorway. "Please," I said with all the politeness I could muster. "After you."

I judged him to be in his forties. He had to duck under the door lintel as he led us into what seemed to be part living room part kitchen. It was colder inside the house than out. Damper too. I could feel the floorboards bowing under my weight.

"Sit," he said, indicating a three-legged stool and an

armchair with horsehair poking through cracks.

We both remained standing.

"Suit yourselves."

"You haven't learned to blend in," I said.

"Who are you?"

"It's the rudeness," I said. "How long is it since you left the Kingdom?"

The belligerence written on his face turned to surprise and then to uncertainty. He paced to the window and looked out as if checking the lane, though I could see he was just buying time to think. I braced myself. If he lunged towards us I could grab the stool and fling it at him.

"I'm from the Kingdom too," I said. "I've been here five years."

"How did you know?" he asked, still looking out of the small window. "Was it really my manner?"

"Not just that," I said. "Yellow sheets as well. No Republican would use them."

He swore under his breath but his shoulders had dropped. The fight had gone out of him. He stepped wearily to the fireplace and propped the poker in the hearth. When he turned to look at us, I noticed the shadows under his eyes. I wasn't the only one who had difficulty sleeping.

"They're French," he said. "The sheets, I mean. Should've dumped them before I crossed."

"I don't understand," said Julia.

"Here, it's white sheets for the living and black for the dead. But in the Kingdom…"

He dropped himself into the chair. "It's like sleeping in sunshine. Didn't want to let them go."

"I would have found you anyway," I said. "I followed the lawyer. He led me here."

"Do you want money too?"

"I want information."

"You're not on an errand from the bailiff?"

"Women here don't do such work," I said.

It seemed we had both fled the Kingdom to get away from debts. But where I had run from the threat of indentured servitude, I guessed he had run with the funds of a failing business. Or, more likely, the savings of gullible investors. I wondered what kind of man would choose to live in poverty to hide a hoard of gold.

"Did you pay the lawyer?" I asked. "Ten guineas for two months of his precious time?"

"I beat him down to five," he said, his eyes narrowing. "You want to know what he told me? It'll cost you."

Royalists do not blush when they display their avarice. But even hearing it made Julia put a hand in front of her mouth. I did a quick calculation. I could afford to go halves on five guineas. But if I let him beat me once, I had a feeling he would try again and again. Exile had left him little power, but he'd cling to it all the more for that.

"I don't pay for information," I said, holding his gaze, waiting for him to blink. When he did, I added: "If you tell me what you know, I'll consider it a kindness. And naturally, when I find out more, I'll tell you in return."

He stared into space for a moment, running the tip of his tongue over his lip. Then he nodded. "There's to be a treaty. That's what Romero told me. Or, there might be a treaty. It's not set in stone. But if it happens, it'll not be safe for the likes of me and you. That's what he said. Unless we pay him to help us. But he would say that, wouldn't he?"

"What kind of treaty?"

He gave me a look. "An extradition treaty, stupid. When it's signed, they'll get us all. Drag us home in chains."

CHAPTER 4

No action shall be aimless. Each gesture and movement must have its motive. And each motive must be hidden.
THE BULLET-CATCHER'S HANDBOOK

The first I saw of the rally was an airship descending at a steep angle behind the trees of Abbey Park. Landing would not usually have been allowed within the city, even though the weather was calm. But since the event was expected to gather an audience from far afield, bringing prestige to North Leicester, certain bylaws had been suspended.

"Slow down," I said to Julia, who was edging ahead once more.

"We don't want to be at the back," she said.

"Someone must be."

My mood had been troubled since Syston, my outlook more cynical than usual. I did admire Julia's ideals, but had less faith in this particular enthusiasm. Having borrowed a pile of old newspapers from Mrs Simmonds, the wharf keeper's wife, I had spent the last evening reading reports of Mrs Raike. She organised soup kitchens, Sunday schools and other works of benefit to the poor and needy. Her volunteers cared for piteous creatures living in the gutters of the city, men and women so deranged they could not dress themselves, let alone find work. I could not fault her virtue in anything I read. Yet I found myself suspicious of the publicity. Did goodness need to be spelled out in newsprint?

I threw in an extra step and drew level. "It's too hot to be hurrying so."

"You don't understand how lucky we are," she said. "Mrs Raike rarely speaks in public these days."

"I'd been hoping to spend the holiday in comfort."

There was no point in arguing. Perhaps it was a cultural thing. In the Kingdom, people boasted of wealth rather than good deeds. And since women were permitted to run businesses and attend universities, they had less need to pour their energies into voluntary works.

We hurried through the ironwork gates and into the park, joining a stream of others, mostly women. Charcoal grey and ivory appeared to be the colours of those enthused by volunteering. My burgundy twill seemed extravagant by comparison. To judge by the size and crispness of the hats on display, the city's milliners had been working overtime.

The thrumming of an engine and propeller overhead grew suddenly loud and a shadow passed over us. I looked up and saw another small airship, its carriage just clearing the top of a pine tree. We hurried around the curve of the path to see it descend into a wide grassy space next to four craft that had already been tethered.

The bandstand lay ahead – an elevated platform with a pointed roof in the Chinese style. Blue and white bunting had been strung between its pillars. Hundreds of people mingled on the grass. Julia took my hand and led me through until we were standing at the very front. I could hear the chink of glassware over the murmur of voices. Standing on tiptoe, I caught sight of trestle tables laid with white cloths and jugs of lemonade.

The crowd was growing by the minute and as it did, I found myself pressed up closer to those around me. I tried to relax my shoulders. My heart had begun to beat faster. I took a deep breath and let it out slowly, trying to identify the source of my sudden tension.

Then a thrill of excitement shifted through the crowd. A tall woman standing next to me whispered: "She's here!"

The murmur of conversations dropped to nothing. I could hear carriage wheels approaching. Then the Mayor of North Leicester was climbing onto the bandstand from steps at the back, his chain of office catching the afternoon sunshine. Two young women climbed up after him, dressed identically with pale green sashes slung from shoulder to hip. And finally Mrs Raike herself.

Wearing a black straw hat, black jacket and black skirt, she had outdone even the most austere of her congregation. A black veil covered half her face. The only colour in the outfit was a pale green ribbon pinned to her lapel. She had been wearing the same outfit, so far as I could tell, in every newspaper illustration.

The Lord Mayor had started addressing the crowd already, though I doubted many were listening. He was saying something about the people who had helped to bring the event about and how it would enhance the city's already shining reputation. But my gaze, like those around me, was on the woman we had come to see and her two sash-wearing attendants, arranged centre stage in symmetrical formation. It was with some relief that I heard the mayor say: "Without further ado..." Then he was stepping back to a smattering of applause.

"Ladies and gentlemen," Mrs Raike began, in a voice surprisingly loud, "I am deeply moved that so many of the fine people of North Leicester have gathered here on this festival day. When I started my mission, we used to meet in the front room of a modest house. We were a handful of well-meaning ladies. Determination was our only resource. At first we collected funds for charitable causes. But for every ten pounds we raised, inefficiency would devour six. Therefore we decided to risk disapproval and do the work ourselves. With only our household staff to help, we purchased soup bones, vegetables and kettles of the kind used in regimental cooking.

"As women, we know the running of a household. Whereas men..." She paused and cast a smile around the crowd, which must by now have numbered a thousand, "... men are more suited to the commercial world. When we funded kitchens run by others, thirty pence was needed to feed a family. But through our endeavours, we found thirty pence sufficient to feed ten.

"We could not have guessed how the fame of our endeavours would spread. I could never have imagined standing in North Leicester on Ned Ludd Day addressing a gathering such as this."

At this, the crowd burst into applause. As our speaker waited for quiet, I glanced across and saw Julia clapping with gusto. But all I could feel was irritation. The uncomfortable heat, the pressure of the crowd and anxiety about my future had combined. How was it, I wondered, that a nation so averse to speaking about money could be barefaced in the display of its charity?

The Lord Mayor was standing towards the back of the stage, fanning himself with the programme. The two young women in sashes were obliged to remain still and were glowing with perspiration. Mrs Raike raised a hand and the last whispering of the crowd dropped away to silence.

"What would I have felt had I known our efforts would yield this wondrous fruit? I would have been overjoyed. I would have worked still harder. And if we have achieved so much in the last twelve years, what will the next twelve bring? Consider this – could you be part of our great movement? Will you be able to look back in amazement on great works that your own hands have wrought?

"A few of you may have the skills to help us. Most will find other ways to give. And in return, you will receive the satisfaction of knowing that you are transforming our great nation."

The crush had increased as she spoke. From my position at the front, I could not now see how far back the crowd went. All eyes were fixed on her. Except mine. A photographer had set up his camera on the bandstand platform and was inserting a glass plate. I noticed reporters there also, scribbling down her words.

The Lord Mayor stepped forwards. "Mrs Raike will now take questions."

I could not see how many people raised their hands. The Mayor pointed and from somewhere close behind me, I heard a woman's voice.

"Why do you organise from Derby?"

The Mayor nodded then repeated the question, loud enough for all to hear, adding: "If you would consider moving to North Leicester, we would welcome you with open arms."

"Early in our mission," she said, "we received a generous donation of property. A disused warehouse in Derby which we adapted to our needs – offices, dormitories, kitchens and a yard for our wagons. Perhaps in time, someone will donate a property in North Leicester also."

The Mayor was pointing to another part of the crowd. The next question was too distant for me to hear. The Mayor cupped a hand around his ear, nodding as he listened.

I brought my eyes back to Mrs Raike. There was something about her that seemed unreal to me. Her clothing was too heavy for the weather and the arrangement of young women to either side unnecessarily theatrical. It is hard for the daughter of a conjurer to take any performance at face value. And I will never trust a veil.

I had missed the Mayor relaying the last question, but now Mrs Raike was speaking again. "Men can help," she said. "But their role is in the workplace. They are the providers. They are naturally competitive. We are homemakers. Our inclination is to nurture and protect. The work of charity suits our gentleness."

I turned to Julia, expecting annoyance at this characterisation. But she remained under Mrs Raike's spell.

I should not have raised my hand. Indeed I hardly knew I had done so. But the Mayor was pointing in my direction and I found myself speaking: "I hear it said that in the Kingdom women run businesses. They study in university. Shouldn't we aspire to the same freedoms?"

Mrs Raike stared at me. For a moment the Mayor seemed about to relay my words to the crowd but then he was pointing to another questioner.

Afterwards, the photographer stepped in and tried to position the dignitaries. But Mrs Raike would have none of it and organised the group into a formal line with the camera far back on the edge of the stage. It was the same arrangement I had seen in every picture of her – the star of the show a small figure in the middle, dwarfed by her surroundings.

An accordionist clambered up onto the bandstand and played the opening bars of the national anthem, whereon everyone joined together in chorus as more young women in green sashes descended with collection plates.

Oh pristine skies and cities of good industry
Protect us now from all those dark machines
We will with upright conduct strive for liberty
And set perfection over dreams

I mouthed the words. Julia did not seem to be singing either. Knowing she would be cross with me after my question, I dared not meet her eye.

Instead, I focussed on Mrs Raike, trying to see the face under the veil. I had imagined her to be perhaps fifty years old. But much of that impression came from the way she moved. From this angle, looking up, I was closer than the camera. To guess her age more accurately, I should have liked to see the skin of her neck, but that was covered by a high collar. Conveniently covered, I thought. The dark mole on her right cheek drew the eye. It was a skin blemish exaggerated in the cartoons I had seen of her. Her skin seemed strangely dry.

A loud clinking of coins alerted me to a collection plate being juggled in front of me. The woman proffering it smiled encouragement. Her brow glistened in the heat. The image so struck me that for a moment I couldn't move. Again, she shook the plate.

Julia glared at me and pulled some more coins from her purse. "This is for my friend," she said. "Forgive her. She's overcome by the occasion."

The volunteer moved on.

"You're doing this on purpose!" Julia hissed.

"I... I wasn't."

"You don't approve of Mrs Raike, and you're displaying your ill feeling like a child!"

The Mayor had begun speaking again, gushing a great list of thanks. Mrs Raike and her entourage climbed down from the back of the bandstand. Presently an engine chugged into life and her small airship rose into the sky, lifted, it seemed, by the applause of the multitude below.

We walked away through the thinning crowd, still not speaking to each other. A bizarre suspicion was incubating in my mind. It was something that Julia would not want to hear. And I would certainly have kept it to myself, but she had once made me promise openness. Therefore, having put some distance between ourselves and listening ears, I cleared my throat and spoke.

"I have something to say concerning Mrs Raike."

Julia turned on me with such a look as might have shrivelled a field of thistles. "Then I hope it's an apology!"

"For what?"

"Isn't it enough that the newspapers turn everything she does into a joke? If a childless man does charity, they don't say it's because he's barren and unfulfilled! I had good news to share and you've spoiled it."

"News?"

"I don't want to say it now!"

"Please. I'm sorry. I want to know."

I could see the conflict written in her face. Though she wanted to stay angry, bitterness was not in her nature. After a moment the frown softened.

"Very well," she said, the corners of her mouth curving into a smile. "When I applied to be a volunteer, they asked me of my experience. When I told them of my lessons, they wanted to know about you – my teacher. I was discreet, don't worry. I simply mentioned your brother and his work. Then, this morning, a message came from Mrs Raike herself, asking if you and he – the siblings Barnabus – would help also."

"*Pro-bono publico*?" I asked.

She blushed. "Must you talk of money? It's the case of the Derbyshire ice farmers that I mentioned to you before. They're badly served by the law."

"If I *had* money, I wouldn't need to talk about it."

"But don't you see – it's perfect. The extradition treaty that's so alarmed you – if it does come to pass, then you too might be helped by Mrs Raike and her lawyer friends. This is your chance to do good for her."

"You wish me to be the deserving poor?"

"Please don't twist my words."

"I'll think about it," I said, not wanting to refuse without the appearance of consideration.

She beamed. "I knew you'd see sense. Now – you had something to say?"

"Oh," I said. "It's nothing." For it didn't seem the right moment to reveal my suspicion to Julia – that her hero might not be a woman at all.

CHAPTER 5

Nothing soothes the troubled brow of a patriot quite as readily as a colourful uniform and a prominent flag.

FROM REVOLUTION

The morning after Julia departed for Derby, two constables arrived on the wharf. The younger one was a spindly lad with a shaving rash. The older one carried a clipboard. Both wore custodian helmets and jackets of midnight blue.

"You live on this boat?" the older one asked.

"It's my brother you'll want to speak to," I said.

"And he is?"

"Away on business."

"What's his name then, this brother?" His set smile did not match the sharpness of his voice.

"Edwin Barnabus," I said, feeling a shiver of fear brush my shoulders.

"You're alone then?"

My interrogator turned to the lad. "Have a scout round. See what you can find."

The boy was off like a dog after a rat – up the towpath, bending to look in through each of *Bessie*'s portholes. Then he jumped onto the crutch and before I could complain he'd ducked through the forward hatch and disappeared inside.

I would have leapt down into the galley to head him off. But the other one grabbed my wrist, wrenching me to a stop.

"The boy won't take nothing," he said. "We just got to make sure, that's all. And while we're about it, I'll have your name too. Miss?"

"Elizabeth Barnabus," I said, pulling my arm free of his grip. "What's this about?"

I could hear the lad inside, opening doors and closing them. Moving things.

"It's a list, is all," said the constable, as he printed my name. "If you haven't done nothing, it won't disturb you."

"I haven't. We haven't."

"There you go then. And you'll have to sign the register at Police House in Syston. It's not just you. It's all the immigrants."

There was a crash inside the boat – the chair in my cabin falling, I thought. I shifted my weight, ready to rush back inside. The constable shook his head. His eyes tracked down to my waist. "It's just signing a bit of paper," he said. "Once a week. You and your brother will both have to do it."

"Why?"

His only answer was a flicker of distaste. Then he was wearing his professional smile once more. The young constable clambered up the aft steps into the sunlight. "All clear," he said. Then he hopped down to the towpath. There were muddy boot prints on the deck where he had been standing.

"Here you go then," said the older one, peeling two carbon copies from the clipboard.

I looked from sheet to sheet. The name *Elizabeth Barnabus* had been printed on one and *Edwin Barnabus* on the other. Reading the details of the appointments, I tried to swallow but found I could not.

"Can't this be changed?"

"It's the law, miss." He pushed back his helmet and scratched at his hairline with the blunt end of the pencil.

"But we can't... come at the same time."

"Everyone thinks they're special," he said.

The young constable sniggered. They turned to go. My mind whirled with a chaos of possibilities.

"It's in our contract," I blurted, stopping them. "Our contract with the wharf keeper. Someone must look after the boat. At all times."

"Contract," he said, as if the word had gone off.

I found myself holding my breath.

"Law is law, I suppose," he said at last, pulling the papers from my hand. "Can't force you to break a contract. What time would suit?"

From the day that I bought her as a derelict hulk, *Bessie* had been a passive thing. Her only movement, a tilt as I stepped from one side of the cabin to the other or when the wind made her pull at the mooring ropes. I loved her that way. The limitation was part of her charm. But in her working life men and women had stood by the canal side just to see her churning past. Julia's father and Mr Simmonds, the wharf keeper, being enthusiasts for mechanical things, had expressed an interest. They came to inspect her one day and leaned their shoulders against a paddle wheel, turning it to expose the corroded portion from below the waterline. It wasn't too bad, they said. And the engine must have been left well greased, for it all felt smooth. She might be mended. To me it had felt like an insult.

On my knees, working from the galley towards the cabins, wiping away the young constable's muddy footprints, I found myself wishing for the first time that the engine was not frozen with rust. If only I could fire up the boiler, let steam to the pistons and hear the paddle wheels slapping the water on either side of the boat.

I righted the stool in my cabin. Refolded my linen. Found grubby fingerprints on a pair of cotton bloomers.

If the extradition treaty was signed, they would know exactly where to find me. I did not believe that Yan Romero could help, even if I had the money to pay him.

As for Mrs Raike – I had to find a way to tell Julia that the woman was not what she seemed. If indeed she was a woman at all. There had been a disguise, sure enough, plastered so thick that no sweat showed through. As for her covering the neck – that is what any performer must do who wishes to pass for the opposite sex.

If Mrs Raike wanted Julia and the siblings Barnabus to help the ice farmers of Derbyshire, she would be waiting a long time.

●●●

My brother's appointment was for six o'clock. But having heard that the Police House remained open into the evening and not wishing to expose my disguise to full daylight, I waited until half past the hour before pulling the curtains across my cabin porthole and exchanging corset for binding cloth.

By the time I stepped out of the boat, the sky above the horizon had paled to duck-egg blue. Mrs Simmonds waved from the top of the embankment, trying to attract my attention. A conversation with the wharf keeper's wife being never less than an inquisition, I pretended not to notice and launched myself away from the quayside, planting my heels in the towpath and mud.

"Oh, Mr Barnabus…"

Her call was distant enough to ignore.

As I walked, I hummed. A continuous mid-pitch note, lowering it by stages until I could feel that familiar tickle at the base of my throat. There is an art to speaking like a man. And also a discipline. The tissue that vibrates to achieve it lies a fraction below the voice box. When I was a child, my father had told me that nature did not intend it for this use. Thus, I must hone the skill. The first time I achieved it, I coughed until I retched. It had felt as if a bee was buzzing inside me. But each time after that, I could do it for longer. At the age of twenty, I merely needed to go through the warm-up routine. The voice was never perfect. But it could pass.

The land was dark by the time I reached the bridge, but the canal still reflected the last light from the sky. I climbed the first step then froze. It seemed there had been a footstep behind me. I had found myself imagining the sounds of someone following several times of late but had put it down to growing paranoia. But this time it seemed real. I turned slowly but could see no one behind me. A loud splash made me start, but it was only a bird landing in the water. Ripples spread from the deep shadow under the far bank.

Without the blue lamp on the wall, Syston's Police House would have looked the same as any other building in the row. I let the knocker drop three times and stood back to wait. Presently there was a scuffing sound and the report of the bolt being drawn. The door opened, splashing the yellow light of a gas lamp onto the road.

"We're closed," said a man silhouetted in the hallway. Regulation police braces dangled on either side of him.

"I was told to come and register," I said, satisfied that the pitch of my voice sounded true.

He pulled spectacles from his trouser pocket and held them up to peer through. "Are you one of them?"

"Edwin Barnabus," I said, taken aback by his corrosive tone. It seemed my place of birth was pushing me beyond the pale of Republican civility.

He gave a cursory glance at my proffered hand, then turned on a heel. "You're late," he said, as I followed him inside.

We entered the room, which should have been a front parlour had it been an ordinary house. But instead of domestic furniture it had been fitted out as a waiting room. Wooden benches ran along two walls. A high counter occupied the opposite corner, seeming like a pulpit. It was behind this that the constable stationed himself. He snapped his braces over his shoulders, opened a ledger and started to write. I made to step forwards but he waved me away. Feeling a growing disquiet, I stared at the scuff marks on the wooden board that fronted the counter.

"Right," he said. "Reason for the lateness?"

"My watch stopped."

I saw him transcribe the lie into his ledger.

"Papers?"

This time he did not object when I stepped forwards. I placed Edwin Barnabus' forged identification documents on the counter, together with the carbon copy I had been given earlier. The constable read each sheet, taking his time, occasionally writing.

Then, without a word of explanation, he came out from behind the counter and disappeared through the door. I could hear the opening and closing of drawers. When he returned he was carrying a folded paper.

"You're to come back in two weeks and sign the register. And every two weeks after."

"What if I'm sick?"

He was behind the counter again, leafing through the ledger for no apparent reason, avoiding eye contact. "A note from your physician. Don't leave it more than a week or you'll be arrested. And you'll need to put this in a window of your house. Facing the street."

He pushed the folded paper across the counter top.

"I live on a boat," I said.

"You have windows on your boat?"

"Portholes."

"There you go, then. But make sure it can be seen."

I opened out the paper. It was a roughly printed black crown on a red background – a crude representation of the flag of the Kingdom of England and Southern Wales.

"It's so we know who's a Royalist," he said. "In case there's trouble."

CHAPTER 6

*Each takes meaning from what he sees. But no two
will be found to have seen the same.*

THE BULLET-CATCHER'S HANDBOOK

I awoke already sitting up, my fists bunching the
cotton of my nightgown above my breasts. There was
a vague sense of something loud snagging in the last
moments of my dream. Then I heard running feet and
an urgent whisper outside the boat.

My father's pistol was too well hidden to lay hands
on in a rush. Leaping from the bunk, I snatched a
shawl and slipped down the gangway to grab the
sharpest knife from the galley.

Holding my breath, I listened. The only sound was
blood rushing in my ears. Pulling the curtain an inch I
peered through the porthole. Two figures stood a few
yards away, leaning together. One whispered with
a cupped hand to the other's ear. Then they stood
straight and I recognised them as my neighbours, the
coal boatman and his eldest son.

Sliding the bolt on the hatch, I climbed a step and
peered out.

"Miss Barnabus?" whispered the coal boatman.

Gathering the shawl closer around me, I stepped up onto the aft deck. "What's happening?"

"Thieves, miss."

"Almost had them," said his son.

"How many?"

They looked at each other. "Could have been two," said the coal boatman. "Three maybe?"

"We heard them though," said his son.

"Knocked a painted jug from off the roof."

I felt the muscles of my arms loosening. My heart began to slow. "What did they take?"

"We scared them off before they had a chance."

"You don't think it could have been an animal?" I asked.

The men looked at each other. In the gloom I couldn't make out their expressions. But there was uncertainty in the way they stood. I relaxed some more. The thought of the two of them blundering around in the dark might have been comic. But the misadventures of vigilante groups often caused tragedy. I silently thanked providence the coal boatman didn't own a gun.

"They've taken stuff before," said the son. "The thieves I mean."

"What sort of stuff?"

"There was a quarter loaf of bread on Sunday."

"And two good rashers of bacon gone last week," added the father, though with less certainty. Perhaps he had needed to hear himself say it to realise how it would sound. The bacon thief who knocked over a jug then doubtless found a warm spot to lie in, licking the grease from its paws.

The silence became awkward.

"I could ask my brother to look into it," I suggested, trying to help them save face.

"That would be grand." The coal boatman seemed genuinely relieved. "He could come now. A fresh trail better than a cold one."

"He's out. I'm sorry."

"Ah yes. His work, I suppose."

The two men looked at each other.

"In any case," I said, "the thieves'll be long gone now. They'll not trouble you again tonight, for sure."

"Right you are." The coal boatman lifted a hand, as if to touch his cap, though he must have rushed from his bed, for he had forgotten to put one on. "I'll say goodnight, then."

They started walking back towards their boat, but the son broke step and turned. "The bacon was locked in the pie-safe," he said. "Tell your brother that."

To be lonely is a sorrow. And worse when the world believes you have a brother for company. Such was the necessity of my double life. But until recently, I had Julia to confide in. Now we had been separated by distance and by the argument that had tainted our parting.

I opened the stove door, still warm from the evening. With a spill of twisted paper in one hand I blew on the coals brightening them from grey to orange. First there was a thread of smoke, then flame on the tip of the spill. From that I lit the candle lantern.

Soon fresh sticks were crackling. Though it was a

luxury I couldn't afford, I put two shining lumps of anthracite among the flames. There was no milk or sugar on the boat. But even a cup of black tea can warm the hands.

I had not been sleeping well. The visitation of the constables and the hanging of Florence May had somehow become tangled in my mind. Bad dreams woke me more often than sunshine.

The crude Kingdom flag was now gummed in place in Bessie's porthole window. No one on the wharf had mentioned it. But I'd detected a coolness from some of my neighbours. And weekend tourists whispered to each other as they passed. One family even shifted to the other side of the towpath.

In the daytime I could banish such thoughts and turn my mind to matters that needed attention. But at night it was not so easy. Seeking distraction, I fetched pen, ink and paper from my cabin and placed them on the galley table next to the lantern.

Dear Julia,

By now you will have arrived in Derby and I do hope sincerely that you are settling. I am imagining you meeting a string of eligible lawyers in the days to come. It is only a fancy, but the thought of you crossing them off a list one by one is making me smile. For I do not think you will find any to compare to your friend in London.

Here, things continue as always. The coal boatman believes all manner of brigands abroad on the wharf at night and has begged for my brother's help in detecting them. But I think a saucer of milk is more likely to catch this burglar than any search for clues!

   I am longing to hear of your adventures. Please write when you have time.

   Your friend,
   Elizabeth

CHAPTER 7

That immigrants bring disease, crime and immorality
is a truth so universally accepted as to require no proof.

From Revolution

Secularism was the Republic's answer to religion. And the Secular Hall was a church in all but name. A flight of low steps led to its magnificent central doorway where a bust of Jesus looked down alongside likenesses of Plato, Socrates and Voltaire. On Sundays the faithful gathered there to hear sermons on temperance, honesty and the rewards of tolerance. Small congregations, to be sure. Stripped of the irrational, there seemed less to draw a crowd.

On other days, community groups could hire out the space.

I had timed my trip to arrive as the meeting began. But stepping along the squeaky floor and through the wooden doors, I found the meeting hall almost empty. A family was sitting on one of the rearmost pews. Two young men were huddled in conversation near the front. And at the side three women, who might have been a mother and two daughters, were arranging glasses and bottles of cordial.

All turned as I entered. For a moment I thought it must be the wrong day. Then I looked more closely. There was a glint of red garnet from the end of the mother's hat pin and one of the young men had turn-ups at the end of his trouser legs.

An older woman strode towards me from the side of the hall. "What are you looking for?" she asked, with an easy rudeness that I instantly warmed to.

"The meeting should start at two," I said.

"If I needed them to be here at two, I'd have told them it started at one." She ran her eyes over me from hat to boots, assessing. "You must have been in the Republic a long time. Punctuality's still a dirty word for most of us."

She held out her hand, which I took. "Tulip," she said. A solidly Royalist name.

"Elizabeth," I replied. "You're the organiser?"

"Officially? No."

It seemed I had found a kindred spirit. "I fled the Kingdom five years ago," I said.

She cast me a dubious look. "You'd have been a child. You came alone?"

I nodded. "And here I am."

"And wish to stay," she said. "I assume we share that same goal."

In truth I wished to return. But that was a long and complicated story. Not one to share with a stranger, though it seemed we shared much else.

People arrived in ones and twos after that. Most had assimilated to some degree. But taken as a group there could have been no mistaking them. However hard an exile tries to blend in, there is always something to give him away. Even the way a man swings his arms as he walks can place him on one side of the border or the other.

I saw nods of recognition between some of the newcomers. Handshakes and shifty glances. Conversations were hushed – the habit of wanting to be invisible, hard to drop. The man from the labourer's cottage in Syston was one of the last to enter. It was he who had told me of the meeting. But now he seemed keen to keep his distance and slunk off to the other side of the hall.

At a quarter to three, when it seemed the meeting was at last about to begin, the doors banged open. The murmur of whispered conversations fell to silence as Yan Romero made his entrance. From our first meeting, I knew he was a performer, someone who liked to shock. But his appearance still took my breath away. He wore moss green wale cord trousers, a mustard waistcoat and a pale pink top hat of outrageous height. The outfit would have turned the heads of London dandies.

We were hiding in the Republic. He could come and go as he pleased. We tried to avoid second looks in the street. He had dressed to make an omnibus crash. Everyone stared. Mouths hung slack. No display of power could have more perfectly shaken this particular audience. He was doing what we could not.

"Afternoon," he said, speaking into the sudden quiet.

He flourished a handkerchief, blew his nose loudly and marched towards the lectern. Tulip intercepted him with a handshake then turned to address the room.

"I call this meeting of the Association of Kingdom Exiles to order. If you would all take your seats we can–"

But Yan Romero had already climbed the pulpit. "You all know why we're here," he said. "So let's cut to the chase. Then you can all get drunk. Or whatever it is you people do."

Gone was the effete charm he had used to insinuate himself onto my boat. Here was a different man – more debt collector than lawyer. Even the accent had changed. Sing-song trills replaced by a steely edge. I felt myself shudder. I knew not to trust a man who could change his face to suit the day. But with that opening sentence, I and the rest of the hotchpotch audience, wished to be as free as him. And as rude.

"I'm supposed to be addressing clients only. Half of you haven't paid. Thought you could sneak in? Forget it! When the treaty gets signed – and it will – you'll be hauled back over the border to face whatever it is you ran from. I won't lift a pinkie to help – unless you're a paid-up client."

The silence that followed his statement was awful. It was Tulip who managed to break it. "How do we know you'll be able to help? You give some guarantee?"

"What are you?" he demanded. "Whores and fraudsters. Killers and runaways. Half of you'll be hanged within the year. That's the only guarantee.

Save your money if you want. Give it to Clarence Hobb before he puts the rope round your neck.

"I'm going for a drink now. I'll be in the Three Cranes. If anyone wants to commission me, bring your money and I'll put your name on the list of the saved."

That was it. He marched out. I felt the air waft as he passed close to me. A breath of rose-scented perfume. The door slammed and he was gone.

I waited for Tulip to speak again, but she seemed paralysed.

The squeaking of shoes made me turn. The family who had been sitting on the rearmost pew were heading for the door, shamefaced.

"There are other lawyers," said Tulip. "If we band together…"

But more were on the move, heading for the Three Cranes. Better the lawyer you know.

CHAPTER 8

*A man will eat until full. But no amount of gold will
ever be enough. And no amount of love.*

THE BULLET-CATCHER'S HANDBOOK

Our letters must have crossed *en route*. My approach
had been to write of pleasant things – to dilute the
bitter taste of our parting argument. Such evasion was
not in Julia's nature.

> *Dear Elizabeth,*
> *I have not heard from you since arriving in Derby.*
> *I fear that when we parted on Ned Ludd Day, it was*
> *under a cloud of feeling quite alien to our friendship.*
> *The thought of it has been gnawing at me. Please*
> *write and say all is as before.*
> *Julia*

She had been sixteen when we first met. Then,
I thought her directness a remnant of childhood.
Two years later it had, if anything, grown stronger.
Speaking one's mind was held to be a virtue in men
but a vice in women. It caused friction in Julia's

family. It alienated would-be suitors.

The single exception was her lawyer friend from London, who seemed enchanted by her boldness. Nothing could better have proved his suitability for her – in my eyes at least. My own situation made romance impossible, but I hoped Julia would achieve it and one day find happiness in marriage.

Knowing she would by now have received my letter, I put off writing a reply. Romero's alarming threats had been consuming most of my energy. I needed something other than that to put on paper. The detection of the bacon thief suggested a suitable diversion.

If I arrived at the coal boat dressed as a man, some of the family might be fooled. But I was to see Mary, the coal boatman's wife. And she had the kind of eye that saw to the truth of things, especially in daylight. She usually wore practical clothes, so I chose an outfit that would not look out of place in her company – a grey cotton walking skirt and a full sleeved jacket of the same colour.

The coal boatman's sons did not hide their disapproval when I arrived.

"Where is he then?" asked the younger one. "Your brother, I mean."

"Business keeps him away," I said.

"But that's no good," said the older one.

They were standing on the heaped coal in the hold of the boat, black smudged and frowning.

"I'll see whatever he would have seen," I told them.

"But you're a woman!"

"True."

"A woman can't–"

His complaint was cut short by the slamming back of the hatch and a swish of skirts and knitted shawl as Mary jumped onto the steering platform.

"Billy! Josh! Mind your manners!"

"We was just saying–"

"What were you just saying, Billy? What were you just saying? A woman can't do what?"

The older boy seemed about to answer, but seeing her expression, snapped his mouth closed again. Wisely, I thought. Then they were both clambering away over coal and tarpaulin, across to the boat moored alongside.

"And don't think you'll be eating before all them sacks are filled!"

She winked at me. "Boys! But they'll learn. If I can find strong wives to teach them. Now Lizzy, I've a pot on the boil. Won't you come in?"

There were six of them in the family. Husband, wife, two sons, two daughters. And two boats – the larger, a barge for the fetching of coal from Nottinghamshire or Coalville, whichever was cheaper at the time. The smaller craft was an ancient wood-hulled narrowboat from the time when locks were only seven foot wide. This they used for delivery runs, selling to houses and businesses that flanked the canals. The girls and parents slept in the cabin of the barge. The boys in the narrowboat.

"I'm a disappointment," I said to Mary. "They were hoping to see my brother, Edwin."

"Didn't think he'd come," she said. "Keeps himself to himself, that one."

"Your husband told me something was knocked over. And food stolen before that."

She pointed to a painted metal jug on the cabin roof – roses and castle design. Though wide at the base, it would not have taken much to shift it.

"A person did it you think?"

"What else?" she said. "A ghost?"

"Mrs Simmonds' cat perhaps?"

"Maybe," she said. "Maybe it was." Then she led me up onto the steering platform where the cabin roof overhung a small cupboard with walls of finely perforated metal. She selected a small key from the loop on her waistband and turned it in the lock. The cupboard door swung outwards. Inside was a shelf made of the same perforated metal sheet. On it rested a parcel of butcher's paper with hock bones sticking out at the side.

"Soup tonight?" I asked.

"Soup every night, when we can afford," she said.

"Why are you showing me your pie safe?" I asked.

"So you see how clever was this cat that you say did the thieving. That's where the bacon was stolen from."

I sat on the cot in the crowded cabin, watching Mary laying a lace-edged tablecloth. On this she arranged her best china, wiping invisible dust from each piece before placing it. The teaspoons and sugar tongs were silver.

I had examined the pie safe. The lock was crude. I could have picked it one handed and I claim to be no expert. But whoever had taken the bacon, one thing was now certain – it had not been the cat.

Mary took down the Measham teapot from its display shelf, the brown glaze dotted with white daisies.

"You had a disturbed night," I said.

She made a "Hmph" sound.

"Your husband and son patrolling the wharf."

"They're fools, the two of them," she said.

"You didn't hear anything yourself?"

"Oh, I heard, yes. I heard. And if there's a thief, then he heard too – them crashing about like a football game. What did they think they'd find out there? And then they went and woke you too, Lizzy. Men! But your brother's not like that, is he? Doesn't go off like a dog after a rabbit, without thought or plan?"

"Edwin's much the same as me," I said.

She examined me then, as if searching for some tiny mark. I found myself looking away.

"It's a shame he couldn't come today," she said, handing me a cup of tea. "There's no biscuits. Sorry."

I sipped. She had made it strong and milky. It seemed clear to me that a thief who kept returning to the same place could not live far away. But there was delicacy needed in suggesting it. Mary might not take it well if she thought I was accusing one of her neighbours.

"If my brother was here," I said, "he'd be wanting to know if the thief came from outside the wharf."

She shook her head. "Who'd trouble for such scraps? It's one of us for sure."

I felt relieved to hear her say it. "You'd have made a good detective," I said. "If women were allowed such work, I believe you'd find the thief yourself."

"It's not the finding that's the problem," she said. "It's what happens after. I'm not saying there aren't people on the wharf who'd lift or dip pockets. Not every boatman has a clean nose. But what good comes of knowing it for sure? The men give chase. But what if they'd caught him and it'd been one of the Biggins boys? How would we live with them after that? Or what if it was old man Harboro? Some things is best not knowing. That's how feuds start, that is."

"Do you not want to know?"

"If it could be just me doing the knowing, that'd be grand. I could whisper in an ear and it wouldn't happen no more. But I'd rather not know if the men had to know too."

"Why do you think he only stole from you?" I asked.

"Not just us. The Carters lost a block of cheese two weeks back. And Mrs Biggins had a jugged eel took."

"So it's probably not the Biggins boys after all," I reasoned.

"She could have just said it to put me off the scent. And then there's Alice, the washwoman, she lost a pair of pig's ears. And there's Mrs Simmonds too..."

I started losing track of the list of names and stolen items. "It might be simpler to tell me who hasn't had anything taken," I said. "Then, if everyone was telling the truth, we'd have narrowed the search."

"Ah, well," she said, embarrassed. "That's the thing. Everyone's had something nicked. Everyone except you of course. And your brother."

•••

Afterwards, I could not let go of Mary's words. It hadn't occurred to me before to ask why her husband and son ended up outside my boat that night, when they did not know which way the thief had run. Now it seemed that Mary might be warning me what others on the wharf were whispering. Or perhaps she was thinking it herself. I kept coming back to what she had said about stopping the thefts with a whisper in an ear. Was it my ear she meant? Had that been the whisper? And worse, I wondered whether I would have been a suspect at all had it not been for the Kingdom flag stuck inside the glass of my porthole window.

A second letter was waiting for me when I arrived back at my own boat. Mrs Simmonds must have slipped it through the crack at the edge of the hatch.

Dear Elizabeth,

Your message had arrived when I returned from posting mine. I should have known not to fret over a few cross words. Indeed, if you were here, you would see how wrongly you judged Mrs Raike. She has made great strides to promote the freedom to choose one's own path in life – an ideal we both hold dear.

I am in a dormitory with three other girls. One helps to prepare food for the benefit of the deserving poor. A second ministers to those wretched creatures who cannot gain access to the city's overflowing asylum. Indeed there are many such living in derelict buildings hereabouts. Little more than wild beasts they seem. She is very brave. The third teaches letters and reading in the prison.

For myself, I have this day met a lawyer who has knowledge of the ice farmers and their grievance. He has provided me with volumes of law books such as I have not seen before. They are quite different in character from the Intelligence Gatherer's Guide to Legal Process. The words are harder to understand and I need make frequent use of the dictionary, but the ideas make plain enough sense.

Ice is being stolen by one unknown. But as to who is responsible for carrying the financial loss, this I cannot understand. Is it the farmers themselves or the boatmen who carry the cargo or the ice factory in Derby, where it is processed and stored? I can find no case in the law books that matches the particulars of this one.

Mrs Raike has set great priority on the resolution of the case. She was disappointed that you and your brother could not be here to help. You know I am also.

Your friend, Julia

At first, all I could feel was irritation that she insisted on blaming me for the argument. But on reading the letter again my annoyance softened. By the third reading, I had grown curious. If I replied directly, I could catch the evening postal collection.

The ice theft sounded petty. More a dispute over payment than a deliberate crime. The most singular question was why Mrs Raike had made it such a priority. But that, I could not ask without testing Julia's friendship once more.

Dear Julia,

    No one will accept financial responsibility until it is proven where the ice is being lost. Lawyers will look for the answer in books. Each will find differently, depending on the side they represent. Is it simply melting?

    If you want truth, travel to the high peaks where the ice farmers live. Let them show you how they work. Ask questions. Observe. You know my methods.

CHAPTER 9

It was to dispel the smog of superstition and prejudice
that we pulled the churches down. Now that work is
done, let us build libraries in their stead.

FROM REVOLUTION

Having done battle with the steam taxies and wagons
that jammed the roads around Belgrave Gate, I
headed west to St Margaret's Library. After the bustle
and noise of those densely packed streets, stepping
into the building felt like entering a tomb. The cold
dry air smelled of dust. My footsteps echoed under
the high ceiling.

"Can I help you?" asked the man behind the
reception desk. He seemed to have spent too long
indoors, for his skin was as pale and veined as the
marble floor. His sleeve protectors were smudged blue
with ink.

"Do you take the Derby Herald?" I asked.

For a moment he seemed confused. Then he said:
"We are not a newsagent."

"You're a reference library. I thought–"

"For scholars. We are a reference library for scholars."

"Good."

He glanced around him, as if looking for help in explaining some obvious truth. I followed his gaze. In the reading room beyond, men sat bent over desks, browsed shelves, conversed in whispers.

"Perhaps you are foreign?" he suggested.

"You're denying me access?"

"I... don't have that authority."

"Then I'll have the Derby Herald please. Everything you've got from 1996 to 2001."

He ushered me into a side room almost filled by a walnut table. There was just space to walk around the outside and pull back one of eight high-backed chairs. Having settled myself for a long wait, I was surprised when the door opened after only a few minutes. A younger librarian entered, hauling a book trolley on which rested twenty huge volumes. He manoeuvred it along the narrow gap and parked it next to me. I angled my head to read the gold leaf lettering.

Derby Herald   1996   Jan–Mar

He cleared his throat. "I'm... uh... sorry to be shutting you away like this. Dr Bowers – you spoke to him – he said it was for safety."

"Mine or his?" I said, failing to keep the edge from my voice.

The young librarian chuckled. "He fears some of the older patrons would be overcome with shock. There won't have been a woman in the reading room for – well, since it was a church."

"But it isn't forbidden?"

"No one's pressed the point before. But I fear they'll draft a rule after today. Dr Bowers is probably trying to gather a quorum of the trustees as we speak. It's a shame. I should have liked to see you stride into the reading room. It would have been entertaining. Apoplectic seizures and the like – we have books on the subject if you cared to deepen your knowledge."

"Perhaps another day," I said. "Or maybe not if the rules change. But thank you."

"If you need anything else, I'll be directly outside."

Once the door was closed, I hefted the first volume onto the table and lifted the cover. The paper was foxed with brown spots. A musty smell wafted up as I turned the first page and began scanning the headlines. The information I was looking for would be buried somewhere on an inside page.

The wall clock ticked laboriously as I worked. When the first volume was finished, I slid it across the table and replaced it with 1996 April–June.

Skimming old newspapers is difficult for someone curse-blessed with an excess of curiosity. So many stories were hinted at by each headline. Murders, marriages, missing persons, patents rejected and notices of surgical demonstrations. Several times I found myself reading articles I should have brushed over. But soon I had moved on to July–September. A large stain ran through the pages, speaking of some accident in the past. A leaky roof, perhaps. October–December showed more of the same damage. But the beginning of 1997 was in better condition. And it was here that I found my first clue.

Under the heading, **FEEDING THE DESERVING POOR**, I read:

The households of several of the city's leading families have banded together to lend assistance and education to the deserving poor. Using the best nutritional science and spare food donated for the purpose, seventy-five destitute but deserving families were fed on Sunday by volunteers, including the wives of several prominent businessmen.

There were no names and little more information except the recipe – an unappetising pea and barley soup, fortified with carrots, potatoes, onions and cattle bones. But the date and the description of the event matched the story Mrs Raike had told at the Abbey Park rally. I licked my finger and turned the pages, searching more carefully now. The next report came two weeks later.

DERBY SOUP KITCHEN BOOMING
Crowds gathered, Sunday, for the distribution of food to Derby's deserving poor. The new soup kitchen on Upper Wharf Street has become a lifeline for many of the city's destitute.

Again, there was no mention of Mrs Raike. Indeed, women were only referred to in terms of their relationships to named men. I sat back and stretched my neck which was becoming uncomfortable.

The following weeks yielded three more articles. The local businessmen were now calling for donations of food to help with their work. An empty warehouse had been procured. There was even a photograph of men and women standing next to a wagon-load of onions. The picture was of poor quality, the faces little more than smudges. I looked from one to the next, vainly searching for any similarity to Mrs Raike. The caption read:

> *Cllr Wallace Jones with the volunteers of the Upper*
> *Wharf Street kitchen.*

I hurried on to the next volume and discovered Mrs Raike's activities reported on the front page for the first time. The same photograph had been reproduced next to an article headlined: **WHARF STREET SOUP KITCHEN CONTROVERSY RAGES**

A petition is calling on the city council to toughen its stance on the Upper Wharf Street soup kitchen. The association of grocers and food retailers has been leading calls for tax exemptions from which the charity benefits to be withdrawn, claiming the businesses of hard-working people were being damaged.

"There's thousands being fed at Upper Wharf Street," claimed Gerald Hackworth, association chairman. "Before the kitchen opened, they had money for vittles. Now, that money is spent on alcohol and horses."

At the time of going to press 1700 citizens had added their names to the petition. "There are hundreds asking to sign," Hackworth claimed. "The City Council will ignore us at its peril."

Another complaint against the soup kitchen is that it is taking women away from their work in the home. "They're out of their element," claimed one association member. "Women can't understand the damage they are doing because they don't know business."

I examined the photograph again. The image was less smudged in this reproduction. The caption read:

Cllr Wallace Jones (centre) and the Upper Wharf Street organising committee

A man stood on the councillor's right hand side, a woman on the left. The woman was too close to him to be anything but a family member – a sister perhaps, or his wife. I judged them to be in their twenties.

A week later and the Herald was reporting that the petition, now numbering 2800 signatures had been delivered to City Hall.

After that there was nothing.

I moved to the next volume – August–September 1996. I had my eye in now and it took only fifteen minutes to skim through. October–December was similarly devoid of mention of the soup kitchen.

I had to work through all of 1997 and half of 1998 before I found what I was looking for.

MINISTER OF PRISONS PRAISES DERBY WOMEN

The work of Mrs Raike's girls, an organisation of local women, was recognised last week by Gordon Carlson. On his visit to the city, the Minister for prisons met Mrs Raike and some of her volunteers in their offices on Upper Wharf Street.

There was no photograph and little of substance in the report. But after a year and a half of obscurity, the organisation had re-emerged, and now in its familiar form.

Articles followed in train after that. Hardly a month went by without some new endorsement or report. There were occasional letters of complaint. Gerald Hackworth wrote in from time to time. Always there was a swift response, well-reasoned and amicable, in contrast to the attacks.

And there were photographs – Mrs Raike flanked by the great and the good standing at a distance from the camera. Eleven years had made no alteration to her appearance. She wore the same austere outfit that I had seen in Abbey Park, the same hat and veil. Nowhere was there a photograph of Councillor Wallace Jones and Mrs Raike together. Indeed, the articles did not mention him again.

I closed the last volume and tucked my pencil and notepaper into my sleeve. When I poked my head from the door, the young librarian jumped up from his chair and was at my side in three long strides. I wondered if he had been watching all the while.

"I'll be leaving now," I said.

He walked me back to the main entrance, the click of our shoes echoing from the veined marble walls. Of Dr Bowers there was no sign.

I thanked him as he held the door for me. And then, as an afterthought, I asked: "Whatever happened to Cllr Wallace Jones?"

"Something has happened to him?"

"I was reading about him. But that was twelve years ago. Is he still alive?"

The librarian began to laugh, as if I'd made a joke. But on seeing my confusion, he pulled himself up. "Forgive me. But it's common knowledge you see. His star has risen. He was appointed Minister of Patents last year."

I stepped out of the door, as one born into sudden sunlight, dazzled by the revelation but unable to resolve it. I had begun to suspect that Mrs Raike might be Wallace Jones in disguise. But now to learn that he was Minister of Patents – one of the foremost officers among the Council of Guardians. He would surely not risk a public deception on such a scale. Perhaps I had made the mistake of projecting my own double life onto another.

My thoughts were cut short by a voice close behind me.

"Are you Miss Elizabeth Barnabus?"

I turned to see a uniformed constable standing next to the library door.

"Elizabeth Barnabus?" he asked again.

"Yes, but it's all resolved," I said, thinking at first that he had come at Dr Bowers' request. Then it came to me that the old librarian did not know my name. "What's this about?"

"Just come this way, miss."

He gestured down the library steps. I looked. Two more constables stood next to a black Maria, parked on the roadside. He grabbed my arm before I could run.

CHAPTER 10

One who can escape from a locked safe for the entertainment of the audience will never trust his secret to paper and ink. For where would he find to keep it?

THE BULLET-CATCHER'S HANDBOOK

I was not alone in the maw of the black Maria. Three others sat on benches running along the walls. All looked at me as I clambered in, shielding their eyes or squinting against the daylight. One I recognised.

"Tulip?"

The door slammed shut behind me, blinking us into near darkness.

"Who's that?" she asked, grabbing my hand just in time. The engine had clanged into gear, and I would have been jolted off my feet but for her support. I half fell onto the bench next to her.

"I'm Elizabeth," I said. "We met–"

"At the Secular Hall. You crossed as a child."

"You remember."

"I'd hoped to see you again. But not like this."

A slit high on the side wall allowed a little light and air into the cell. It would have been too narrow to squeeze an arm through, let alone shoulders and hips. A memory of once escaping from a locked carriage came back to me. That time, I had been led by instinct. There had been a clutter of objects. I had found a way. This chamber was bare. I reached a hand to feel below the bench. It was merely a plank fixed along the wall. There could be no hiding here.

My eyes were growing accustomed to the gloom. The floor was a single sheet of metal. Other than the two benches, the only fixtures were leather hand straps dangling from the metal ceiling. The vehicle was purpose built – a prison on wheels.

"They must have signed the treaty early," said Tulip, her voice small but close.

"It's not due yet. And we'd have heard."

"Signed in secret maybe?"

The black Maria had been steaming through a series of turns, throwing us first forward and then back. Now it started to accelerate. Steadying myself with a hand on Tulip's shoulder, I clambered up onto the bench and looked out of the slit window. It took me a few moments to understand where we were. Then I recognised a landmark – the ruins of a Roman wall beside the road – and knew the canal must be close ahead.

"We're heading west," I said, lowering myself back to the bench. "If they were taking us to the border, we'd be going to the main crossing by the clock tower. That's south."

"Not if they want to keep it quiet," said Tulip. "They'd want a crossing where no one would see."

I listened, trying to pick up more clues, but our

prison reverberated with the boom of the engine and the clatter of its wheels. All I could know for certain was that we travelled over cobbles.

I tried to think, to reason out the tumble of events and new knowledge. But panic was rising in my chest. If Tulip was correct we would be across the border in a few hours. I imagined the iron collar and chains that would be waiting for me on the other side. My skin crawled as if seething with lice.

Someone must have told them where to find me. For days, I had been nagged by the sense that I was being watched and followed. But the thought that a spy might be on my trail was comforting compared to the more likely truth. They had gone to make the arrest at the wharf where one of my neighbours had informed on me, telling them I had set off towards the library.

There was a screech of brakes and the engine noise changed. Our movement came to an abrupt stop, throwing us towards the front of the wagon. I could hear voices close outside – two men exchanging greetings. A bolt clanged, the door swung outwards and daylight streamed in. I could just make out three figures climbing up, then the door swung closed and darkness swallowed them. The after-image stayed with me though – the silhouette of a woman and two children. The boy had been holding her hand, the girl clinging to her skirts.

We made three more stops after that; the last prisoners in were two men. The benches were full so they had to stand, gripping the leather straps to keep balance.

Since crossing the canal and the river, there had been a few miles of steady climb before the land levelled out again. The bench below the slit window being full, I could no longer climb up to look out. But once, as we stopped for water, I heard beyond the sound of the tender being filled, the throbbing hum of twin airship engines passing low overhead.

The only airship terminus for miles was the international hub at Anstey. That meant we had veered somewhat north of west, taking us away from the border not towards it. We were being taken to a place of confinement pending deportation. They wished to guard us so that we could not drop into hiding as the signing grew closer. I silently berated myself for underestimating the foresight of the Republic's government.

The sound of running water stopped and I heard the squeak of the filling arm being retracted. Then the engine noise picked up and we jolted into movement once more. Tulip's shoulder bumped against mine. I wondered what had made such a strong woman take refuge in the Republic.

After Anstey, the cobbles gave way to a dirt road, softening the din inside our cell. But here the carriage began to sway and lurch. Every pothole threw us one way and the other. Heads bumped on walls. The children were crying and one was sick on the floor. The journey slowed. The light through the slit window became egg-yolk yellow. Shadows passed more frequently across the small window. The sun outside was getting low.

Then we stopped. This time the engine stopped

also, with a long whoosh of venting steam.

The door opened. Outside, a line of uniformed constables stood shoulder to shoulder. Beyond them I could see trees and a row of green-painted huts. I searched for a perimeter wall but could see none. It was an army camp, I guessed. Not a prison. I felt my heart accelerate. Unlike the black Maria, this place had surely not been designed to prevent escape. And with forest all around, getting away would be easy.

"Come when your name's called," said one of the constables. He read from a sheet of paper: "Fredrick Morison."

One of the standing men shuffled to the door and was helped out.

"Happy Rathsphere."

A man on the opposite bench got up and followed.

"Arthur Purling. William Fotheringham. Thomas Thatcher."

When the carriage was empty of men, the constable who had been calling the names followed them out of view. Another constable took his place, holding another list.

"Sunshine Turner, Angeline Turner, Drake Turner."

The mother pulled her two children to their feet and headed out.

"Tulip Slater. Elizabeth Barnabus."

After the vomit smell and body odour of our confinement, the first thing that hit me was the cool freshness of the air. There was birdsong and soft light. And then I saw the men walking away in a line towards one of the huts. The left ankle of each had been shackled. Each leg iron was linked to a long chain which they carried between them.

"Left arm out," a constable said to Tulip.

She obeyed, meekly. He snapped a shackle around her wrist, shut it tight, tested it then gestured her along and turned to me.

"Left arm out."

There is a technique used by the escapists, whereby they flex their muscles and inhale deeply as they are tied. When they later breathe out and relax they can wriggle free, because the chains and ropes have fallen loose. But the wrist is bone and sinew. There is nothing to flex.

The constable grabbed my arm and snapped the manacle in place. I felt the iron grip. Then he shoved me in the back and I found myself stumbling towards Tulip.

Behind me, he instructed the next in line. "Left arm out."

Each of our manacles was connected by a short length of chain to an iron ring, through which a longer chain had been threaded, linking all together, just as the men had been. Except that they had been joined by the ankle.

Tulip leaned close to whisper. "Too shy to tell us to raise our skirts?"

"They're Republicans," I reminded her.

The constable folded the list of names and stood back to survey the line. "Lift the chain!" he called.

After a moment's confusion we had each gripped part of the length with our manacled hand and were being led over the grass towards a hut some distance from the one the men had entered. The young girl was crying. Not able to lift the chain, she let it drag along the ground next to her.

The constable counted us in through the door of the hut, though it seemed unlikely that any could have wandered off since being shackled. An iron ball had been padlocked to both the front and back of the long chain, too big for our manacle rings to pass over. But once we were inside the hut, the ends were also locked to ring-bolts in the floor.

"Food will be served before sunset, courtesy of the Council of Guardians. I suggest you wash and make yourselves comfortable." So saying, he closed the door. I tried to listen for the sound of a lock or bolt being shot, but everyone was suddenly talking at once and I had no chance to hear.

There were ten of us on the chain, including the two children, but only nine beds along the wall of the hut. A pot-bellied stove stood on a rectangle of slate, the chimney pipe heading straight up through the roof. Jugs and bowls for washing had been placed together with chamber pots in the corner of the room. The windows were not barred. Chain and ring bolts notwithstanding, this place had been built for some other purpose.

Somehow we arranged ourselves along the room and everyone moved as one towards the beds. The poor mother and her youngest child were obliged to squeeze together furthest from the door. The rest of us had a bed each, though the chain allowed comfort to none. It could either lie heavily across the chest, or uncomfortably under the body. In this, the men would have an easier time. Had it been attached to our ankles it could have lain on the floor along the foot of the beds.

"We could turn around," I said, reasoning that if our heads were at the bottom of the bed, we too could lay the chain along the floor. No one else seemed convinced of my idea.

"Listen," said Tulip. A notice was pinned to the wall next to her bed. She read out the title: "Rules for patients." Below was a long list, with some words and phrases underlined. I scanned the regulations for clues.

5.*No tobacco – chewing, smoking or snuff.*
6.*No spitting.*
7.*Name badges to be worn at all times.*
8.*Opium to be administered by medical staff only.*

"Then it's a hospital," said Tulip.

"Not a hospital," said the woman with the children. "A sanatorium."

Tulip shifted around, making the chain clank against the iron bed frame. "How do you know?"

"I came last summer. But for a holiday. There was a camp for children from the city. We walked in the woods. It was... different. No prisoners. They told us the history of the place. Before anti-tubercular medicines, people with consumption came here."

"To die," said a woman further up the row.

Sunset came without sight or smell of food. Nor did we have lamps. There wasn't much speaking. Just a few apologies when people had to move to use the chamber pot and ended up dragging the chain. And soothing words from the mother to her children, who were crying from hunger.

Lying in the dark, panic churned in my stomach. I had examined our confinement from all angles but found no possibility of escape. The more I focussed on the problem, the faster and more disorganised my thoughts became until they were bouncing off each other, little more than a blur.

In a moment of clarity, I realised what I was doing. I took a series of deep breaths then started to recite the thirteen times table in my mind. After one hundred and ninety-five I became lost, but the exercise had done its work. My thoughts had slowed. In an effort to divert them from my imprisonment, I focussed on the puzzle of Mrs Raike.

It was only a few hours before that I had been reading through old volumes of the Derby Herald. Her organisation had started twice. The first time seemed natural enough. Councillor Wallace Jones had been at the helm. They had made some mistakes in dealing with local businesses and ended up in a controversy that reached the front page. The second time had been very different. 'Controlled' was the word that came to mind. Unnaturally smooth. Mrs Raike had made her appearance and Wallace Jones had vanished from the scene.

My thoughts were interrupted by the door banging open. A young constable entered with a tray, on which rested three loaves, a saucer of butter and some knives.

"Why did you turn out the lamp?" he asked.

He seemed taken aback when Tulip told him that no lights had been given to us. But he left without offering help.

It was Tulip also who organised the distribution of the food, tearing the bread into portions and making sure everyone had their share of the butter. I chose to eat my bread dry, though it proved hard to swallow. I also managed to end up with one of the butter knives, which I slid into my boot. The knife was too dull to be used as a weapon and would probably prove useless. But the act of stealing it comforted me. A taste of defiance. The illusion of control.

After the others were asleep, I reached under my bed frame and dipped my finger in the butter I had hidden there. I greased the skin of my wrist and started to work the manacle, pulling first one side and then the other, feeling it bite into my flesh. Discomfort turned to pain. The pain became unbearable. But however hard I pulled, the iron would not slip over my hand.

CHAPTER 11

The tyrant has ever held law to be synonymous with justice.

FROM REVOLUTION

Our gaolers were constables with no experience of prison work. That much was clear from the start. Just as it had been no one's job to bring us lamps, we soon discovered that it was no one's job to empty the chamber pots. We had to beg the man who came in the morning with our breakfast. He relented at last. Our chain was unlocked from the ring bolts in the floor and we were allowed to walk in procession, carrying the soiled and stinking porcelain out to the latrine hut to be emptied and rinsed.

Everything about the prison was haphazard except the chain itself.

With the arrival of the noon meal – more bread – we had another chance to make demands. This time it was for our water jugs to be re-filled and to be allowed a few minutes exercise in the spring sunshine.

"How long will this go on?" Tulip whispered to me as we walked circles around the hut.

"Till the treaty's signed, I suppose."

"And then?"

"They don't want us in the Republic," I said. "But I guess they'll be shy of being seen to help the Kingdom. We're an embarrassment. They'll get rid of us as quietly and quickly as they can."

"And after that, home," said Tulip. "Back to the Kingdom." She stared at me for a moment, as one might assess a horse before placing a bet. "I never asked what you ran from to end up this side of the border. You don't, do you? Ask I mean. Not that sort of question. It's private business."

"There's not much private when you've slopped out the night soil together," I said.

She laughed. Such a joyful sound felt out of place.

"I like you," I said.

"You might not have liked me in the Kingdom."

"Why not?"

She did not answer.

"I was born in a travelling show," I told her. "Grew up there learning the bullet-catcher's trade."

"You surprise me."

"Travellers shouldn't be so pleasant?"

She blushed. "You seem too well spoken. Well educated. I thought..."

"You can't win an audience unless you understand them," I said. "And you can't do that unless you can think like them. My father taught me to read from an encyclopaedia. One page a day. He'd won it in a bet. The well-schooled speech I learned from others in the show."

"You make it sound idyllic."

"It was the way it was. I had nothing to compare it to. Until the Duke of Northampton saw me one day. Decided I'd make a diverting plaything. He dropped backhanders to some officials so the law court would award me as payment for a debt that never really existed. That's what I ran from."

"Oh," she said, her expression blank.

"Why did *you* cross the border?" I asked

"I'm a bad person," she said. "But you can't run from that."

The manacles were rubbing our wrists sore by the time we filed back into the hut. I asked for them to be loosened a notch. This request was refused.

It was after the evening meal that one of the constables stepped into the hut holding a slip of paper. We had been given a lamp at last. He angled the paper to its light and read: "Elizabeth Barnabus?"

"Here," I said.

Flourishing a key, he marched to my bedside and unlocked me. Where other guards had stared unabashed, this one would not meet my gaze. Perhaps he had not found it so easy to cast civility aside.

"Out," he said.

It was the first moment when I could have tried to escape. If he hadn't been following quite so closely, I could have slammed the door between us and run. The mere thought of it set my heart to a double time beat. Not that I could have got far.

"What's happening?" I asked.

"Walk," he said, shoving my shoulder in case the instruction had been unclear.

The sun had just set and the windows of the huts were dark, except for the men's hut and one other at the very end of the row.

"I'm to be tried?"

No answer.

"I want to see a lawyer."

"Walk," he said again.

We approached the last hut. He pushed me towards the door. When I climbed the steps he did not follow.

From the outside the hut had looked identical to all the others. But inside it had been furnished as an office with desks instead of beds and box files instead of chamber pots. At the end of the room stood a man wearing a homburg and a long tailed jacket. Even before he turned, I knew him. He was an agent of the International Patent Office and our paths had crossed before.

I spoke his name. "John Farthing."

"Elizabeth."

"If you had something to do with this, I'll–"

"No," he said, cutting in before I could embarrass myself with an impotent threat. "The Patent Office has no jurisdiction here."

"Yet, it's to blame."

He knew what I meant by that and I saw in his expression that my words had stung. It had been an agent of the Patent Office who had accepted a bribe and set in train my family's bankruptcy and my own indentured servitude to a lecherous aristocrat. But for that man, I would not be living in exile.

"I've offered before to help you seek justice," he said. "I could still try."

"We both know it wouldn't work."

"If you change your mind, all you have to do is send word. I'm based at the High Pavement office in Nottingham. They'll always know how to contact me."

He sat down and gestured to the chair opposite. "Please."

"I'd rather stand," I said. "It's a luxury – being unchained."

Discomforted, he got to his feet again.

"How did you find me here so quickly?" I asked.

"Your name is on a list. Any legal action concerning you and I'm informed."

"*You* are informed?"

"Is there anything you need? Anything I can get for you?"

"Why am I on a watch list? I thought you were done with me."

"Must you be like this every time we meet?"

"Why am I on your list?"

"You ask that now?"

"It might be our last chance to talk. Once the treaty's signed, I'll be shipped off to the Kingdom. I might be rather busy after that. The Duke will have special work for me, don't you think?"

John Farthing slammed his palm against the desk making the lamp jump. "Enough!" I had never seen him so angry. But just as quickly, he had his emotion bottled and corked. "If there was anything I could do. Anything..."

"Then why are you here?"

"I want you fairly treated. Are they feeding you?"

"Bread and water."

"This we can change. There should be fruit or vegetables at least. I'll speak to the commander. Do you have enough warmth? Can I bring you anything?"

"A set of lock picks?"

"You are proud, Elizabeth. Do you think yourself so well provided that you can throw back in my face all kindness?"

He didn't deserve my taunts. In part of my mind, I knew that. He was a man who would always do his duty. He had helped me in the past – when my needs had run in parallel with his narrow loyalty. But he was first and last a servant of the Patent Office, an institution I detested.

I knew no way of letting go my anger. And thus our meetings seemed always to run this way. Yet once it was over, I would be led back to the hut and chained. I massaged my left wrist where the shackle had left a bruise.

I lifted my foot and flexed it. An idea began to form.

"Would you turn your back for a moment?" I asked.

"I'd happily see you escape. But there are guards outside. Not that I doubt your capacity. But–"

"I'm not going to run," I said. "I just want to adjust my underwear. There is no privacy when I'm with the others."

"Oh. I'm... I'm sorry. I thought..."

"I can trust you not to look?"

"Of course." He turned to face the window.

Choosing a chair near the wall, where I would not be seen from outside, I sat and began unlacing my boots.

Agents of the Patent Office were sworn to poverty and celibacy. Detached from loves and possessions, they were supposed to exercise their powers with priest-like detachment. Bawdy cartoons and music hall jokes told a different story. But John Farthing, I judged to be without feelings in those areas. He might tell lies in the course of his work. But he would not sneak a look at a lady undressing.

"Thank you for visiting me," I said, slipping off my boots and lifting my skirt and petticoat.

"Thank you for... for agreeing to see me," he said, somewhat flustered by the situation.

"I do appreciate your concern."

"It's good to hear that."

I unrolled my right stocking and stretched the bare leg out in front of me, working the foot up and down, feeling the Achilles tendon moving out and in.

"Why does the Patent Office still watch me?" I asked.

"It's... nothing. Nothing to concern you." Still that fluster in his voice. He was hiding something – and with an uncharacteristic lack of finesse. "The case of Florence May... it's yet to be closed. That is all."

I peeled my left stocking half way down leaving my thigh bare but two layers over my lower leg. Then I doubled it again so that my calf and ankle were loosely covered by four layers of material.

"I saw her hanged," I said, trying not to let the horror of that day into my mind. For I needed to have my wits sharp.

"There was uhm... in Florence May's possession... an item that remains undiscovered," he said.

"A machine?"

"An artefact. It was in... that is to say, it belonged to... to her father. We cannot close the case until it's recovered."

I pulled the stocking from my right leg up over the layers of stocking that now covered my left ankle, and then up all the way to my thigh. Thus it held the bunched material tight.

"Two patent crimes in the same family?" I asked, testing my freedom of movement by stretching the foot up and down again.

"A... a coincidence."

"What artefact?"

"I can't say."

"Can't or won't?"

"It's not for you to question me." His voice was strained.

"But a coincidence? You trust coincidences? Two patent crimes in one household?"

"It's not so strange," he said. "Not from a bullet-catcher. The only people more trouble are alchemists."

Trouble. As the daughter of bullet-catchers, that is what I would always be in the eyes of the Patent Office.

I had my boots on, and was lacing the left one carefully to hide the bottom of my artificially thickened ankle.

"May I look now?" he asked.

I stood and brushed down my skirts. "Yes."

He turned, but kept his gaze lowered. First the young guard had not met my eyes. Now it was John Farthing. Good, I thought. Let them feel shame for what they have done.

"This is goodbye then," I said, and stepped towards him, hand extended.

He took it and at last looked at me straight. The intensity in his expression took me aback. "Goodbye, Elizabeth," he said.

It was as I turned to go that I caught sight of myself reflected in the black mirror of the window. And behind me, a perfect reflection of the chair in which I had been adjusting my stockings.

I turned and marched to the door.

The young constable was waiting for me outside. We marched back in the light of a thin moon. Somewhere in the forest an owl shrieked.

John Farthing had been watching me. He had seen everything – my preparation to escape, my stockings, my bare thighs. In the darkness, I blushed with anger.

The constable pushed me up the steps into the women's hut, where the lamp had been turned low. One of the women put a finger to her lips. The children were asleep.

"Arm," instructed the constable.

"My wrist's sore," I whispered, pulling back my cuff to show the bruise.

"Other hand then."

"Can't you put it on my ankle?"

He looked down. I saw him swallow. No rules covered this, I guessed. Under the uniform, he was a young man. Not waiting for his answer, I sat on the edge of the bed and lifted my skirt a few inches, making sure to keep my bare right leg out of his view.

He knelt. "Thank you," I whispered. Then even quieter: "Please look away as you put it on."

He did so. I felt his hand encircling my padded ankle and the pressure of his shoulder against my knee. I flexed my foot, making the tendon stand. The iron clipped into place. Then he was out of the hut, as fast as he could move without running.

Tulip gave me a look that said she knew I was up to something. But it wasn't until the lamp was out and the sounds of sleep breathing could be heard on either side of us that she reached across the gap between the beds and touched me on the shoulder.

I shifted my head closer to hers.

"Seducing the guards?" she whispered.

I pulled back the blanket to reveal my leg. I had already worked the two stockings off from under the iron, which consequently hung loose. But not loose enough to slip over the heel. I held up the bunched stockings so that a splash of moonlight touched them. Tulip nodded slowly as understanding came to her.

From under the bed, I took the remains of the butter, now fluffy with dust. She watched as I greased the skin then started trying to slip the shackle. It slid, becoming tighter the closer it got to the heel. The more I pushed the harder the other side of the metal loop pressed into the top of my foot. When I could no longer bear the pain I pulled it back onto my ankle, tears pricking at the corners of my eyes.

I lay back, breathing hard.

Tulip slipped out of her bed and knelt next to me. "You were almost there," she breathed.

I shook my head.

"How much do you want to escape?"

She pulled the nearest jug across the floorboards. I watched as she half-filled a wash bowl. Then gently, ever so gently, she guided my foot into the water.

I gasped at the sudden cold.

She shuffled back to the head of the bed. "Your foot's swollen," she whispered. "Wait now. It'll go down."

I closed my eyes. "Even if this works, I can't get you out."

"I know," she said.

"I'm sorry."

"I've always been going back. To the Kingdom, I mean."

"But if you could run?"

"Some things you can't escape." Then, after a silence, she added: "I thought we were all rogues. All us exiles. What did that lawyer Romero call us? Thieves and murderers? I was going to tell you why I'm here. But then you told me your story and I was ashamed."

"It doesn't matter what you did."

"Are you religious?" she asked.

"I don't know. I've never had the time to think about it much."

"Some people believe that if you're sorry enough, everything you did before gets wiped clean. All you have to do is confess and that's it. But what if you're not sorry? What then?"

She did not wait for me to answer, but turned her attention back to my foot, which had started to ache from the cold. She lifted it out of the water and slid her fingers over the skin, which was still slick with butter. I felt her working the shackle towards the heel until it started to hurt.

"Put the blanket in your mouth," she whispered. "Bite down."

She watched me do it. Then hard and sudden she pulled the shackle. Pain sliced through me. I squeezed my eyelids closed till lights shot across the blackness. She pulled again, harder this time. I tried not to cry out. Then my foot was back in the water and Tulip was rubbing the skin, causing new jabs of pain with every touch.

I spat out the blanket and dragged air into my lungs. Then I opened my eyes and looked. The water in the bowl was dark, as if ink had been poured into it. I blinked, trying to clear the tears from my eyes. Blood welled from the top of my foot. Tulip was holding something up for me to see. It was the shackle.

CHAPTER 12

Control the light and you control the shadow. Place
your illusion in one and your trick in the other.

THE BULLET-CATCHER'S HANDBOOK

There is no misdirection more fully compelling than
a lock. The escapist in the Circus of Wonders taught
me that. He showed me a trunk he used on stage and
asked me how I thought he could get out of it. The
padlock was huge to me, just a child, and heavy. It
filled both my hands. I pulled on it, leaning back with
all my weight. Only after I had given up did he show
me the secret. Smiling, he tipped the trunk on its side.
The base hinged inwards like a door. It was no prison
at all.

Having bunched my blankets so that it seemed a
person might be lying in the bed, I took Tulip's hand
and kissed it. She touched my cheek then gestured
towards the door.

There was no lock. There was no guard.

I limped down the steps and followed the inky
shadow of the huts all the way to the edge of the

camp. Once in the trees it was too dark to see the ground and I had to feel my way.

Tulip had torn a strip from the sheet to use as a bandage. It cushioned the pressure of my boot against the wound. But every time I flexed my ankle, pain like a needle of ice stabbed through the throbbing ache. Every time I stumbled, I had to stifle a cry.

Money and spare clothes were at the wharf, together with my gun and the means of disguise. I reckoned there to be seven hours before dawn. Then perhaps another hour after that until a constable carried breakfast to the hut and found me gone. Even at a slow walk, my boat was in range.

Unless John Farthing decided to intervene. He had watched my preparation to escape, shame putting a stopper in his usual eloquence. I had no means to judge whether he would report what he had seen. Now more than ever, I needed a clear head, but when I thought of him my mind clouded with anger.

At last, I found my way out of the thickest part of the woods and was able to make out the line of a path. Soon I came to a road with fields to either side. There was a hill to my right. Recognising its profile against the starry sky, I reckoned the village of Cropston must lie ahead. After that would be Anstey and after that again, the suburbs of North Leicester and the wharf that had been my home.

But having walked less than a mile, I was limping so badly that I had to stop and lie in the verge with my boot loosened. Blood had soaked into the leather and the laces were sticky to touch. When I stood again, the pain was sharper than ever. I hobbled on for another

but the hour was early and the wharf still deserted. I stepped off the path and into the grass so that my footsteps would be silent.

Drawing level with Bessie, I crouched low to look in through a cabin porthole. I could see nothing but my own reflection, which was that of a wild woman. My hair hung in rats tails. My boot leather might have been too dark to show the blood but somehow my sleeve and the side of my face were streaked with it. No wonder the boy had been afraid.

The crude Kingdom flag was still gummed to the inside of the glass.

Climbing onto Bessie's deck I saw that the hatch had been forced – the hasp ripped free leaving splintered wood behind. My pursuers had beaten me home. They could have left already. But they could also be hidden inside, waiting for my return. I stepped back onto the towpath, trying not to let my movement disturb the stillness of the boat.

"Elizabeth!"

It was Mrs Simmonds, the wharf keeper's wife. She looked down at me from the top of the embankment, her mouth hanging open in shock. Then she glanced around. For a horrifying moment I thought she was going to call for the police. But then she put a finger to her lips and beckoned.

When she got me inside her house and closed the door, she did something entirely out of character – that woman who pried unwontedly into my affairs, that old gossip, that meddler. She enfolded me in a hug.

I was so taken aback that I burst into tears.

•••

I could not stay at the wharf. Indeed, that had not been my plan, though for an hour as the Simmondses had fed me and painted my wounded foot with iodine, I had allowed myself to think otherwise. But someone had given me away to the constables – else I would not have been found at the library that day. The only people who knew where I had gone were my neighbours. Nothing on the wharf remained secret for long. Every hour increased the danger to my friends.

Mrs Simmonds filled the tin bath from the copper. Then she took my clothes one by one as I stripped, holding them well away from herself as she carried them to the sink. I watched her spooning salt into a basin of cold water for my blood-stained blouse.

When I was down to my chemise she averted her eyes.

"The soap is lavender scented," she said in a house-proud tone that made me smile despite my desperate circumstances. "Wash and then sleep. The bedroom is upstairs."

When she had gone, I shed my innermost layer and stepped naked into the bath. The sensation was indescribably wonderful. I had heard of the pleasures of lying with a man, but at that moment it seemed to me they could never compare to the sensation of being enfolded in the arms of steaming water.

A small bundle of letters had arrived during my absence. With the hot water doing its work on my aching body, I dabbed my hands dry and began sorting them. The first was a demand from the lawyer, Yan Romero. I had been to the meeting in the Secular Hall. I now needed to make good with payment of ten guineas. I scrunched the paper in my hand and tossed it to the scullery floor. The second letter was from a man whose son had gone missing two years back. All hope had been abandoned but he had received report of a sighting of the boy living like a wild animal on the street. Could my brother be commissioned on a pay-by-results basis? It was not through heartlessness that I crumpled that letter and sent it to join Romero's. The hope of a parent is sustained long beyond reason.

The final letter was addressed in Julia's hand.

Dear Elizabeth,

Today I met with the lawyer of the boatmen who transport the ice, and also with the lawyers of the warehouse in which the ice is stored. They are each as bad as the other! Indeed, they both claimed in different ways that others were at fault. I have no recourse but to follow your advice. As soon as can be arranged, I will depart for Ashbourne, which they call the Gateway to the Peaks. There I must meet a guide, for the ice farmers' homes are of necessity remote. I travel without chaperone. Whatever happens, please do not tell mother.

Having dried myself, I slipped into a borrowed nightgown and towel-turbaned my hair. Writing paper, pen and ink had been left out for me as requested. I pulled back the lace cuffs for fear of smudging them and then scratched out a hurried reply.

Dear Julia,

The ice farmers, boatmen and warehouse must surely keep records. An innocent man will not

withhold his accounts. Are they kept in ledgers? Can
pages be removed and replaced? Is the handwriting
the same throughout?

It is ever thus – when clients have eliminated the
obvious and whatever remains seems impossible, they
call on the intelligence gatherer for help. We are left
to sift the fine detail for the inconsequential. Therein
the devil hides.

Having climbed the stairs as directed, I entered the
bedroom, a place of chintz and porcelain figurines, a
boudoir with no hint of Mr Simmonds.

The room being warm, I lay on top of the covers.
In any case, it did not seem right to get into their bed.
Though I had been on the move all through the night, I
held no hope of finding sleep. It was mid-morning and
bright. My stomach was busy digesting a breakfast of
bacon, eggs and strong tea. Thoughts shuttled through
my mind like receipts through a department store.

I closed my eyes to rest from the sunlight that
streamed through the net curtains. Just for a moment,
I thought, then I would open them again and start to
focus on the problem of hiding.

When I did open my eyes it was dark. For a moment
I could not remember where I was. Then the sound
that had woken me repeated and I sat bolt upright – a
fist hammering on a wooden door.

"Open in the name of the law!"

Mrs Simmonds answered from the hallway below,
her voice high pitched with alarm. "How can I know
you're a constable?"

More hammering.

I was off the bed like a dog out of a trap, feeling a stab of pain from the forgotten wound as my left foot touched the ground.

"My husband isn't home. I can't let you in."

"You'll open the door or we'll break it down!"

There was nowhere in the bedroom to hide. I grabbed the towel, which had worked loose from my hair, and half ran down the stairs, using the banister rail to help support my weight. Mrs Simmonds pleaded to me with her eyes. I could see a light moving through the dimpled glass of the window in the back door. A man with a lantern. There was steam in the scullery. My wet clothes lay piled in the tin bath, waiting for the mangle. There were not enough of them to hide below.

"This is your last warning."

The banging on the door was even louder.

"Wait," squeaked Mrs Simmonds. "I'll fetch the key."

I opened the door to the coal store, lifted the nightgown and climbed inside. Then I closed the door behind me and started excavating a hollow in the heap of anthracite.

The front door slammed open with a boom. "Out of the way!" Heavy feet pounded up the stairs. Cupboard doors opened and slammed.

Lying in the black hollow in the windowless room, I started burying myself, lump by lump. I could taste coal dust. I had not finished when the door swung open. For a second, the light flooded in. I froze – face half turned towards the side. Then the door slammed and I was in blackness again.

While the search was going on, Mr Simmonds returned to the cottage with Julia's father. I could hear them remonstrating with the officer in charge. At last it was done and nothing had been found.

"I'm sorry, sir. And ma'am," the constable said. "But there've been sightings. The fugitive's a Royalist so we have to take it serious. If you see her, you must contact us." And then after a pause: "It's prison for harbouring a fugitive... you know that? And worse for a Royalist spy."

The door slammed closed.

I waited.

"Where is she?" asked Mr Swain in a low voice.

"Elizabeth?" That was Mrs Simmonds calling in a half-whisper. "I thought she was downstairs."

Lumps of coal clinked against each other as I sat up. The door opened and I saw the three of them staring in. All their mouths fell open at the sight of me.

"Hello, my dear," said Julia's father.

"Oh my," said Mrs Simmonds. "I think you'll need another bath."

Later, when the house was back in order and I was clean again, I joined Mr and Mrs Simmonds and Mr Swain who were waiting in the living room. They all watched as I seated myself.

"I can't stay here," I said.

Relief spread over Mrs Simmonds' face.

"Then you shall come to our house," said Mr Swain. "There's space in the attic. I can build a bed for you. There are no windows, but by that same token you can have lamps and no one outside will see."

Mr Simmonds nodded, but I could see his anxiety.

"I can't walk yet, but as soon as I can, I'll be away. The swelling's starting to go down. I can move my ankle already."

"Where will you go?" asked Mr Simmonds.

"If you don't know, you won't be called on to lie."

"Is there anything we can do?"

"You've done too much already. I feel guilty to ask..."

"Ask anything," said Mrs Simmonds.

"I need to borrow your husband. And Mr Swain also."

I watched from a hidden place at the top of the embankment as the two men used boathooks and a towrope to manoeuvre Bessie away from the quay, then along the cut and into the boathouse. Though they both lived on land, they did not bump her once.

I slipped in after them before they closed the boathouse doors.

"She'll be safe here," said Mr Simmonds.

"Thank you. But I was going to ask if you thought, while she was here, you might... mend the engine."

Mr Simmonds sucked his teeth. Mr Swain stroked his chin. Neither spoke.

"You've each spoken of it in the past – how good it would be to see her on the move again."

"They say she was a fine sight," said Mr Swain. "And I've seen a photograph from when she carried the post. Her paddles frothed the water to buttermilk. But to fix the engine... I'd have loved to see her running. But it's been… how many years?"

"Too many," grunted Mr Simmonds.

"A boat sitting idle that long. You can't expect it to be easy."

"You said her engine had been left well-greased," I said.

"Metal is metal," said Mr Simmonds.

"I have money. Not a fortune. But if parts were needed… My purpose would be to steam away and hide among the waterways. She'd need to be disguised as a working boat. Perhaps it's too difficult?"

Mr Swain steepled his fingers "Well, having a look could do no harm. Was she built in the Kingdom or the Republic do you suppose?"

"Kingdom," said Mr Simmonds. "I'll get the Imperial spanners."

Smoothing my skirt under my knees, I knelt by the hatch in the floor. Then bending low, I reached in shoulder-deep and felt underneath the axle to grasp my father's flintlock pistol. It was the only possession that still connected me to my family. The emblem of a leaping hare on the stock had been fashioned from inlaid turquoise. I laid it next to me and reached below the floor again to retrieve a cloth purse. I had gained two hundred Guineas through the sale of a jewel-inlaid box some months before. Most of that had been spent paying off debts. I weighed the purse in my hand, hearing the last few gold coins chink against each other.

A flicker of movement snapped me from my thoughts. Something dark had passed outside the porthole. I held my breath, listening. There was silence, then the clang of the boathouse door and the sound of the men returning.

Mr Swain lowered a lamp through the access hatch and clonked a spanner against the axle. "Caked with grease," he said.

"Is that bad?" I asked.

Mr Simmonds tutted as he bent low, getting his head and shoulders deep into the hole in the galley floor. He sniffed noisily.

They both got to their feet. Mr Swain brushed invisible dust from the knees of his trousers. Mr Simmonds paced the distance between the access hatch and the galley's aft wall.

Bessie had once been a postal boat. Workers had sorted letters and parcels as she sped through the night. The pigeonholes that lined most of my galley were testament to that past. But the aft section was different. Unlike the fine joinery that characterised most of the fittings, this had been constructed from cheap pine. Painting it over had been one of the first tasks in making the boat habitable.

"What's behind here?" Mr Simmonds asked, rapping his knuckle against the pine boards.

"I think it was a coal bunker," I said.

Mr Simmonds pulled a face that said he disagreed.

Mr Swain had joined him and was running his fingers around the edge of the aft wall. "A crowbar do you think?"

"I'll get one."

I watched through the porthole as the wharf keeper

hurried away. "What's happening?"

"Did you ever wonder why they put the aft hatch on the starboard side of your boat instead of dead centre?" He nodded towards the panel. What drove this fine craft, Elizabeth? What sent it at such speed along the waterways of our nation?"

"Paddles."

"Which were driven by?"

"An engine."

"Indeed, yes. And where do you suppose that engine might reside?"

I looked to the access hatch in the floor. Bessie had been sold to me as a decommissioned hulk. I had vaguely assumed her workings were concealed below my feet. But there must have been a firebox, and that would have had to be accessible. It would also have had to be far away from the precious cargo. A conjuror's daughter should be more interested in hidden things.

"What you see beneath the floor is merely the drive mechanism by which power was transferred to the paddle wheels on either side."

The boat tilted and Mr Simmons clambered back down into the galley. I looked in alarm at the crowbar resting on his shoulder.

"Couldn't find a smaller one," he said.

"This might become a trifle noisy," said Mr Swain. "Perhaps you'd like to wait outside?"

"No," I said, then seeing Mr Simmonds placing the end of the crowbar against the wall, I changed my mind. "Yes. I'd better..."

But it was too late. My words were lost as the

crowbar bit and the wood squealed like an animal in pain. Mr Simmons shifted his body around, bringing the bar level with the aft wall, levering a plank out of position. It crashed to the floor, throwing black dust into the air. A second plank wobbled for a moment then fell after it.

The silence that followed was abrupt. I grabbed a tea towel and held it to cover my nose and mouth. But instead of backing away from the evil looking cloud, Mr Simmonds manoeuvred himself level with the hole he had created, his boots crunching on the debris strewn floor.

He clicked his tongue. "Well, look at that!"

While I stood frozen, trying to comprehend the devastation, Mr Swain stepped forward.

"Oh my goodness," he muttered.

They met each other's gaze for a moment and then turned as one towards me. They seemed excited, I thought, but embarrassed also.

I advanced towards the ruined end wall. At first the men just stood staring, but as I approached they parted to let me through. I had been expecting pipes and pressure gauges, but as my eyes adjusted to the gloom, I saw something so entirely out of place that at first I couldn't resolve it. There, inside the cavity, was the torso and head of a woman leaning forwards, breasts jutting towards the light. The same black dust covered everything, but I could discern a gleam of silver on the shoulder and arm where metal showed through. In scale it was perhaps half life-size, but eerily life-like.

"What's... that?" I whispered. "And what's it doing in my boat?"

"She's an engine," said Mr Swain. "Or rather, an ornamental plate. The engine itself is further back."

"Richmond-Ellis," said Mr Simmonds.

"Who?"

"Not who, but what!" said Mr Swain. "Karl Richmond and Christopher Ellis set up an engine works in Coventry in 1920. They never turned a profit. Went bust... must have been..."

"1931," said Mr Simmonds.

"They ran out of capital in 1931. The uh... statue – that was their emblem. She's called the Spirit of Freedom. Unmistakable really."

Unmistakable was one word for it. The head and shoulders leaned free from a vertical plate but lower down the figure had been rendered almost flat – the narrowing of the waist merely an outline, the navel a crescent pock mark on the metal.

"The point is these engines are rare. And marvellously powerful for their size. And you might not realise, this one's older than your boat. Bessie was built in... What would it have been? 1960?"

"1962," said Mr Simmonds.

"Precisely. So this engine must have been salvaged by someone. And they knew what they were doing, too. Richmond and Ellis weren't great businessmen but no one's matched the workmanship, even today."

"Rare as hen's teeth," said Mr Simmonds. "Got to be fixed."

The grit scrunched under my feet as I stepped back. "She's naked," I said.

Mr Swain's beard hid the colour of his cheeks, but I could see that his neck had reddened above the collar.

"I hope you aren't offended," he said. "She was... that is, it was manufactured in the Kingdom. You know how those Royalists are. Of course you do. What am I thinking? And, well... we admire her from an engineering standpoint."

Offended is exactly how I'd felt. Not because of the nakedness itself – I was content to see my own body or the bodies of other women when I visited the bathhouse. But this thing had been made just so for the gratification of men. And to discover that it had been hidden all these years in my home – my sanctuary.

I shifted my gaze from its breasts to its face. For a moment I was caught by the serene expression. Ridiculously, I found myself waiting for it to blink. Whoever the model had been, she had knowing eyes. I imagined the sculptor positioning her, telling her to lean forwards, push out her chest. No doubt he thought himself master of the sitting. But that half-smile – it told a different story.

"The Spirit of Freedom, you say?"

"We could board it up," said Mr Swain. "That is, if you think it improper."

"No," I said. "She's been in the dark too long."

CHAPTER 14

A young man's eyes are keener, far. But they will never
pierce the illusion that is age itself. For none care to see
what they will become.

THE BULLET-CATCHER'S HANDBOOK

Ice brought down the swelling. Mrs Swain purchased
a block of it. They broke it into pieces which they
wrapped in towels and packed around my foot. For
two days I lay with my leg raised, being fed chicken
soup, which Mrs Simmonds pronounced the most
strengthening of foods.

Occasionally, Mr Swain came to sit by the sofa
where I was obliged to remain. At these times he would
tell me how the work was progressing and school me
on the operation of the engine. He drew diagrams
of the controls, making me memorise the sequence
of operations to start and stop. His fingernails were
blackened from grease and rust.

"You'll make mistakes," he said. "It's more art
than science. But if you keep watch on the boiler
pressure and the water level, you won't go far wrong.
Remember that – always watch the gauges."

Through long hours of waiting, I stared at the ceiling, imagining a journey south. I pictured myself dressed as a man, crossing the border into the Kingdom. Oh the sweet air of those rolling hills. I would ride in comfort along the lanes I had travelled as a child. In my mind, the May blossom was so plentiful that under its weight the branches bowed low. From South Leicestershire I would cross into Northamptonshire, passing Naseby where the old civil war was ended.

Then on via narrower tracks until I could overlook the grand masonry of the stately home wherein lived the Duke of Northampton. It was hard to decide if it would be better to wait in a hedgerow until he passed, or perhaps climb the wall and steal inside to the place where he slept. I pictured it each way, taking time to imagine the moment when I raised my father's gun and shot him in the heart.

I wept as I pictured the scene because I knew it would not happen. My father had given everything to let me escape. Whilst there was a chance of living free, I could not take that step. And there was still one possibility. Julia had offered it to me before she left but I had been too stubborn to accept.

At five in the morning on the third night of my stay, I got up and dressed in my walking skirt and coat. I packed gun, powder and shot, money, clothes and such disguises as would fit into my battered travelling case. Then, without waking my hosts, I slipped from the house and walked away from the wharf that had been my home for five years.

By dawn I had flagged down a dairy boat. Five pence bought me a slow ride to the River Trent.

There I was able to buy some simple food and wait for another boat whose captain would take passengers. I caught my second lift on a barge loaded with Bedford bricks. We chugged up the Derwent to the Link Canal. The sun had long set by the time we arrived in the city of Derby.

"Do you know Upper Wharf Street?" I asked.

The captain nodded.

"Then could you tell me where it is?"

"You'll not be wanting to go," he said.

"Nevertheless – if I did, what direction would I walk?"

He pointed along a street running away from the canal. "That's Wharf Street. Beyond that, Upper Wharf Street. But a girl on her own shouldn't risk it. You don't know the creatures that sleep in the gutters there. Leave it till morning." So saying, he gestured to the cabin of his boat and gave me a smile, unnervingly false.

From his description, it seemed I was close, so I decided to risk it. After fifty paces, I fancied there might be feet following and thought to step back to the boat. But when I listened more closely, there was nothing to be heard but water trickling in an open drain so I pressed on along Wharf Street. However, after five minutes, I was regretting the decision. One amorous boat captain seemed a small risk compared to the various shapes that I could now see moving on the edge of my vision.

Lamps there were, but not one of them lit. Such illumination as there was came from the half moon, which seemed to me like an axe blade. Half of the street lay concealed in inky blackness. Growls and grunts issued from deep doorways. They could have been made by animals, except that I caught the occasional word slipped in among them.

Fatigue burned in my arm, but I lifted the travelling case higher and quickened my step. Here and there, cobbles showed through the mud and filth. Puddles of water reflected the clouds. Stepping into one, my foot had already gone ankle-deep before I realised my mistake and jumped clear.

Ahead, I could make out a warehouse building with a quarter-circle of low steps leading to a curved door at the very corner. A single gas lamp hissed and spluttered above it. A painted sign read:

MRS RAIKE'S CHARITABLE FOUNDATION
Mon–Fri 8am to 6pm

"Pretty girl!"

The sudden shout came from behind a water trough to my left.

I ran the last twenty paces and yanked the bell-pull. The lamp above the door, though feeble, now blinded me to anything beyond its sickly yellow circle.

Unclipping my travelling case, I snatched my father's pistol from inside. The mechanism made a crisp click as I pulled back the hammer full cock. The shuffling of feet beyond the lamplight abruptly died.

But now there was another sound – footsteps approaching from within the building. A scrape of metal on metal – a spy-hole cover being slid. Then three bolts slid one after the other. I half turned, not daring to present my back to the street. The door opened a crack.

A woman stood within, dressed in a nightgown and cap. By the candle lantern in her hand I could make out a great length of grey hair falling forwards over one shoulder.

"Who are you?" she asked.

"Let me in."

"It's after hours. There's no entrance after hours."

"Please."

"It's not allowed."

"I need to see Julia Swain."

This time she hesitated before responding. "I can't discuss our members. You'll have to come back in–"

"There's someone out here!"

"I'm sorry."

"Then I need to see Mrs Raike. Tell her it's Elizabeth Barnabus!"

The woman seemed to be examining me through the crack. Then it closed. Three bolts scraped back into place. Footsteps hurried away.

I pressed my back to the door and tried to peer beyond the gas-light, but found no definition in the darkness. There was a sound though – something scuffing over the cobbles, circling left. Then a figure resolved. It was a man, shambling towards me without lifting his feet. His lips were drawn back like a snarling dog. But his eyes stared blank as if he was not seeing me at all. So compellingly inhuman was his expression that it took me a second to realise he was naked.

"Stay back!"

My shout made no change in his expression.

"Mother!"

The word came grunted from the right hand side, away from the naked man. Movement flickered there on the edge of the black. I swung to face it and raised the gun as if taking aim, my finger pressed to the trigger guard. It was loaded and primed, but a knife would have been more use. With my foot, I slid the travelling case closer to the door.

"Strumpet!"

My aim was wrong entirely. I spun thirty degrees and took aim again, touching the cold metal of the trigger itself. "Step into the light and say that!"

The naked man stood staring at the wall. A string of saliva ran from one side of his mouth. He swiped a hand at the air, as if trying to hit something that was invisible to me.

Through my back, I felt a vibration. Then there were footsteps coming at a run and the scrape of the bolts being drawn. I half-fell backwards into the building. It was the same woman as before. She dragged my case in after me and slammed the door closed. I leant against it as she locked up against whatever those creatures were.

We stood panting, looking at each other. I now saw that her grey hair was flecked with a few strands of black. Her eyes tracked down to the gun in my hand.

"You can have no firearms here."

I was reluctant to give my father's pistol to anyone. But liking even less the thought of stepping back outside, I half-cocked it, pulled back the steel and blew the powder from the pan. The woman seemed alarmed when I held it out for her to take.

"It's safe," I said.

With the lantern raised in one hand and the gun dangling from the other, held between finger and thumb, she led me away from the door along a wide, bare corridor.

"There were men out there," I said.

"Unfortunates."

"Then they're known to you?"

"At this time of night, anyone out there is a lost soul. You shouldn't have come."

"One of them shouted things."

"The asylum is full."

"But the other was worse. His face... it seemed not human."

She did not respond.

"You know these creatures? What's wrong with them?"

"I know that all need food alike. Our kitchens provide. There are many such of late. They've nowhere else to go. Thus they find their way to Upper Wharf Street."

"He was naked."

"We give them shirts and trousers and coats, donated through the generosity of those more fortunate. But some won't abide cloth against the skin. Or don't know what it's for and rip it off. You saw one such creature."

We had passed many doors already, each banded with metal. Some were padlocked, the hasps bolted directly into brick. Whatever had been warehoused here must have been seen as valuable. Or dangerous.

We reached a corner and set off along another stretch.

Though I did want to see my friend, if just for the familiarity of her face, it was Mrs Raike who I hoped would have the power to help me. Julia had mentioned the woman's influence, her access to lawyers and money. My own research had revealed a connection to the Minister of Patents, one of the most powerful men in the Republic. And my suspicions went further.

"Are you taking me to Julia Swain?"

"I can't discuss our members."

"She's my friend. My pupil."

No answer.

"Then am I to see Mrs Raike?"

"She isn't here."

The woman stopped walking so abruptly that I had passed her before realising and had to backtrack. She slid open a concertinaed metal gate and ushered me into a small chamber, panelled with wood. Two ropes ran taut between a hole in the ceiling and one in the floor. It was some kind of elevator. She slid the gate closed, placed gun and lantern by her feet and then began hauling down on one of the ropes. We began to rise to the sound of creaking pulleys.

I could not count the floors we passed, but guessed we had reached the top of the building by the time she took back the lantern and led us outside. This floor was less sparsely furnished. As we walked, the lantern reflected from the glass covers of paintings hanging on the walls. The air smelled different. On the ground floor corridor, carbolic soap had failed to cover the stale smells of boiled bones and cabbage.

Here I detected wood polish and something fainter – a musky scent.

The woman stopped in front of a door.

"What's your name," I asked.

"My name isn't important."

She didn't follow me into the room but closed the door behind me. I took in my new surroundings – a study it seemed. Bookshelves ran from floor to ceiling. A set of library steps on wheels had been parked to one side. Leather armchairs were arranged around a hearth in which no fire burned. Such light as there was came from two wall-mounted gas lamps.

It was with a start that I realised I was not alone.

"Come here," said a woman, who had been sitting stock still in one of the chairs.

Leaving my suitcase by the door, I took the chair opposite her. "Thank you."

"It's not that new arrivals are unwelcome," she said. "But the time of night... I'm sure you understand."

Her hair had not been brushed. I guessed the tea gown she wore to have been pulled on hurriedly over nightwear.

"I gave my name at the door," I said. "But I don't know yours."

"Here, I'm known as Housemistress," she said. "You may call me Ma'am if it sits more easily."

"The tradesmen and professionals you deal with call you this?"

"They do."

Unsettled, I let the question of names lie. "I need to see Julia Swain. I believe she's here."

"You're mistaken."

"Then may I ask where she is?"

"We don't discuss–"

" – your members' business. That's what the other woman told me."

"And yet you ask again."

"I'm her friend. And her teacher. I feel responsible."

"Girls come to serve here for many reasons," the housemistress said. "Not all want it known. To have worked – even in a charitable cause – can damage their prospects of making a good match. You're a Royalist, I believe. It may be hard to understand."

"Being born in the Kingdom doesn't make me a Royalist."

"I've read that south of the border women pride themselves in money-getting."

The tone of her voice made me want to deny it, though it was true enough. I took a breath and looked for some clue to strengthen my position. The woman's hands were folded on her lap. The way they lay would have hidden a wedding ring had she been wearing one. I felt as if I was trying to pry open an oyster with my fingernails.

"Mrs Raike asked for my help," I said. "And my brother's. We were invited."

"Circumstances change."

"Then the case of the ice farmers has been resolved?"

"It has not."

"Mrs Raike was insistent that I come with Julia."

"But now you are sought by the law," the housemistress said. "On the run, isn't that the common term? Did you think the news would not have reached us?"

"I... wasn't trying to deceive you."

"I can give you a choice," she said. "A bed for the night and in the morning we hand you over to the constabulary. Or you may leave now – if you wish to take your chances on the streets."

"You'd be so cold as to do that?"

"What choice have you left us? Do you have any idea the number of our enemies – men and women too – who wish to see us brought low? They'd seize on any scandal to harm us. Didn't you think of the trouble you'd bring by coming to our door?"

"I'd be taken back to the internment camp."

"Very likely."

A game of guesses and long odds had brought me here. On the turn of a wild eight, all the agonies of my escape could come to nothing. But I had no other card to play.

"There'll be an extradition case," I said.

"We're not responsible for your misdemeanours."

"I'll be called to answer for my movements."

"And the court will learn that we behaved impeccably. You're in deep folly if you hope to blackmail us with innuendo."

"It'd be consequence not blackmail," I said. "Under cross-examination, they'd make me say why I came."

Her eyes narrowed.

"Which was to ask why your leader goes under the name Mrs Raike when no such person exists."

I released the words, still not knowing if they were true. The housemistress neither blinked nor flinched. Her expression was one of a tourist to the asylum – sadness and pity.

"I think you'd better go," she said.

"It's a disguise–"

"Enough!" The housemistress pointed to the door, her cheeks colouring with anger.

I stood, feeling as if an iron collar was tightening around my neck. But as I turned to go, a hollow click sounded and a door-sized section of the bookcase swung out. Framed in the new opening stood the aged figure of Mrs Raike.

CHAPTER 15

*The vexed question of woman's suffrage has ever been
the cause of discord. But when put to the test, the
electorate have found no enthusiasm.*

From Revolution

Unlike the housemistress, Mrs Raike showed no
signs of hurried dressing. Her immaculate plaits were
wound and held up under a cream house cap. Her
dress and shawl were the same bombazine that I had
seen in every photograph. I would have called them
widow's weeds – though if she was in mourning the
period must have been indecently long.

I followed her through the opening into a smaller
chamber, insufficiently lit. A single oil lamp rested on
a table carved in the Chinese style. I could make out
comfortable chairs and lace antimacassars. The fire
in the grate crackled reluctantly, suggesting a fresh
shovel of coal on the embers of the previous evening.

Mrs Raike pulled the bookcase door closed and we
were alone. From this side it was wood panelled.

"They told me you weren't here," I said.

"You are excessively determined, Miss Barnabus.

Persistence is a virtue only in moderation."

At the rally in the park, there had been noise and distance between us. But I was now close enough to hear every subtle layer of her voice. There was nothing false about it. And though the neck of her dress was high, it would not have concealed the Adam's apple of a man. My theory had been dashed.

"May I sit?" I asked, trying to process the flood of new information.

She nodded. I chose the chair nearest the fire and watched as she lowered herself into the other one, moving as if her limbs were dry sticks.

"I overheard some of your conversation with the housemistress," she said.

"Overheard?" I glanced at the wood panelling, unable to see a spy hole but certain it would be there – behind one of the hanging pictures perhaps. A secret room is not built without the means to look out unobserved.

"You spoke loudly," she said. "I found myself listening. Forgive me, but you seemed to be saying that I don't exist."

Her tone of voice mocked me. For a moment I forgot the opening of the speech I had prepared.

"Well?" she prompted.

"I... was brought up in a travelling show."

"How singular."

"My father made me disappear. On stage."

Her eyes were boring into me. "A charming story. Though perhaps less than ideal as an upbringing. We run orphanages, did you know that?"

"No."

"Yes. And we feed the destitute, for which we're criticised. We rescue women who have fallen. Girls younger even than you were when you came to the Republic."

It seemed I wasn't the only one to have rehearsed a speech. And her words were having an effect.

"Do you know how I disappeared on stage?" I asked, trying to get back on track but no longer comfortable with the place I was driving towards.

"Would you have those girls sent back to their bawdy houses?" she asked.

"No. Of course. But–"

"Can you imagine what they suffer?"

"But–"

"Then why are you attacking me?"

I took in a deep breath and asked again, with more force: "Do you know how I disappeared on stage?"

No answer.

"I didn't. I was still there. In full view. But disguised. That was my art – appearing to be someone else. I recognise the same art in you."

Her hands gripped the arms of the chair. "Stop!"

But I pressed on. "You *are* in disguise. There *is* no Mrs Raike."

Seconds ticked past. Then her rigid shoulders dropped and I knew a barrier had been crossed.

She stood. As she stepped across to the table, her movements were already changing from a brittle shuffling to the smooth-limbed gait of a woman in her prime. I watched her adjust the lamp, letting out more wick. The flame grew and the room brightened.

"I don't want to harm you," I said.

"Then why have you done this?"

"We can help each other."

"Indeed?"

Her voice was smoother than before. It still had an edge, though its nature seemed different, more dangerous perhaps. It came to me that the only people to have seen me enter the building were some poor insane creatures on the street and the two women from within the organisation who conducted me to this secret room.

She sat back in the chair. "Tell me – who do you think I am?"

"The first time I saw you, I figured you for a man in disguise," I said.

"Ridiculous!"

"I'm sorry. It was from a distance. You were speaking in Abbey Park."

Recollection flickered across her face. "You asked a question."

"Yes."

She nodded. "And now what do you think?"

"Your work divides opinion. You've enemies. Your disguise is to protect a reputation from scandal. I'd thought you were Wallace Jones, Minister of Patents. But now I know you're a woman... I believe you're his wife."

"You're wrong."

"Then his sister."

She acknowledged the truth with an almost imperceptible nod.

"So much makeup can't be comfortable."

I watched as she took off the cap. Then she picked

at her cheek and started peeling away the wrinkled skin, revealing a rosy glow beneath. She must have painted herself with some kind of rubber solution. In moments the false mole was removed. A woman of perhaps thirty-five years sat before me.

"There was no perspiration," I said. "The other women on stage looked set to faint but you weren't even glowing. And the haste with which you left the stage. The mayor was still speaking. I think perhaps it could not have lasted longer."

I wondered what the price of this revelation would be. My gun had been taken. But there was a horn of black powder in the travelling case. I resisted the temptation to glance at it.

"You are not only persistent, Miss Barnabus. Astute also. I wonder if your brother has these qualities in such measure."

"Perhaps," I said. "But what of *your* brother?"

"If my work is loved by some it's loathed by many. As a Councillor he may frame our laws, but he has voters to thank for his position. My supporters are overwhelmingly women. Thus they have no say in the elections."

"You mean he'd be voted out if the truth were known?"

"It's certain. And without the protection that his office allows, this whole enterprise would crumble. Thus I hide."

The more plainly she laid out her situation, the clearer it became that I wouldn't be allowed to leave. The risk I posed to her was greater than anything I had to offer in exchange.

"You hide in full view of the public eye," I said.

"And you hide doubly. The newspapers covered your recent adventure. None of it made sense until I imagined the story turned around with you as the private intelligence gatherer and your brother perhaps helping from the background."

I had made the mistake of projecting my own deception onto her – thinking she was a man in disguise. Now she pictured me with a brother less able.

"We're victims of our sex," I said. "Both of us. We have minds to think but aren't supposed to use them."

"And that means I should help you?"

Her question had a mocking tone. I wondered if she would have the stomach to kill me, or if she intended to lock me away. There would be many secure rooms in a warehouse such as this.

She stiffened as I got to my feet. "Help will come running if I shout," she said.

"I simply want to show you something."

Keeping eye contact, I reached down and unclipped the case. With my right hand, I flourished Julia's letters, a distraction from the work of my left hand. One smooth movement and I was back in the chair, feeling the sharp angles of the powder horn hidden beneath my thigh.

"Letters?" she asked.

"From Julia Swain."

I needed enough smoke and confusion to make my escape. But even if I plunged the horn into the heart of the fire, it might take several seconds to detonate.

"What have Miss Swain's letters to do with me?" she asked.

"They speak of the ice farmers."

The explosion would not kill. I would shout a warning. We could shield ourselves behind the chairs.

"What of the ice farmers?"

"I could still help you solve their case."

I inched my hand from my lap towards my side, ready to grab.

"And in return, you wish me to hide you from the authorities?"

My hand stopped. I had not expected her to take my feeble bargaining position seriously.

"I don't need help in hiding. But your brother is on the Council of Guardians. The treaty isn't signed. He could–"

"He's one minister among many. The treaty can't be stopped."

"It could be... amended," I said. "An amnesty for those who crossed the border before it came into force."

The fire popped and crackled as new flames broke through. We both jumped.

"It wouldn't be easy," she said. "The law change is popular. Forgive me, but Kingdom exiles aren't looked on kindly."

"But you'd try?"

"In return you'd investigate the ice farmers?"

The conversation had taken such an unexpected turn and so quickly that I was certain I had missed something important. "I... that is, yes. The investigation would take me further from the border. That would be a blessing."

"If you'll do that – and no mention of your

connection to me – I will ask my brother to try."

My hand inched away from the powder horn.

That night we made the most insubstantial of bargains. I promised to not reveal her identity. She promised to ask her brother to attempt an amendment of the treaty. And all the while, I tried to understand why the little I had to offer was of value to her.

Money was the only solid thing that passed between us – expenses for my journey. As she took it from the housemistress and signed for its receipt in a ledger, I slipped the powder horn from under my thigh and back into the travelling case. She placed the purse in my hand, reminding me of the promises we had undertaken to honour. Later, I would check them for forgeries.

"There's one more thing," I said, before leaving. Someone's been watching me for the last two weeks – ever since Julia made contact with you. I've caught glimpses of him. Will you now call him off?"

She shook her head. "I know of no such man. If you're being followed, it is nothing to do with me."

CHAPTER 16

There is no such thing as half a bluff.
THE BULLET-CATCHER'S HANDBOOK

Deceptions, like coaches, seldom singly come. Though I had uncovered Mrs Raike's disguise, I could not trust her. There were surely more layers to be peeled back before I knew the whole truth of the woman.

Yet our motives seemed inexplicably in alignment. She wished to avoid a scandal. I certainly did not wish to cause one. She wanted me away from Upper Wharf Street. I wanted to be further from the border and constables who could recognise me as a fugitive. She wanted to have the case of the ice farmers resolved – though I still did not understand the reason. And I wished to see my friend again.

Thus, with a purse of money from the charitable foundation and with my father's pistol returned to me, I set off to Ashbourne, where Julia had gone to gather information on the ice trade. I would help solve the case and Mrs Raike would pull what levers she could. If the extradition treaty was amended, I could be free again. If not, perhaps I could hope that the weight of my knowledge might motivate her to hide me.

The walk to Ashbourne would have taken less than a day unencumbered. But I was hauling a travelling case and my foot had not fully healed. I dared not risk opening the wound again. Neither would I dare the coach station undisguised for fear of the constables, who might well hope to acquire me at such a place.

Fugitives are fated to make slow progress.

Having left the warehouse via a courtyard and a flight of brick steps, I set out in the pre-dawn gloom. Dew beaded the metal railings of the empty street. There were no more animal noises from dark doorways. But once I thought there were footsteps following. And another time, hearing a metallic scrape, I swung my head to see a sewer covering askew that before I hadn't noticed. After that I left the wharves and warehouses behind me. The streets were still shabby but my heart calmed with the lessening of dread.

Presently I found guest houses of the kind where a single woman would be asked no questions on taking a room. There were food stalls on the street outside, selling to men who trudged towards morning shifts. Most of the food looked as filthy as the hands that served it. But needing to eat, I bought two flat loaves griddled before my eyes, over a fire of smashed up furniture. I chose the middle of a row of three guest houses and paid for two nights, though I intended to stay for only a few hours.

The room was unclean, the linen stained and crawling with mites, the lock broken. I hefted the iron bed frame across so that it would stop the door from being opened. Then I settled myself on a wooden chair, injured foot raised on my travelling case.

I supposed it would be impossible to sleep, propped as I was. My mind darted over dark thoughts and suspicions too quickly to dismiss any of them. When fatigue at last won out, I carried those half-formed fears with me into sleep. My dreams were stalked by monsters.

I awoke stiff-necked having slept through most of the day. Motes of dust drifted in the air before my face. In the gloom earlier I hadn't noticed the moth holes that patterned the curtain. But with the evening sun outside, each hole allowed a pencil of light to penetrate the darkened room.

The gas lamp offered but a feeble splutter. Come dusk it would be too dim to work by. So I half drew the curtain and began my transformation while the sun was still over the roofs. Working with the mirror inside the lid of my travelling case, I darkened my skin tone, laying down the gum and fake facial hair that would alter my appearance to that of a young man. I thickened my eyebrows, replaced corset with binding cloth, blouse with shirt, skirt with trousers. I let the flattened top hat pop out on its springs and extended the telescopic walking cane.

In the *Bullet-Catcher's Handbook* it says that of all disguises, expectation is the deepest. It was only eleven hours into the two days for which I had booked the room. Whatever suspicion the landlord entertained as he watched a young man stepping out of the door, it was not that the young woman tenant had chosen to leave. I read the thought behind his smirk – *Under*

that respectable dress she was no better than the others. He
didn't look at the travelling case in my hand.

Ignoring him, I walked out onto the cobbled street,
leaning on my cane to hide the limp as best I could.
I had to force myself to keep my eyes on the road
ahead and not to look back in the give-away manner
of those who fear themselves followed. Paranoia
breeds in the mind when you are on the run. And I, a
double fugitive, running from the law of the Kingdom
and the Republic.

The coach station was silent in the night. A grand
iron framework supported the arch of the high roof.
Underneath ran a wide road. Here, coaches would line
up during the day. It would bustle with the loading
and unloading of such goods and people as could not
afford to travel by air and were in too much of a hurry
to go by boat.

Sheltered under the canopy of the coach station
was a row of squat and functional structures – the
porters' lodge, ticket and overseer's offices, strong
rooms, feed store, pigeon house, news stand, tea shop
and the waiting room in which I would be spending
the night.

The ticket office was empty. I pinged the counter
bell and presently a sleepy young man emerged from
the back and asked if I had read the opening hours.
I slid a tenpence across to him by way of an apology.
Having palmed it with practiced sleight of hand, he
gestured to a plaque on the wall.

Derby Coach Station is recognised for
— excellence in passenger care —

"Timetables aren't everything," he said.

I would have saved Mrs Raike's money, but the 3rd class waiting room would be locked until morning. So I walked away with a 1st class ticket and a copy of the timetable, which told me that the first coach to Ashbourne would leave at half past eight.

The waiting room was warm, though it smelled faintly of sausage. The chairs were clean and comfortable. I chose one furthest from the door and next to a pot-bellied stove. With my back to the wall and my case next to me on the floor, I ate the last of the bread from the street vendor and settled down for a long wait.

With the stillness pressing, my anxieties began to return. In the filthy guest house, troubles had flitted through my mind on dark wings, moving so fast that I had no way to fix onto any of them. But now, fortified by some hours of sleep during the day, I plucked one from the air.

Mrs Jones, sister of Councillor Wallace Jones, was pursuing the rights of women as she saw them. Hers was a distinctly Republican approach – liberation through labour. Let us work as volunteers and our status will rise. That was the argument. Our talents will be recognised and we will enter into a more balanced partnership with men. Mrs Raike was a fiction created to drive the movement forwards and take the criticism, so that her brother could quietly support the same agenda from within government. In secret they were both lobbyist and lobbied.

I instinctively disliked Mrs Raike's sanctimonious displays of virtue. But the illusion itself – its audacity – this I could not help but admire. I knew the ways

of the bullet-catchers. I had been with the greatest
alchemist of the day and seen through his tricks. But
here was a woman who wished to change more than
lead into gold – she had set about the transmutation of
the entire Republic. It was a goal which, had I thought
it possible, I might have shared.

But I did not trust her.

She had claimed to know nothing about a spy on
my trail. This was the thought I kept returning to. For
weeks I had been noticing movements and sounds
where there should have been none. At first I'd put it
down to paranoia. Then, just as I'd begun to entertain
the idea that I was being watched, the constables came
to arrest me. Whoever was following, it seemed they
had lost my trail at that point. But when I returned to
the wharf, I was found again. The flicker of movement
I had glimpsed through Bessie's porthole after she was
moved into the boat house – there was no explanation
for it, but that someone had been outside watching.

Then I had been followed from the canal to the
warehouse on Upper Wharf Street. "The asylum is
full," the woman had said. Poor creatures, she had
called them. I had been too panicked to think clearly
at the time. But it came to me, there had been more
than one shadow following me along the street. When
I disembarked from the boat, before the madness,
there had been the sound of stealthy footsteps.

It was the next step of logic that I'd not been able
to think about until now. Perhaps it had been too
disturbing to entertain. When I walked to the police
house in Syston, I'd heard a noise from the bushes.
And now again, walking to the coach station. But

these times, I was in disguise. If the same person was following me when I walked in the guise of a man, the secret of my double identity had been pierced.

My thoughts were interrupted by the opening of the waiting room door. A man in uniform peered inside. But for the peaked cap, I would have thought him a constable.

"Evening, sir," he said, glancing around the room and sniffing the air.

Without my voice warmed up, I didn't trust myself to speak, so I nodded to return his greeting.

"Where would you be travelling?"

Digging in my jacket pocket, I retrieved my ticket and held it up for him to see.

He stepped across to me, releasing the door to swing back on its spring. It closed with a creak and a thud. I could read his badge now. *Anglo-Scottish Republic – Transport Police*. He bent to examine my ticket.

"Ashbourne, is it?"

I nodded.

"Gateway to the Peaks," he said. "On holiday?"

I pointed to my throat and then my chest. He frowned.

"Recovering from influenza," I whispered. "A rest cure."

He straightened himself. "Anyone been here? A woman on her own, perhaps?"

I shook my head.

"Well, I won't disturb you any longer."

I watched the door creaking closed after he was gone.

•••

The fire shifted in the pot-bellied stove. Outside the waiting room, the station clock ticked laboriously. More distant and fainter still was the sound that every city makes as it breathes, even in sleep.

If I had been tailed from Upper Wharf Street, then the one who followed me must be near. I stood and moved silently to the waiting room door. Through its single glass panel, I could see the wide roadway and the arch of the high roof above it. Two barrels had been left upright next to a small pile of crates on the far side. There wouldn't be space behind for anyone to hide. I shifted my head across to see further around the station, searching for places in which I might have positioned myself to keep watch. If I was tailing someone alone, I would need to take what sleep I could. The question was – where could a person sleep and still be sure the target would not slip away?

I gazed at the ceiling, trying to remember the appearance of the building from the outside. It was single storey, for sure. Flat roofed, I thought, with a low balustrade. That is where I would have gone, perhaps lying with one ear to the ground. A light sleeper might be woken every time the waiting room door thudded closed on its spring.

With great gentleness, I twisted the door handle. The latch clicked, sounding like a gunshot to my ear, though it can have been little louder than the clock ticking. Pulling the door inwards, I propped it open with my travelling case.

Cold night air reached into the room. I held my breath and listened.

Nothing.

If my watcher was up there and awake, he was keeping still and silent. Because the door opened inwards, he would not be able to see it. Indeed, if he wished to avoid giving himself away, he would need to keep his head back from the edge. Or she. Whoever it was had been light footed and probably small.

I counted the seconds by the ticking of the station clock. After five minutes of silence I slipped through the door and began to side-step, following the wall of the building as closely as I dared – for a touch of fabric against brick would be loud enough to give away my plan. At the first corner, I thought I heard something so stopped to listen. The sound was faint and it took me a moment to identify it as a tuneless whistling. I scanned the other side of the station and saw a movement – the transport constable in his peaked cap ambling from the back of the animal feed store. His path would bring him in my direction.

I was around the corner of the building in one quick movement. He would be with me in under a minute. He would want to know why I had left my suitcase propping the door.

Quickly now, I stepped down the side of the waiting room and round behind it. Turning the corner, I saw an iron ladder, fixed to the rear wall.

Aware of the sound of my clothes moving, I started to climb. Two rungs up, I remembered to remove my top hat. There was no one else to see and anyone who had followed me thus far must already know my sex.

Two more rungs and my head was just below the cornice of stonework that projected from the top of the wall. I took a final step, bringing my eyes to the edge. And there crouched a figure with his back to me. He peered out from the front of the building. It was a teenage boy. A ragged coat hung loose from his malnourished frame.

I did not need to see his face to recognise him. His name was Tinker and we had met before.

But the constable would be returning. I was down the ladder in three steps and dashing back towards the waiting room door, knowing the boy would hear. Braking hard, I rounded the final corner in the semblance of a relaxed stroll.

I had misjudged the time. The constable was standing barely two paces away.

"And what," he said, "might you be doing?"

CHAPTER 17

*Wealth flows from the grinding mill of industry. And
from wealth comes refinement. But nothing upsets
the refined quite so badly as the smell from a factory
chimney.*

FROM REVOLUTION

Tinker – a small-framed boy in outsized clothes, self-
orphaned, adrift in a world of men. A year before
he'd been a stable hand on a grand estate in the
Kingdom. His mother had a fondness for drink and
his father was free with the belt. So the boy latched
on to a kinder man. And when that man ran away
to join a travelling show, Tinker followed. It might
have worked out, but Tinker's adopted parent had
been spiralling towards destruction. Thus, for a time,
the boy mistakenly latched onto me. When we said
goodbye, I'd not thought to see him again. But there
he was, on the roof of the waiting room.

In front of me stood the constable, running his
fingers around the peak of his cap. "Well?" he
demanded.

I coughed into my fist, trying to loosen my throat.

"Air," I whispered.

"Air? What?"

I coughed again. "I needed air."

He leaned forwards and peered into my face. Expert though I was, my disguise wouldn't stand the long scrutiny of suspicious eyes. He stepped closer. I tried to get past him and back into the waiting room but he put out his arm to bar my way.

"Let me through."

"Where're you from?"

"North Leicester."

"Whereabouts in North Leicester?"

"Glenfield," I said, picking a pleasant suburb at random.

"And what do you do in Glenfield?"

He was so close now that I could smell his breath and knew who had cooked the sausages in the waiting room. He was tall. Even with the lifts in my boots, I would've had to angle my head upwards to look him in the eye. And that I couldn't do without letting the lamplight shine fully on my face.

I took a step back. He closed the distance again.

"What do you do?" There was iron in his voice.

"Tinker!" I blurted, the word coming too loud from my mouth. Too high pitched.

There was a faint scuffing sound from the roof of the waiting room.

"What did you say?" demanded the constable.

"I tinker," I said, hoping that the boy would understand my message.

"I'm going to have to ask you to open your case, sir."

He gestured towards the waiting room door. An image flashed into my mind – the bloomers and skirts that would expand outwards as the lid lifted.

"Why?"

"We're searching for an escaped prisoner."

"Who?"

"Doesn't matter who. You're behaving in a suspicious manner. I'm an officer of the Transport Police. I–"

"Is he dangerous?"

"It's a she not a he. And yes, she's dangerous. Royalist spy named Elizabeth Barnabus. Now – open – your – case!" He pushed me between my shoulders and I stumbled towards the waiting room door.

It was then that Tinker chose to act. There was a loud thud from above – the stamping of a foot on the flat roof. The constable froze. His eyes darted upwards. I could see the thoughts tumbling over each other in his mind. Then he turned on his heels and sprinted around the building to the back. His boots clanged on the iron ladder.

A sack thumped to the ground next to me, followed directly by Tinker himself, landing cat-like. For a fraction of a second, wide blue eyes shone up at me from a face that would have made a coal miner seem clean. His white teeth flashed in a broad grin.

"Ashbourne," I whispered.

He grabbed the sack and sprinted off down the road.

Seconds later the constable had scrambled down the ladder and was sprinting back around the waiting room. The last I saw, he was pounding away in hot pursuit. Watching him go, I wondered why I'd blurted my destination to Tinker instead of taking the chance to slip away.

The coach rattled along Derby Road towards Ashbourne. Ignoring the other passengers, I peered hungrily through the mud spattered window glass. I was further north than I had ever travelled. Every detail was of interest to me.

The air had sweetened as we left the city. Now, having passed through the rolling countryside for some ten miles, I could again smell the occasional tang of smoke, though more from wood than coal. The shops and houses displayed virtuous modesty, their fronts narrow and understated. Many were built of uneven grey stone instead of terracotta brick. They lacked the resolute order of the city. I liked them more for that. Plainly but expensively dressed women and men were out taking the air. They strolled between tubs of scarlet geraniums, which dotted the roadside. Nature, it seemed, was allowed to flaunt.

I saw but one factory as we rolled through the main street. The sign proclaimed it to be a manufacturer of corsets. The workers around the gates were neatly clothed and clean. The streets grew narrower but there were none of the signs of poverty I had witnessed in the city. Window glass reflected the liquid gold of the morning sun. Even the black painted doors and window frames were bright.

The coachman reined in his horses and we slowed to a stop under a signboard hanging from a gallows-style beam across the road. *The Green Man and Black's Head*

Hotel. The porter carried my case inside. I resented his assumption but still had to pass over a coin for his trouble. Ashbourne was going to be expensive.

At the desk I found myself yet again navigating my own web of deception. I was still presenting the appearance of a young man. This being a very different kind of establishment to the guest house in Derby, I couldn't ask to see the un-chaperoned Julia Swain. Nor had I been given so much money as to be able to make free with it by booking rooms of my own. Instead, I wrote a message on the hotel's notepaper and folded it.

"Miss Julia Swain asked for the address of my children's nanny," I said. "It's for her sister. Could this be given to her?"

The desk clerk pocketed the coin I had passed with the note and said that he would see that it was delivered. I watched as he slipped the paper into one of the rack of pigeon holes behind the counter. Under it was the number 203 and a hook from which no key dangled.

"Thank you," I said. "And may I trouble you to direct me to the rest room?"

He hesitated until I had passed yet more money, then pointed out to the back. It did not matter whether or not he believed the charade. Unseemly conduct was like sewage – everyone knew it existed, but no one wanted to be reminded of the fact. So long as virtue remained plausible, Republican morality would be satisfied.

I picked my way through the bar, empty at that time in the morning, and out to a coach yard. Crates of empty brown bottles were stacked around the outside. A tradesman's entrance took me back into the building. Unseen, I made my way up to the second floor.

Julia opened the door to my knock. On seeing me she seemed temporarily incapable of speech. Her appearance suggested a beached carp rather than a lady detective.

"Let's protect your reputation," I whispered, not waiting for her to unfreeze, but slipping into her room before anyone could happen upon us in the corridor.

"I... I thought... that is..."

I cut her mumbling short by wrapping her in a sisterly embrace, as I'd done a thousand times before. But after a moment she was struggling away from me. "Please change first," she said, blushing. "I'm too taken aback by surprise to greet you properly."

She watched intently as I peeled the false hair from my chin and changed into female attire. She didn't smile until I had wiped away the last of the makeup and was brushing out my hair.

"Better?" I asked.

"I don't think I'll ever grow accustomed to seeing you like that."

"I'm sorry if it offends."

"It's just that when you're dressed as a man the world seems upside down. And you being here – it was a shock. I only received a letter from you this morning – and that postmarked North Leicester."

"Events," I said, "have overtaken me."

She sat and listened as I related the trials that had beset me since we parted. The colour drained from her usually rosy cheeks as I described my internment and escape. I chose not to dwell on the brutal details.

"Will they come looking for you?" she asked, alarmed.

"They don't know to look for me this far north."

"They shall not have you!"

"If by force of indignation they could be stopped, you'd have saved me already."

She smiled at that. "And what of Mrs Raike?"

"What of her?"

"She told you where to find me."

"Yes."

"And anything else?"

I didn't fancy my chances of keeping Mrs Raike's secret without Julia realising I was holding something back. So I said: "There's something I can't tell you."

Her expression clouded. "Explain."

"What did Mrs Raike say when she sent you here?"

"That I should talk to the ice farmers. But not to use her name. Discretion is the watchword, she said. But you're avoiding the point!"

"I once promised you openness," I said. "But now another promise holds me back."

"What can't you tell me?" she asked, before seeing the illogicality of her words. "I mean what manner of thing?"

"It regards Mrs Raike..."

"But now you've met her, surely your misgivings are gone."

"I'm more convinced of her sincerity," I admitted. "But she told me something in strict confidence. Would you have me betray her trust?"

Julia got up and started pacing in the way she did after an argument with her mother. I braced myself for some expression of anger or frustration. But after two times back and forth across the room, the frown left her face and her shoulders relaxed.

"I'm hungry," she said.

"Oh."

"There's a tea shop across the road. They do scones with cream and jam."

"That sounds lovely."

Nothing more was said on the matter of Mrs Raike. Not that day.

The thing that infuriated me about Julia was the absence of nuance in her thinking. A statement could be true or false. A person good or bad. Though I'd taught her for two years, she still had trouble comprehending that the world of the intelligence gatherer is coloured in indistinguishable shades of grey. The morals and motives of crime and deception can't be resolved through arithmetic.

But certainty cultivates contentment. Though she often missed the subtlety of things, her attitude gifted her with a marvellous ability to divide wakefulness from sleep. Seconds after I had turned off the gas and plunged the room into darkness, her breathing became deep and regular.

"Julia?" I whispered.

But she was gone.

I lay, looking at the line of moonlight on the wall. Julia was happy. So should I have been. For once, I was well fed and warm. She had presented me as her cousin, unexpectedly arrived, and the hotel had provided a cot bed for me to sleep on. Though lumpy where wooden slats pressed through the thin mattress, it was luxury by the standards of my recent experience.

Circumstances had taken a turn for the better. I had escaped and was safe for the time being. They would never think to look for me in Ashbourne. Julia was content to not know a secret and Mrs Raike would lobby for my cause.

The mystery of the figure that had been following me was resolved – insofar as I had discovered his identity. It seemed that Tinker was still focussed on me after our adventures a few months before. In his chaotic world, he had mistaken me for a substitute parent. His was an unhappy knack of betting on the wrong horse. The question of why he'd not revealed himself had been tumbling in my mind. Possibly he feared that I would send him away. Yet whilst he hid close, he could believe there was hope of me taking him in.

And then I had made a mistake. Without thinking, I had let him know that I was travelling to Ashbourne. He would surely try to follow. But with my life lurching from one disaster to the next, he was a responsibility I could not accept.

Slipping out of the bed, I padded to the window. Under moonlight, the rear courtyard appeared like a woodcut illustration. I vainly tried to pierce the shadows, searching for a boy in a ragged coat, hoping he would not be there.

•••

When I awoke it was already daylight outside. Julia was gone and her bed made. I found a tray with half a rack of cold toast, butter, chunky marmalade and a cup of tea, also cold. A considerable number of crumbs and a used butter knife told a story.

Not having felt properly clean since leaving the wharf, I filled the basin, stripped and washed vigorously with flannel and soap. By the time Julia returned, I had dressed and breakfasted and was sitting in the sunshine by the window.

I could tell from the fast beat of her approaching footsteps that something had alarmed or excited her. Once inside, she stood with her back pressed against the closed door.

"We must leave," she said.

"What's happened?"

"Pack now. I'll pay the bill."

"What has happened?"

"I... I went to send a report to Mrs Raike. In the post office there's a wall pinned with official notices. And... a picture of you. I nearly fainted."

"Someone who looked like me, perhaps?"

"Your name was on it. Printed. I didn't want to stare, but I did. I couldn't help myself. I really couldn't. And now I think maybe I was seen staring. And if I was seen–"

"Julia, for heaven's sake, slow down."

"We must go. We must leave as quickly as–"

"What did the notice say?" I spoke slowly and firmly.

"Elizabeth Barnabus. Wanted fugitive. One hundred guineas reward for information leading to her apprehension."

"One hundred!"

"And four hundred guineas for her capture and extradition to the Kingdom of England and Southern Wales. Claimants will be required to provide proof of their contribution, witnessed by public notary. The sum to be paid by his grace the Duke of Northampton."

I felt my heart constrict. I watched Julia rush to her travelling case and then away to the dressing table and then back to the case without having picked up any of her things.

For one hundred guineas, I understood why the transport constable in Derby was so focussed in his search. But four hundred would transform the life of a working man. Everyone seeing the notice would dream it might be them to claim the prize.

"Was it a good likeness?"

Julia stopped, mid-stride, her hands full of brushes and tooth whitening powder. "Not a photograph. Yet not unlike."

"Was it the image itself or my name that made you stare?"

"I... can't say. But once I looked closer, I saw clearly it was you. There was a description also. Your height. Your eyes."

"What about my hair?"

"I can't recall. Black, it must have said."

"Long or short?"

"The picture showed it long but I can't remember the words."

"Then put down those things and help me plait it. We'll pin it up. And while we do that, think of the clothes in the picture, and the hat. All the details we can change. And then I will go."

"We," said Julia. "You'll not be going alone."

"There are penalties for harbouring a fugitive."

But her face was set and I knew her mind would be also.

CHAPTER 18

Wink to one who has come to see a trick. But never let
the winkbe seen by those who have come to see magic.

FROM REVOLUTION

The Circus of Wonders was a paradise for a child
who liked to play dress up. There were wagons full
of clothes, hats and shoes – anything and everything
that would show brightly in the limelight. There were
belly-dancer's veils and paste jewellery and skirts with
little mirrors sewn in and wigs of natural colours as
well as colours that nature did not intend. Under the
tabernacle of the big top, all excess was benediction.

But when Julia returned to the hotel room and
unwrapped the package she had brought, I discovered
that the wig maker's art in the Republic was somewhat
different.

She said: "I told them you tried to cut your own
hair and had an accident."

"You did tell them my hair was red?"

That had been the idea – to change my colour
to something conspicuously different from the
description on the wanted notice.

"They don't do red."

"Are there no red headed people in Ashbourne?"

"He said they're not 'that kind' of wig maker. And there was something about 'proud colours' and modesty. It seemed he was insulted that I'd asked. This one was the lightest tone they had."

I took it out of the box and stepped to the window the better to see. The hair was a light mousy brown and would hang to the shoulder.

"He had longer ones, but it would have been too expensive."

For a moment I wondered where blonde and auburn women in the Republic went if they wanted to raise money by selling their hair. There would always be willing buyers in the Kingdom. The more striking the colour, the more they would pay. I had never considered it before, but there must be people who earned a living trading 'modest' hair north and 'immodest' hair south.

"Will it do?" Julia asked.

I placed it on my head, deliberately askew and pulled a face. "Do you recognise me?"

She giggled, but it seemed more from nerves than happiness.

The staff of the Green Man and Black's Head had already seen the natural colour of my hair. If I were to venture out with my new wig, it would surely raise their suspicions. Thus, I had to hope they wouldn't go to the postal office and see the wanted poster.

I was obliged to remain closeted in the room all through the day whilst Julia went to buy food and make arrangements. Guides would be needed for our journey up into the world of the ice farmers in the Peak District. Julia had been waiting for them when I arrived in Ashbourne. Each day she had been told they would come the next. But now she dispatched a more strongly worded message, telling them she could delay no longer.

One more loose end remained to be tied. That was Tinker. I had said goodbye to him the previous year, assuming he would go back and resume his place among the wagons of the travelling show, which was still touring despite the disruption it had suffered. He had not been my responsibility. But Tinker was far beyond the conventions of society. That made his actions unpredictable. Unwontedly, he had attached himself to me.

The coal boatman's wife had told me of food being stolen from the wharf. It had been going on for months, she said. It was now clear to me that Tinker had been the thief – stealing to eat. He had feared discovery by me, so had avoided taking from my boat. But his actions had pointed the suspicions of the community in my direction. When I left, he must have left also. The thefts would have stopped, confirming suspicions that I was a Royalist ne'er-do-well and better gone than living among them.

I wondered where the boy had slept during his vigil. There were places enough to bed down unseen along the far bank of the canal. But he couldn't have survived January without warmth. It had been bitter. Mr Simmonds kept a stove burning to stop the water in the boathouse from freezing. Tinker could easily have found his way in there.

Things would be different for him now. He knew
I had seen him in the Derby Coach Station. I had
spoken his name. Having followed me so far, he
would surely have travelled on to Ashbourne. But
secrecy is a hard habit to break. Even if he had found
his way to the Green Man and Black's Head, I didn't
think he would try to make contact. I imagined him
hiding somewhere outside, keeping watch.

The fugitive poster meant that I was going to have
to disappear again. Tinker had once seen through my
full disguise and not even broken step. That a woman
should dress as a man and do a man's work seemed no
stranger to him than any other part of his chaotic life.
A simple wig was never going to fool him. If I didn't
do something, he would continue to trail behind me.
And that would leave us both vulnerable.

The sun had set and the small town grown quiet. After
a day indoors, I was itching to walk under the stars.
I pulled the curtain aside and peered out at the rear
courtyard of the hotel two floors below. There was
no prospect of seeing Tinker. But if he was keeping
watch, he would certainly see me.

Turning down the lights, I headed out.

Night hides a multitude of indiscretions. But any
watcher would have had no doubt that I was leaving.
The most revealing detail would have been my travel-
battered case – proof of identification, had they
known me.

Across the yard, past a stack of barrels, then out
towards the road at the front. There would be no

looking back – such a gesture might scare away one following. Then a brisk march away into the night.

Three seconds passed. Then Tinker emerged from his hiding place. Not stealing from behind the crates as I had anticipated, but dropping down from the slant roof of the privy. More like an animal than a boy.

That is when I stepped out of my own hiding place – the shadowed doorway of the tradesman's entrance. He froze, confused. I didn't wait for him to think it through – to understand that the woman he had seen dressed in my clothes carrying my case was in fact Julia, that he had been tricked into revealing himself. His head flicked from one side to the other. I launched myself across the space between us. I saw his shoulder drop and knew he was about to spin and run.

"Tinker! Stop!"

He hesitated. It was enough. I had his arm. He stepped back, taking me with him. He wriggled and squirmed trying to get free. I tightened my grip. He twisted and threw all his weight to the left almost pulling me off my feet.

"It's me," I hissed.

Another slight hesitation betrayed his uncertainty.

"I've got something for you."

He tugged once more at my grip. Then the tension went out of his muscles and he flopped to the floor. I laid his arm down on his lap then slowly let go. The black of his eyes reflected the light from the hotel windows. I brought my other hand forwards so that he could see what I held – an apple. It was hard to buy an apple in spring. I'd tried three shops with no success. Having almost given up, I asked at the front desk of the hotel. The clerk said that his brother had a few left, packed in a barrel of straw. I paid three times what the price should have been. The skin was wrinkly and slick with wax. But the apple was still good.

I held it close to Tinker's nose. I saw him inhale.

"It's for you," I said.

He took it and sat up, leaning his back against the brick wall of the privy. He held it in both hands close to his nose. He filled his lungs with the smell of it. I knew he wouldn't eat it. The last one I had given him – which had won his misplaced loyalty – he had carried like a talisman. The knowledge of the gift had been more precious to him than the taste.

"It's good to see you," I said.

"You tricked me." He mumbled the words into the apple.

"It was the only way. You're too good at hiding."

His white teeth flashed in a grin.

"Now," I said. "We'd better get some food into you."

We sneaked him in via the back stairs. He wasn't keen and seemed to mistrust everything about being indoors, placing his feet as if he expected the carpeted floor to give way at any moment. Once in the room we opened the window wide, for the smell of him would have made an undertaker faint.

I watched him as he gobbled down a bowl of cold oxtail soup and a hunk of cheese which we had discovered in the kitchen. Julia, now returned, looked at me aghast. The boy had the manners of a puppy. He finished off by licking out the bowl. Then he sat back and sighed, as might a king after a fine feast.

"Now," I said. "What have you been doing all this time?"

"Watching," he said, wiping away the remnants of the soup from around his mouth with the back of his sleeve. In doing so he inadvertently cleaned a patch of skin, which now showed pale through the surrounding dirt.

"So you've been spying on me?"

He pulled an indignant expression.

"Then what?" I asked.

"Keeping watch," he said. "Looking out for you."

"Looking out for you?" Julia repeated, confused.

"Protecting me, he means."

Tinker nodded.

"Thank you, Tinker," I said. "But we'll have to find you something else to do now. New clothes. Somewhere to sleep."

"Somewhere to wash," Julia added, earnestly.

At this, Tinker took offence. "Don't want new clothes!"

"You're in rags, Tinker. They look like they'd fall to pieces in the wash."

"Then don't wash them!" he said.

I admired the logic.

"What's to be done?" asked Julia. "He needs to go to school."

Her intervention was unlikely to help our cause. I decided to change tack.

"Why didn't you tell me you were watching?"

He gave me a look that seemed to say I was stupid.

"I could have fed you."

"Fed myself."

"In the winter you could have come in."

"Then I couldn't have seen."

"There was nothing to see."

But as soon as I said it, I knew I was wrong. The way his eyes flicked to Julia, calculating, then back to me. The way his lips thinned as he clamped his mouth closed, stopping the words from spilling out. The boy had seen something. And he wouldn't say it in front of Julia.

"Well you're here now," I said. "And that means you're going to be washed – like it or not."

I am amazed by the power of a bowl of water and a block of soap. Tinker did struggle at first but, once we had his arms pinned and the wet flannel on his face, he seemed to give up the fight. Having seen the transformation, I understand the satisfaction that must be felt by a man restoring an ancient painting. Layers of dirt rubbed away to reveal pink skin beneath. The boy who had appeared as a monochrome illustration was revealed in beautiful colour. Sleeping rough and living off stolen scraps, he had no right to look so healthy.

His shirt more or less fell away in the struggle to hold him still, so we continued washing his neck and arms. One hour and three bowls of water later we had done all within our power. His hair had proved impossible to comb. And his legs we had not dared to investigate. But his top half at least was washed. Perhaps the smell of him was less or perhaps our noses had grown accustomed to his proximity. All in all, Julia and I were satisfied.

"What about his clothes?" she asked.

"I've got clothes," the boy said, pouting.

"Tomorrow we'll find new ones," she said.

I knew full well that Tinker wouldn't still be with us in the morning. Though his piteous state was hard to witness, I understood something of his need for freedom.

"Would you look for a shirt for him tonight?" I asked.

"But the shops–"

"I don't mean to buy one. Perhaps you could find one to borrow. The desk clerk might know someone who could help."

Julia shot me a sceptical look. "Are you sure?"

The moment she was out of the door, Tinker grabbed his old shirt and somehow managed to wriggle into it without tearing either sleeve clean away. Then he pulled on that oversized coat and tied the belt. The scrubbed face seemed incongruous peeping out of that grimy collar. He was about to launch himself to the door when I grabbed his wrist once more.

"What did you see, Tinker?"

He wriggled in my grip for a moment then met my gaze.

"Spy," he said.

It took me a moment to understand what he was saying. "You saw someone following me?"

He nodded.

"At the boat?"

The nodding became more vigorous. "Stayed on the bank, he did. Under the trees. Didn't see me though.

You didn't see me, neither."

I had seen something but not known what it was. He seemed proud of his achievement though, so I decided not to contradict him.

"Can you describe him? If it was a him?"

"Yeah. Thin like a drain pipe. And he moved funny."

I let go of Tinker's wrist and watched him demonstrate, pulling himself upright and swinging his arms backwards and forwards like a marching soldier.

"Three nights, he was there."

"When? Before the policeman came or after?"

"Two nights before. One night after. You come out on deck for a look. Then you go in and he gets out his watch and his book. Then he's scribbling."

It would be less worrisome to think that it had been a constable. But I knew it could not have been so. They had me where they wanted without any use of spies. Nor could it be connected to Mrs Raike and the ice farmers. That all came later. I could think of one explanation only – the Duke of Northampton had been keeping watch on an asset he hoped soon to regain. A shudder started at the nape of my neck and ran down my spine. The boy did not seem to notice.

When I had composed myself I said: "Thank you, Tinker. But now I'm gone from the wharf, I don't want you hiding out in the cold and the dark. Do you understand? There are better ways to be. Safer ways to live. And you won't be needing to steal for food."

"What about the other one?" Tinker asked. I assumed he was speaking of Julia. But then he added: "He's outside now."

I glanced towards the window. Tinker shook his head and gestured towards the front of the building.

"Another spy?"

"Yeah."

"Has he seen you?"

Tinker grinned. Oh, the pride of the boy. If I had not been so alarmed by his revelation, I might have smiled.

"Where is he?"

But Tinker had heard something. I saw his eyes jump around the room, looking for a way to escape. Before I could stop him he'd snatched his apple and was off. The slam of the door was still ringing in my ears when it was opened again by Julia, a man's shirt draped over her arm.

"Was that… in the corridor? I thought…"

"Yes," I said. "He's gone. It was the threat of new clothes."

CHAPTER 19

Smoke is never thick enough nor mirrors so perfect.
THE BULLET-CATCHER'S HANDBOOK

I related to Julia all I had learned. She wanted to go out to the front of the hotel immediately and search – a naive response. She had no idea how difficult it is to observe and remain unseen. If Tinker was correct and someone had been watching, he must be exceptionally good at his job.

"You won't find him," I said.

"Then let's play the same trick we used to catch the boy. I'll walk from the hotel dressed in your clothes."

"If he's out there, he'll have seen what we did. He won't fall for the same trick."

The grandfather clock in the hallway ticked laboriously towards one in the morning. I could hear no other sound in the hotel, guests and staff being sound asleep.

A few minutes earlier I had stood in the empty lobby, scanning the keys hanging behind the desk, memorising the numbers of vacant rooms. Now I worked to pick the lock of one of them, kneeling, eyes closed, probing the mechanism through the twisted wire in my hand. Feeling the resistance starting to give, I increased the pressure and the lock clicked open.

The room smelled of soap and polish. The curtains were closed. In stockinged feet I stepped across the floorboards and sank down next to the window. I then took the small mirror I had been carrying and slid it slowly behind the curtain, bringing it to rest on the sill. With my head pressed to the wall, I could now see the reflection of the houses opposite. And with a fractional twist of the mirror I could scan the street.

The gas lamps had been put out at this late hour. Although that meant less light, it left the shadows softer and as my eyes grew accustomed to the scene I started to be able to see into the doorways and side passages.

We use our eyes to see the world. But, as every conjurer knows, it is the mind that makes meaning. Thus, as I stared into the mirror I tried to lay my preconceptions aside and observe the reality of the shapes and shadows. But all I could make out were the angles of empty spaces.

Perhaps there never was a man watching. Or perhaps he had given up and gone away. I waited, listening to the heavy tick of the clock outside the room. It was not long before the mechanism whirred and a bell chimed the hour.

I listened.

The entrance to the hotel was directly below me but the click of the bolt being drawn was so faint that

I would have missed it had I not been holding my breath. The door did not creak but I saw, through the mirror, a bar of lamplight opening onto the cobbles. For a moment it was obscured by Julia's shadow. All was as we had arranged. Then the shadow was gone and the crack of light closed once more.

I had positioned the mirror to take in a wide area of cobbles opposite, where a small street branched off from the main road. The angles there were deceptive and I thought there space for a man to hide. Also, to the right of the window was a narrow passage between a half-timbered house and a brick building. I stared into these places. My eyes stung for want of blinking. There was no movement. I heard the door bolt slide closed again below me. Julia would be returning to our room to await my report. The tension began to drain away. There was no one waiting on the street. I reached to take the mirror back but stopped mid movement.

I had seen something. A glint of light from an upstairs window of the half-timbered building opposite. I had not noticed before, but there was a small mirror resting against the inside of the glass. It was black but for a fraction of a second it had blinked silver. It was a thing so small as to be of no consequence. Indeed, the movement could have come from the wind shifting a curtain. But now I knew where to look.

I watched until my limbs were going numb. The clock struck two. Several times I imagined I had seen another movement, only to be convinced I had been mistaken.

When the movement came, it was nearly three in

the morning. This time there was no doubt. I saw a hand inching from behind the curtain and twisting the angle of the mirror. While it was still there, I slid my own mirror away from the sill and clutched it to my heart.

My legs were an agony of pins and needles as I stumbled back towards our room, thinking every shadow an assassin poised to strike.

On the wharf I had felt that I was being watched. But here I had felt nothing. This spy was an expert. A different proposition to the man Tinker had described making notes about my movements. That man had stood in view – for Tinker at least.

But to keep watch and not be seen, not even suspected, over a period of days in a busy town – this required focus, experience, talent and detached intelligence. Not to mention the stimulants needed to stay awake and the skill to use them without pushing yourself into madness. It was a dangerous combination of talents.

The man at the wharf must have been working for the Duke of Northampton. I could see no other possibility. But this watcher had to be different. Had he been from the Duke, I would be arrested already and back at the internment camp awaiting deportation. The man spying on me now could not know my identity. That meant he had picked up my trail since I left Mrs Raike in Derby. And that suggested he was watching because of the investigation into the ice farmers. Spies like this one were not cheap. I could see no reason why his rare talents would be directed to a matter so trivial.

I remembered also my question about Mrs Raike. Her interest in this obscure case had never made sense to me. She had done her research, discovering Julia's connection to a private intelligence gatherer. She had specifically invited my friend to come in order to secure my brother's services. Something had elevated the ice farmers in her eyes above the masses of the deserving poor.

I tapped my knuckle on the door of our room, three times quietly. Then I turned the handle and stepped inside.

The gaslight had been extinguished. I could see Julia's form under the bed covers. As the door clicked closed she sat bolt upright. In the same movement she held out her arm, pointing my gun towards me.

"It's me!" I hissed.

Her arm wavered for a moment then dropped. I rushed to her and eased the pistol from her fingers.

"I didn't know what had happened to you!" she said. "You were supposed to come back."

"And so I have."

"When you didn't come… I found the gun in your travelling case."

I held it up for her to see. "Next time pull back the hammer. It won't fire unless it's first cocked." I showed her the movement then un-cocked it again and put it in her hands. "Now you."

I made her do it three times before I took it back. "Tomorrow I'll show you how to load."

CHAPTER 20

It is not in the entrails of doves that the fall of empires can be read, but in the breeding of secrets and the multiplication of lies.

FROM REVOLUTION

We did not sleep that night. I propped a chair under the door handle by way of a barricade. Then we sat with our heads close to each other and I whispered to her my reasoning and my fear.

She would not at first accept the conclusion, so foreign did the idea seem. But her logical brain could not deny it. If the watcher had known my identity, he would have reported me to the constables. Or, more likely, he would have tried to capture me himself and claim the bigger reward. I would already be sitting in the internment camp awaiting deportation. But if he didn't know who I was, there could be no reason for him to follow me.

"You don't mean…" Julia wafted her hand close to her face, as if fanning away a sudden heat. "But he can't be… Why would anyone want to follow me?"

"We should find out, don't you think?"

There was no value in alarming her further, so I didn't unpack my fears. The man following was an expert in his trade. He would not be hired cheaply. Whoever had set him to follow Julia must have a powerful reason. My mind kept returning to Mrs Raike and her strange obsession.

"When you arrived in Derby, had any work been done on the case of the ice farmers?"

"There was a list of names," she said. "People to be questioned. And a ledger of numbers – an account of deliveries of ice to Derby during February. The number of boats, the size of each cargo."

"Who wrote the numbers in the ledger?"

"I didn't think to ask. Why is it important?"

I had no way to answer.

At five o'clock, with the sky turning from black to grey, I slipped out from the back door of the Green Man and Black's Head carrying a hunk of cheese and the end of a loaf of bread, stolen from the kitchens.

I stood in the middle of the cobbled coach yard and turned slowly, searching the deeply shadowed corners. Tinker had made his way to the wharf to hover just beyond my view. And now he did the same in Ashbourne. I couldn't look after him. Nor had he asked me to. But an unfamiliar feeling had begun to ensnare me – the responsibility for a life more piteous than my own.

I wanted to run.

Instead I clicked my tongue. Something moved on the roof of the outhouse. I stepped closer and whispered: "I need your help."

He landed lightly on his feet, dropping immediately into a crouch. His face was smeared with dirt, though not as evenly as it had been. I held out the food to him. At first he seemed suspicious that I might be trying to trick him into a new set of clothes. Only as I started to explain did he relax enough to nibble the bread. By the time I'd finished, his white teeth were a shining grin.

"Easy," he said.

"No. It's dangerous," I said, feeling the snare tighten its grip.

At midday, having packed away every trace of our presence, Julia and I locked up the hotel room for the last time. We carried our cases to the lobby, handed over the key, paid the balance and left. The doorman ran to call a cab for us and then loaded our things. For once I did not begrudge him the tip.

"Where to?" asked the driver.

"The coach station, if you please," said Julia, keeping her voice low, as I had instructed. We didn't look up to the window opposite until we were in the cab. And then only a glance. Any more would have seemed staged, as indeed it was. Even though he was a man of great skill, our spy would have no way of reaching the coach station ahead of us.

On the short journey, I pulled the curtain across the window and positioned the wig on my head. I had been wearing my hair up under my hat that morning. Julia helped me to pin the wig in similar fashion. I'd only just got my hat back in place when we drew up at our destination. The driver showed no sign of having noticed the change.

Once Julia had bought us two tickets for Derby, we walked swiftly to the waiting room, which was conveniently empty, and positioned ourselves out of view of the window. I then removed my hat and let down the wig, knowing that I would not be able to go about without it afterwards. Nor would I be able to return to the hotel or any other place where I had been seen with dark hair.

As for the spy – he would be following. But such a man would never make the mistake of putting his head around the waiting room door. He would observe from somewhere in the distance, anonymous, patient for our next move. Or perhaps, having asked at the ticket office and learned our destination, he would check the timetable and board our coach at its next stop.

Thus, when he did reveal himself it shocked me to the core. We had been sitting perhaps five minutes when the splash of sunlight on the waiting room floor was interrupted by the shadow of a man, his image strangely foreshortened by the angle of the sun. Such was the distortion that I couldn't say if he was stocky or slim. I watched the shadow move its hand and raise its bowler hat, as if in greeting. The gesture was unnaturally slow. Mocking, I thought. Then he tapped his fingertips on the glass, leaving no doubt that the message was intended for us.

In a blink he was gone.

"He knows we know," said Julia.

"Good," I said managing a bright smile, though my stomach churned.

•••

At a quarter to one the Derby coach rolled to a stop outside. We could hear the rattle of wood and brass and the clop of hooves as the horse team was changed. The station master shouted instructions. Porters called to each other as they started unloading.

The waiting room door swung open and a man in a bowler hat looked in. "Tickets for Derby?" Then he was gone. The door creaked closed on its spring. It could have been him. But so could half the men in Ashbourne.

We stepped out onto the platform. Julia handed her case to one of the porters who hefted it up to a second man, perched on the high rack. When he reached for my case, I shook my head.

I kissed Julia on the cheek. We held each other's gaze for a moment. There was no need to put on an act. The anxiety we felt would pass for the significance of a parting. Then I turned my back and walked away, hoping we had been correct and it was Julia he would follow. Hoping also that she would be safe.

I looked out of place sitting on a park bench with my suitcase next to me. But still more out of place was Tinker. An elegant couple taking the air startled as he dodged past them. Having kept to the shadow of the tree line like an insect afraid to be scorched by the sun, he arrived at my side, panting and conspicuous. Aware of disapproving looks, I dipped into my purse as if rummaging for small coins.

"Hold out your hand," I whispered. "No. The other way up – as if you're begging."

He did as he was told, though I had the impression

he would have preferred people to think he was stealing than asking for a handout.

"Did you manage it?" I asked.

"Course I did!"

"Did he see you?"

Tinker shook his head vigorously. "Soon as you's off, he's chasing on a pedal cycle. Found the back way in. Then I'm up the stairs to his room. Door's left half open."

Tinker dipped inside his ragged shirt and extracted a handful of scrunched papers.

"From the waste bin?" I asked.

"Under the mattress."

From which I gathered that the scrunching had been all Tinker's work. The boy was illiterate. Paper was just kindling to him. He would surely have ignored it but for my explicit instructions.

"I'm going away now, Tinker," I said, taking a golden guinea from my purse and trying to place it on his palm. He snatched back his hand as if the metal had burned him.

"Take it! Hide it in your shoe. You won't be able to follow me."

"I can follow!"

"Not any more. I want you in Derby. Go to Upper Wharf Street. You remember the place? You followed me there, I think. But go in the daytime."

"Better at night," he said.

"Didn't you see the man who followed me there – snarling and drooling?"

"Yeah. And more like him."

"Well then."

Tinker tilted his head like a confused puppy. "What d'you want with me in Derby?"

"Mrs Raike's Charitable Foundation feeds poor orphans. And there's a school and–"

"Nah," he said. "Best stay with you."

"It's too dangerous. I can't look after you."

He grinned then, as if I'd made a joke. I tried to grab his arm but he twisted and scampered away. When I looked down, I saw the gold coin still in my hand.

It was a short walk to the Buxton Road, where I easily found the stables which were just as Julia had described them. The stable-master was a man who seemed more accustomed to using his mouth for chewing tobacco than speaking. He wore the peak of his flat cap low, making his emotions hard to read, but I felt comfortable enough in his presence. There were many of his type on the North Leicester Wharf.

His wife offered the use of the parlour in their cottage. Such a small room should have had less china on display. I doubted any of it had been used. She brought me a pot of tea and a cup of more ordinary design.

Alone at last, I retrieved from my travelling case the papers that Tinker had stolen and laid them out on the floor in front of the fireplace. First were air and coach tickets. Some I noted used, others remained open. Taken together they described a journey – first class from Liverpool to Nottingham in early March, then from Nottingham to Derby where he stayed a week before catching the coach to Ashbourne. That final ticket was dated close to the day when Julia had taken the same trip. There was also an open airship ticket for a return to Liverpool, which seemed good for travel from any major terminus.

I slipped the tickets into my purse and moved on to the next sheets – pages cut from the Nottingham Post. I flattened them out, searching for a mark that might indicate which articles he had been reading. There was nothing. I held the papers up to the window, looking for the pinpricks of a secret message. Again, nothing. Yet they must have significance – since the man had kept the pages hidden.

The final two sheets were messages printed on notepaper. The same hand had written each, though with different pens. Fold marks suggested they might have been enclosed in envelopes. As for what they said – this I could not tell, for they were written in code.

It was mid-afternoon before Julia arrived.

"He was with me in the carriage!" she exclaimed as soon as we were alone. "I'm sure it was him. He wore a bowler."

"As do half the men of England."

"But he smiled. It wasn't a nice smile." She pulled back her lips in imitation.

Julia had led a sheltered life. I wondered if experience had yet equipped her to recognise lechery.

"Were you alone with him in the carriage?"

"Quite alone." She leaned forward and dropped her voice. "He had no luggage."

I considered this. Lack of luggage was a stronger indication. We had given our spy no time to prepare for his journey. But I was not convinced that a man of such ability would show his face.

"Did anyone join the coach at the first stop?"

She nodded. "But they wore top hats. I stepped out the other door as they entered. To take some air, I said, as if coach sick. But then I whispered my request to the driver and passed him money for his trouble. It worked, just as you said it would. He drove on without warning, leaving the men no chance to follow me. The next stop was Brailsford! They'll be miles away by now."

I wasn't so confident of her identification. How difficult was it for a man to change his hat? Indeed, showing a bowler might have been the very reason he had allowed his shadow to fall on the waiting room floor. The permutations were endless. Double bluffs. Triple bluffs. Thinking about it made my mind feel tangled. However, I did believe we had now thrown him off our trail.

"Did you meet anyone as you walked back into town?" I asked.

"I came directly to you."

"Our spy will be heading this way by now. And your travelling case will be in Derby. If you don't claim it within the month, they'll auction it off to the highest bidder."

She grinned at that. The beige case had been a gift from her mother. Someone might pay well on a gamble that the contents were as pretty as the calfskin exterior. Their reward would be a stack of towels embroidered with the name of the Green Man and Black's Head Hotel. A brown paper parcel containing

Julia's things had been waiting at the stables when I arrived.

"Was it worth it?" she asked. "Did the boy do his job?"

I fetched the papers and laid them out on the rug. She blanched when she saw the coach ticket from Derby to Ashbourne. Retrieving her own ticket, she laid the two side by side. The date and time of travel were identical.

"Can you remember any of the passengers?" I asked.

"I wasn't really looking."

"And no one on the coach today seemed familiar?"

Seeing her distress, I put the tickets to one side and laid out the coded messages. They were composed of letters and numbers arranged in groups. I cast my eye over the first line, reminding myself of the conclusion I had drawn.

C 7 3. D 1 9. A 22 3. E 31 1. E 8 7.

"I fear we've little chance of unscrambling it," I said.

She picked up the first sheet and scanned it. I had been using a pen and paper, scrawling notes in a vain attempt to work it out. Julia now took the pen and began making a tally of each letter and number used.

"Properly speaking, unscrambling isn't the correct word," she said, her tone sounding somewhat superior.

"It couldn't be more scrambled if it were an egg!"

"No," she said, seeming to have missed my irritation. "The letters will have been substituted rather than mixed."

In my several years of intelligence gathering, I'd never studied codes. From afar the subject had seemed overly mathematical, which had perhaps put me off. And it had not previously impinged on my investigations.

"Some letters are more commonly used in English than others," Julia explained, as if to a child. "These are likely to come up more often in the message. I'm looking for patterns in what's been written. It could be the individual letters and numbers or–"

"I don't remember discussing codes with you," I said.

She blushed. "Oh... this wasn't from our lessons."

I wondered at her words. And at why she hadn't mentioned the subject to me before. She usually found it hard to contain her enthusiasms. But as I watched her work, I began to understand how the subject might resonate with her nature. The mathematical aspect of encryption had deterred me. But she would be attracted by it in equal measure. An uncompromising logic characterised her approach to life. Often it disadvantaged her but here it might work the other way.

She frowned as she copied down number and letter combinations. The tip of her tongue projected from her mouth, curling to touch her upper lip. She tapped her fingers against the pen. "What might he have been writing?" she asked.

"That's what you're trying to find out, isn't it?"

"I mean, what words might he have needed to use?"

"The? And? I?"

"Longer words. With double letters."

"Nottingham?" I suggested.

"That's good."

"Surveillance."

"Very good."

But after twenty minutes, she pushed the papers away in irritation and began massaging her brow. I found myself smiling, though I knew it unworthy. When she looked up, I quickly replaced my expression with a frown of sympathy.

CHAPTER 21

Some weeds are pinched out before they grow. Others are uprooted. But the most pernicious of all must be harrowed from the soils of history.

FROM REVOLUTION

There is nothing good to be said for sleeping in a barn. A pile of hay looks soft enough from a distance, but up close there is always a brittle point to poke into your skin. Julia had fallen asleep directly. But unfamiliar sounds kept me awake. At first it had been the scurrying of small creatures. Rats or mice, I supposed. They only went quiet when an owl flew in to perch on a high beam. I know it was an owl because of its screech, which repeated every few minutes thereafter.

The stable master's wife fussed over us as she served breakfast, apologising that the cottage was so small and that there were no spare beds. I gathered that it was not uncommon for travellers to stay. But they had never had 'real ladies' sleeping in the barn before. Sleep was too strong a word for it.

Breakfast was thickly cut bacon, coarse bread and sweet tea. By the third cup, my mood had softened.

And when the clop of horses entering the courtyard announced the arrival of our guides, I even managed to smile.

"Exactly six days late," Julia whispered, though she was smiling also.

The older of the two guides introduced himself as Gideon. His hair was shockingly white against tanned skin. The other, a boy by comparison, was called Peter. He must have been twenty years older than us. Their clothes were simple, almost identical, except that Gideon had loops of coarse twine tied around his sleeves just above the elbow and around his legs just below the knee.

"I'm Miss Swain and this is Miss Brooke," said Julia. We had decided that Elizabeth was common enough for me to risk keeping, but that even in the wilds it would be foolhardy to use my real surname.

"Happy to meet with you," said Gideon in an accent that was unfamiliar to me.

The men had dismounted and were standing with their hands clasped in front of them, as if they had been ordered to keep from fidgeting by the teacher of a Sunday school.

"Well," I said. "Had we better be going?"

Nodding, Gideon stepped towards the stable block. But as I watched him go, I realised that Peter had remained standing and was looking at me. When I turned to face him again, he quickly looked away and hurried off in the direction of the privy.

I watched him go then whispered to Julia: "Did you see him staring?"

She stifled a giggle. "I think he admires you."

"If he recognised me..."

"There're no Postal Offices on the high moorland," she said. "So no fugitive posters either."

At this point, Gideon returned leading our mounts. Julia touched my arm as if to say I needn't worry then walked around the ponies in an imitation of one who knew fetlock from withers. The stable master placed a sheaf of legal documents and a pen in my hand. These I read as best I could. In short, they seemed to say that we were receiving beasts in good health and would be liable for their condition on their return. But the terminology was arcane so it was impossible to be certain.

"We shouldn't sign without first understanding," Julia said, now back at my side.

It didn't seem the place to point out that, whatever the words meant, I would be committing fraud by signing under a false name. And by adding her own name in knowledge of my deception, she would be an accessory.

"Were you to read it for a month, you'd still be none the wiser," I said, putting the pen in her hand.

She pouted as she scratched her signature next to mine.

Some women maintain the side-saddle to be a wondrous invention. But to me, it is damning proof of the illogicality of our world. The right knee must be hooked over the upper pommel, while the left foot is supposedly supported by a single stirrup, which dangles unnaturally high on the horse's flank. The saddle feels too tall and the sitting position too far back so that the reins must be excessively long.

The stable master had chosen our saddles. Julia seemed comfortable on hers. But mine was a few inches too small with the result that my posterior was extended over the far side of the horse in a manner that was possibly indecent and definitely uncomfortable.

In such fashion we set out. Julia and I bumped along next to each other. Our guides rode far enough ahead that Peter may have thought we would not see the bottle he passed to Gideon. Suspicious, I kept close watch. But the drink passed from one to the other and it seemed each took equal share.

After an hour of steady climbing, I looked back and was surprised to see how far we had come. The valley floor appeared flat between the jaws of the escarpment on either side. Red kites circled high above the ridge. I scanned the line of the track, searching for any sign that we might have been followed.

"This is the life I've dreamed," said Julia, breaking in on my thoughts.

"Riding?"

"The law," she said. "The pursuit of justice. Our journey has confirmed me. These experiences may be commonplace to you, but the circle of my horizon has been spread so far in these last few days that I hardly think I'm the same person."

"Then I'm pleased for you. But this is new to me also. I never saw such hills in the Kingdom."

"You rode through the countryside though – as a child of the circus."

"Not on one of these," I said, patting the saddle. "Back then, I rode as the men and boys did."

Julia blushed. "Isn't that unnatural? For a woman, I mean."

"How so?"

"Our bodies," she whispered. "We may wish the opportunities of men, but we're formed in a different way."

"If it were just for the organs that are different, it's they who should ride side-saddle and us astride!"

At first Julia frowned. But then I saw her blush as she understood my meaning. "You shouldn't talk of such things!"

The steep part of the climb had been wooded for the most part. But as the slope decreased, trees gave way to scrubby grassland. Sheep country. And then the grass was replaced by bracken in patches and hummocked moss. Dry-stone walls had crisscrossed the slopes lower down but here the land was open and wide under the pale dome of the sky.

A feeling of unease hung around me as I rode, like the remnant of an unquiet dream. I found myself replaying Peter's gaze in the theatre of my mind. Standing in the stable yard, I'd thought it an expression of recognition. But each time I returned to the memory, I was less certain. I took to glancing back along the path we had travelled. Once I caught sight of a rider in the distance, but he or she was quickly gone.

The hills rose and fell but the track continued along the same constant gradient, having been cut through the rocky bluffs and built up on embankments over the few small valleys that we crossed.

"Does this path seem strange to you?" I asked.

"It seems perfectly pleasant," said Julia.

"Such a work of engineering. How many use it a day do you suppose?"

"We passed a man an hour ago," she said.

"One drover and a flock of geese in three hours of riding?"

"You find suspicion everywhere, Elizabeth."

"Curiosity isn't a vice," I said.

"It is when scattered in every direction! Turn it to the ice theft and we'll surely have the crime solved in no time."

True words often sting most keenly and I was set to defend myself. But Julia's attention had already moved on. She pointed to a copse of trees at a discreet distance from the path and said: "I need to stretch my legs."

Thus a halt was called while she took herself away for a moment of privacy.

Peter fetched a pouch from his saddlebag and began to roll a cigarette. I caught him stealing a glance at me over his cupped hands.

"Enjoying the ride?" he asked.

"Yes," I lied, trying to dismount but discovering too late that my leg had lost all sensation. It folded under me and I collapsed in a heap by the trackside. Peter offered me his hand but I declined.

"That's them saddles for you," said Gideon.

Feeling began to return, bringing with it an agony of pins and needles. I sat on the ground, rubbing my leg while Peter stretched and strolled away up the path.

I watched until I judged him out of hearing then

asked Gideon: "Why was this track made?"

"Why's any track made?"

"Then who made it?"

"Miners done it."

"Why so strong and level?"

"It was stronger once," he said. "They tied it all together with iron rails. But those got ripped up before my granddad's time. Why's tha want to know?"

"I'm just curious," I said.

"That you are."

CHAPTER 22

You will not trick a man until you learn to read him. But you will never trick a man who has learned to read you.

THE BULLET-CATCHER'S HANDBOOK

We had reached the high moorland. Here and there I caught sight of stone-walled enclosures. Sheep pens perhaps. And once, a derelict cottage, its corner tumbled down. Buzzards mewled overhead in a sky that seemed unnaturally vast. The landscape was stark and treeless. Our progress might be seen from miles if anyone was looking.

"It's strange country," Julia said.

"God's own," said Gideon.

"You believe in a God, then?" she asked.

"Most do that live here. But he can be a cruel bastard, if tha knows my meaning."

Despite the brightness of the day, a shiver ran across my shoulders.

The path had brought us to the crest of a low ridge. A stone cottage lay ahead, set amid a scatter of outbuildings. A trace of smoke scudded from the single chimney. It was the first sign of civilisation we had seen in hours.

"Is that where we're going?" I asked.

Peter nodded, then dug in his heels, leading us off down the slope.

We had to stoop under the low lintel of the cottage door. Once inside, it took time for my eyes to adjust. From the single window, small and deep, a shaft of light pierced the room, revealing threads of smoke in the air. The remains of a fire in the hearth gave no warmth.

"Make tha selves at home," said Gideon.

"Where is everyone?" Julia asked. "We were to speak to the community."

"There'll be time for that," said Peter. "Once they're gathered."

He turned to go.

"Wait," I called. "Are they far?"

"Far enough."

He strode out into the sunshine. The door clattered closed behind him.

"I hope it won't be another six days," said Julia, her tone light-hearted. "What do you suppose ice farmers do when it's not winter?"

I watched our guides through an uneven pane of window glass as they mounted their horses and started off down the track. If Peter had recognised me, this would be his first chance to confide in the old man, unless he wanted to keep the reward for himself. I wondered whether there were any constables in the high mountains to whom they could deliver me. There were too many permutations to calculate.

•••

It didn't take us long to explore the small building. Downstairs was a kitchen-scullery and something that could have been described as a living room. The sleeping loft – a row of straw mattresses under the eaves – was reached by climbing a ladder. Julia scolded me when I opened a trunk of someone's possessions. But she looked over my shoulder to see, just the same. It contained a rabbit-skin coat and trousers, the lining mended with patches of un-matching cloth, a pair of leather gloves with short metal spikes projecting from the palm and fingers, three blankets, a scatter of moth balls and a carved wooden animal that Julia thought a dog but seemed to me more likely a sheep.

Outside we found a pump and a stone water trough. There were slates missing from the roof of one small outhouse. The holes allowed in enough light for us to see a collection of strangely shaped saws, spikes and mallets hanging from hooks in the roof beam. Though most of the metal was brown with rust, the blade edges were bright with sharpening. Other pieces of ironwork lying around, I could not name. They were the tools of the ice farming trade, I supposed.

"It's hard to believe anyone could make a living from harvesting ice," said Julia.

"Not much of a living," I said.

After eating some of our provisions we sat outside, leaning against the wall of the cottage. We talked for a while. There was no one to hear, but I found myself whispering anyway. It felt wrong to announce my presence to that vast emptiness.

Picking up on my unease, Julia said: "You're surely

safe here."

"I don't feel it."

"I saw you looking back as we climbed. Did you see anything out of place? The truth is, no one followed. Not even your boy Tinker – which is a wonder in itself."

"He's not my boy!"

"He has remarkable tenacity," she said, undaunted. "Why is he so devoted do you suppose?"

Feeling the heat in my cheeks, I turned away to survey the horizon once more.

"Tell me about codes," I said.

"What of them?"

"Where did you learn?"

"I found a book in my father's study. Mother wouldn't have approved. It was a collection of pirate stories, merely fiction. But one described a method for breaking codes. After reading it, I... experimented."

I glanced back and saw that it was now she who blushed. She got to her feet and brushed down her skirts. I was about to press her for more information but she headed inside, returning a moment later with the papers that had been hidden under the spy's mattress. Having seated herself again, she placed them on the ground between us. "Let's have another go," she said.

Julia may have had the advantage over me when it came to mathematical equations, but I'd noticed vague collections of information unsettled her. It was as if she needed to understand how they were related before she could entertain them. Thus, while she methodically counted numbers and letters on the coded sheets, I turned to the two newspaper pages.

I started by examining the long vertical edge along which the sheets had been connected to the rest of the paper. They had been cut out rather than torn. Scissors leave distinct marks, of which there were none to be seen. Thus a knife must have been used. A sharp one, for the edge was perfectly smooth.

Tinker's crumpling made it hard to be certain, but it seemed the sheets had been crisp before their time bundled inside his shirt. Thus, I reasoned, our spy had not handled them often. Bringing my eye close, I turned the pages, searching for the kind of indentations left by the pressure of a pencil. I could find none. Having exhausted my examination of the paper itself, I began to read the articles.

The first was a report of a skirmish between two chieftains in the mountains of Gwynedd in North Wales. Those anarchic lands beyond the Gas-Lit Empire were taken as a byword for savagery. The reporter claimed direct aerial observation, though no airship would dare fly low enough to see the details he mentioned – *decorated armour* and *hand cannons with bone inlay*. I guessed the description owed more to an anthropology textbook than to any detail he'd actually seen. The article ended with a homily on our good fortune to be living within the civilised world.

The second story concerned the racehorse market in Chepstow. Prices had doubled in three years. One man had made five thousand guineas by buying a stallion on a Monday and selling it again on the Friday. Nothing pleases Republicans more than a story which confirms their prejudices. This one had it all – Royalists gambling on horses and boasting about financial gain.

"It's the wrong kind of code," said Julia, cutting across my thoughts.

"I'm sorry?"

She passed me her sheet of notes. "I've eliminated the possibilities. It's not a substitution code. Not a simple one, anyway. The triplets on the messages probably represent whole words rather than letters." She tapped a column of numbers on the notepaper. "It means there's probably a code book behind it. A list of words and what represents each one."

"Then how would it be cracked?"

"It wouldn't. Unless you have the book."

Absorbing this setback, I discovered that I was not surprised. Julia's innocent enthusiasm saw the world as more simple and cleaner than it really was. The prospect of her decoding the messages of a master spy had always been remote. Nevertheless, another avenue had been closed to us.

A bird flitted down, alighting on the brink of the water trough. We both watched as it dipped to drink. Then in a flash of yellow and brown feathers it was gone. I sat listening to the hiss of the wind in the long grass and the distant call of buzzards. It felt as if the world was holding its breath, waiting for something that it knew was going to happen. Something just beyond my sight.

The sun began to set and the air chilled. Julia went back indoors, but I remained outside to keep watch. A bank of cloud inched across the sky, obscuring the moon and stars. Within an hour it had become so dark that I needed to feel my way along the wall of the cottage to find the water trough.

Then I made out a line of lights approaching along what must have been the track, though I could no more see it than I could the ground under my feet. I tapped my knuckle on the cottage door. Julia emerged carrying a candle, the brightness of which hurt my eyes. I licked my finger and snuffed it out.

"Until we know who it is," I whispered.

At first the approaching lights were disembodied. They floated above the ground like a line of fireflies. But as they came closer I discerned them to be lanterns held aloft on poles, perhaps thirty in number. I edged along the wall to the corner of the cottage, readying myself to slip away. But then I saw there were children among the leaders and I knew this was the community of the ice farmers after all.

The low murmur of their conversation grew louder as they approached. But when they assembled in front of us, it dropped away to nothing. Arranged in an open arc, they stared at us as visitors to the zoo might stare, had they never before seen a pair of baboons.

Gideon and Peter were the last to arrive.

"This is them," said Gideon to the crowd. "The ladies from Derby."

"We're pleased to meet you," said Julia.

At this several of the adults gave greetings of their own, some murmuring, others nodding and tugging their forelocks.

There shouldn't have been room for half of them in the cottage. But once we had entered and Gideon had followed, they crammed in behind. We found ourselves pushed back until we were huddled in the farthest corner. A few pressed around the doorway or stared in at the window. I could see nothing of Peter, who must have remained outside.

Gideon coughed and made a small nod, indicating that we should begin.

"Thank you for coming," said Julia, annunciating each word, as if her audience might not otherwise understand. I cringed but they showed no sign of feeling patronised.

"We have come to hear about your problems." And then, when no one spoke, she added: "Please begin."

"They's taking the ice," said one, an ancient-looking man with a face so brown and wrinkled he looked like a raisin.

There were murmurs of ascent from the others.

"Who do you think has been taking it?" Julia asked.

"They," he said, spreading his arms as if to indicate everyone beyond the four walls of the cottage.

"Oh," said Julia.

It seemed the conversation might stop there, so I asked: "How do you know the ice is being taken?"

"What they send and what's credited to them don't match," said Gideon.

"And what can we do to help?" asked Julia.

"Get us paid," said the wrinkled man. Everyone nodded.

"And how would you like us to do that?"

Gideon frowned and the raisin man frowned deeper. "Use the law," said a woman's voice from somewhere at the back.

To form a useful question one needs knowledge. This is the paradox of ignorance. I decided to try a different approach.

"They've been stealing your ice?" I asked.

"Ay."

"Could you show us?"

Gideon looked to the wrinkled man. The wrinkled man turned, as if seeking approval from the woman at the back. Others nodded. I heard words muttered under the breath, so thickly accented that I couldn't make them out. Then, suddenly, everyone was moving. Some stepped outside. Through the door, I could see one family group settling down on the ground as if getting ready for sleep. Others seated themselves on the earth floor of the house. It appeared that a decision had been made.

"What's to happen?" I asked.

"They'll show you," said Gideon. "Tomorrow. The beds are for you." He pointed up the ladder to the loft.

CHAPTER 23

Without ice there would have been no cities.

FROM REVOLUTION

I had never been a morning person, even under the best conditions, which these were not. A pot of tea was usually just about enough to get me on my way, not a cup of water from the pump, drunk so cold as to make the head hurt.

Though I had slept in my clothes, the bedbugs had found a way through. I halted in the track to scratch through layers of skirts and stocking at my calf, which was dotted with bites, raised and hot. At least we were not riding – my legs and back were sore from the previous day in the saddle. As should Julia's have been, though she sprang up the path ahead of me, as if returning from a rest cure. With Julia, mood would always rule over physical considerations. And today she was excited.

We'd still not been told whether the crowd leading us was merely a deputised group or the whole community. There had been little talk since we started walking an hour before. For most of that time the path had been rising.

"Isn't it beautiful?" said Julia.

I chose not to answer.

Dark lines had for some time been visible at the top of the ridge above us. I'd taken them to be a phenomenon of geology, but as we climbed I saw that they were too regular to be natural. Closer still, I realised that they were raised above the ground surface, reminding me of the kind of racks that fishermen use to dry their catch. Only when we had reached the top of the path was it possible to see their true nature. They were metal troughs, supported above the ground by a framework of posts. The crowd had stopped and were gathering around the nearest one.

"They grows the ice here," said Gideon.

"We do," said the wrinkled man.

"Grow?" I asked. "How does ice grow?"

Gideon pointed up the next rise. "There's a lake up top. When they raise the sluices water gets to flood the troughs. The ice grows fast."

"Five a night, with good freeze on," said the wrinkled man.

"Five what?"

"Five times it gets filled and frozen," explained Gideon.

"We did eight once," interjected a woman standing on the far side of the trough. Others nodded, smiling wistfully.

I knelt and looked up at the metalwork from below. The base was thick with baffles, looking like black gills. I wondered where the workers sheltered through the night as they waited for the water to freeze.

The wrinkled man rapped a bony knuckle on the metal, making it ring. "Hundred and fifty blocks a trough," he said.

I stood again. Looking along its length, I noticed that it was divided up by lines of projecting metal, and that ice formed within them would indeed break naturally into regular blocks. One hundred and fifty blocks multiplied by – I did a quick count of the troughs – multiplied by twenty then tried to multiply again by five for the number of nightly loads.

"Fifteen thousand," said Julia.

"Seventy-five tonne a night," said the wrinkled man.

The figure seemed extraordinary. I wondered how much of the year it fell below freezing. Being the highest land between the Welsh mountains and the east coast, there would be nothing to stop the wind. It would howl across the tops in winter. Imagining the scene, I found Gideon's belief in a cruel God easier to understand.

"How do they count the blocks?" asked Julia.

"Best shown," said the wrinkled man. Then he set off along the line of a small gully that traversed the hillside. It was a man-made water course, though with only a trickle in the bottom. But in winter I imagined it would be full. And frozen. There could be no better surface to slide a heavy load along than ice. Perfectly flat, almost frictionless. I thought back to the strange implements we had seen in the outhouse. Some of them might indeed have been designed to hook ice blocks and haul them.

I glanced behind and saw that Peter followed on

with the last stragglers at the back of the group. He
had kept to himself all morning, smoking most of the
time. He seemed more isolated than before. If he had
recognised me, I did not believe he'd mentioned it to
Gideon, who remained unchanged in character. Or, if
something had passed between them, the older man
must have brushed it off as ridiculous.

The path now rounded a bluff. Ahead of us it
dipped into a small valley and disappeared into a
dark opening in the mountainside. There were other
people here. Families dressed just like the ice farmers
we'd already met. Greetings were waved. Some shook
hands. But it was Julia and myself who drew their
interest. All eyes followed us as we approached the
hole in the hillside.

Gideon and the wrinkled man each took a candle
lantern from a niche in the wall and led us into a
downward sloping tunnel.

"You dug this?" I asked.

The wrinkled man laughed. "Not us. Miners dug it
long ago."

"The hills are full of holes like this," said Gideon.
"Lead, copper, zinc. They dug it all here."

I thought back to the strange trackway we had
followed, also built by the miners.

The temperature dropped as we descended. Then,
quite suddenly, the chill became intense. The wrinkled
man hauled open a wooden door and winter flooded
out to meet us. "This is what tha come for to see."

He held up his lantern, revealing ice stacked all
around. I was vaguely aware of someone closing the
door behind us as we stepped along a narrow way

between piled blocks. Every few paces there were side corridors, identical to the one we were walking along. I couldn't see the full size of the chamber, which receded into darkness all around.

"What's all this ice worth?" My breath steamed as I spoke.

The wrinkled man chuckled. "It's worth nowt."

"It's worth nowt yet," Gideon explained. "That's the trick. Four month of freezing. One month for mending broken kit. Then seven month for carting ice down to the bargemen. That's the life up here. What's frozen water at Christmas – by midsummer it's treasure."

"Who counts the blocks?" I asked.

"It's family by family. Eldest keeps tally."

"In a ledger?"

"Don't need to write it," said the wrinkled man tapping the side of his head with a crooked finger. He strode off down the passage gesturing to one pile of blocks after another. "Logan, Linnell, Speller, Bradshaw, Mansell, Martin, Williams..."

"The ice farmer families," Gideon explained.

"Men from Derby come to fix the bargain – that's the price. Then we haul the ice down to the canal and the boatmen take it."

"So it's never written down?" asked Julia.

"No use writing," said Gideon. "None of us can read."

It was past noon by the time our guides suggested we take our leave. The wrinkled man shook my hand. His finger joints were distorted and the skin felt like roughly sawn wood. Then he moved to Julia.

"Goodbye," she said.

"Tha knows how it is being poor?" he asked.

The question seemed to unsettle her.

"I know what it's like to be hungry," I said.

He nodded and let go of her hand. "What they take – it's nowt but pennies. But it's bread to us."

"We'll stop them," said Julia. "I promise."

I bit my lip, wishing her words unsaid.

The journey back to the cottage was quicker for being downhill. Peter and Gideon strode off ahead. But to guard against injury, Julia and I were obliged to walk with eyes fixed on the uneven path before our feet. There was little conversation.

At the cottage, Gideon saw to the horses, which had been tethered on long ropes so they could graze circles in the thin grass. As dusk fell, Peter built a fire in the grate. The men seemed immune to the smoke, which failed to properly clear up the chimney. But Julia and I were made of weaker stuff and retreated to sit by one of the outhouses. The sky was so clear that it seemed milky with stars.

"Out here there's no one to know who you are," Julia whispered.

"They might already know."

"Nonsense! You could live in a cottage in the mountains and never be found."

"What would I do for food?"

"It would cost so little. I'd send money."

"And how long before news spread of the eccentric woman huddled by a peat fire in the mountains?"

"You'd see them coming. You could move on."

"And on. And on again."

"Then why not live in secret on the wharf. The boat people would keep you safe."

"They'd turn me in."

"No!"

"You didn't see how they changed when the Kingdom flag went up in Bessie's porthole."

Julia regarded me with a sceptical eye. "You've surely misjudged them. In your distress you've imagined ill-feelings that they don't hold."

"Someone told the constables to look for me in the library."

"As I might have done if I hadn't known the dangers! If you came back to the wharf we'd explain to them. You'd be cared for by those who admire you – who are many."

I shook my head. "There's nowhere in the Gas-Lit Empire for me to hide."

"Well I surely hope you won't be hiding beyond it!"

"No," I said. "No chance of that. There's too little law beyond the Empire. Yet too much law within it."

We had been able to hear the sound of Peter and Gideon conversing inside the cottage. Now Gideon began to sing. I couldn't make out the words but the tune I knew from my childhood as the King of the Faeries. One of the trick riders in the Circus of Mysteries had whistled it to the horses to calm them.

"Have you thought more about the code?" I asked.

"I've put it out of my mind," she said.

"You mentioned a code book. What might it look like?"

"I've never seen one."

"Can such things be bought?"

"You'd make one yourself," she said. "Or rather, you'd make two. One for the sender to put the message into code and one for the receiver to turn it back to plain text."

"It might look like a notebook, then?"

"Perhaps. Or loose sheets. Or anything you could write on. Best put the puzzle out of your mind. There's no solving it."

My instruction to Tinker had been to look for papers. He might not have recognised a book as being important enough to take. Or, if it was a small thing, the man might have kept it on his person. In a pocket perhaps, or sewn into the lining of his coat.

"You're more likely to find answers in the newspaper pages," Julia said, interrupting my thoughts. "At least those we can read."

The truth was I had read through the sheets of newsprint three times already. The only articles that could relate to the case were two that mentioned Mrs Raike, but they were of no consequence. The first being a notice of a fund-raising dinner and the second being an article about charitable foundations in the city.

"Ice is mentioned three times," I said. "There's a list of commodity prices on one page. Tea, coal and the like. And ice. But I can't fathom why that could be important. What difference if the ice farmers have lost ninety-nine pennies or one hundred? It's mentioned once more in the business section – an article on the profitability of the canals through the year. The phrase there was 'ice-bound'. And once in the foreign news – the report of a public execution in Bristol. They hanged a murderer from a low drop so the neck bones would be preserved. The body was quickly packed in ice and transported for medical research."

"Public executions," Julia said, speaking the words as if she had swallowed rancid milk. "How are Royalists so callous?" And then quickly she added: "I don't mean you, Elizabeth. You'd never go to see such a thing."

CHAPTER 24

If you want to be believed, tell them what they want to hear. And if you want to be safe, beware, beware the man who does the same for you.

THE BULLET-CATCHER'S HANDBOOK

Having slept our second night in the cottage, we were woken by our guides moving about below. Julia called down to ask the hour. Gideon shouted back that it was past the time to be off. So we hurried to dress, splashed pump water over our faces, and rode away in the grey light of pre-dawn. As we reached the top of the ridge, I turned for a final look, knowing that every step from here on was taking me back towards the constabulary.

There was little talking as we descended. For a time we followed the mining trackway, but half way down, we stopped and dismounted.

"We'll meet again at the bottom of the hill," said Gideon, who then continued on with the animals and our luggage.

"It's just us now," said Peter, not meeting my eyes.

We set off along a side-path, which grew narrower

as we progressed until it was little more than a goat track. Presently we found ourselves traversing a slope that stretched up to the skyline above and down to woods and fields far below. There was nothing horizontal on which to fix the eye. As the drop grew precipitous, I noticed Julia leaning back into the slope.

"Stand upright," I said. "It's easier to balance that way."

She seemed unable to do so. Such was her vertigo that I began to think we'd need to turn back. But then we rounded a bluff and I saw our destination immediately ahead. Julia rushed the last few paces to the security of a small platform cut into the slope.

Here was a system of pulleys and ropes anchored to the platform by a stout iron post. While Julia rested, I looked up and down the slope, taking in a gully that ran past us from the top. A wagon had been tied in the gully next to us. If the rope snapped it might career all the way down to the tree line below. Looking down, I saw that our platform was merely one station in a chain of similar platforms. A wagon was tethered next to each. Julia took my hand and pulled me back from the edge.

"What happens here?" I asked.

"Wait," said Peter. "You'll see."

There had been no time for breakfast and such provisions as we had were being carried down the mountain by the horses. Peter sat chewing on a strip of dried meat which he'd produced from the pocket of his trousers.

Julia believed the awkwardness of his glances at me came from romantic attraction. I feared he recognised me from the fugitive poster. There had been nothing to prove the matter one way or the other. With no constables in the high mountains, there had been no one to whom he could have turned me over. I'd felt in less danger whilst Gideon was with us. My instincts told me the old man was as straightforward and decent as he seemed.

My thoughts were interrupted by a rumbling sound from up the slope and men's voices calling. I stood and looked around but could see nothing until, without warning, a rope went taut and the wagon next to us jolted into movement, climbing fast.

Descending along the same gully came another wagon, passing the first at the half way point. Within seconds the new wagon had pulled up level with us. This one was full of ice blocks.

Two men jumped down. One of the faces was familiar from the crowd we had met at the mine. They moved quickly, hooking and unhooking ropes, making them fast and pulling levers. Then they beckoned to us. Peter clung on to the side of the wagon, as did the ice farmers. We climbed up on the back, taking the standing positions the men had previously occupied. Clinging on, I looked over to Julia, who had her eyes tightly closed, and was about to speak some reassuring words when I heard the clunk of machinery being set and we lurched off down the slope so abruptly that it felt as if my stomach had been left behind.

Half way down, we passed yet another wagon on its way up. I had a glimpse of a man and a woman riding it before they flashed up the hill to where we had been.

And so our journey continued. I lost count of the stages or the number of ice farmers being raised up the hillside by the weight of our cart descending. The scale of the operation began to sink in. Imagining the flow of ice and wagons and people, I wondered whether some would be left to climb the mountain on foot at the end of the day. It seemed more likely that they would wait until the next morning to get a ride.

Presently the gully was surrounded by trees and the slope decreased. I noticed Julia had opened her eyes and seemed less terrified. The men operating the machinery were sweating, but I was feeling the chill of the ice and had to continually adjust my grip to stop my fingers going numb. Then, quite suddenly we emerged from the trees and the wagon stopped. We had reached flat land. There were no more ropes and no more pulleys.

Inhaling the unmistakable scent of standing water, I jumped down. A wharf lay immediately before us, complete with hand cranes for loading and unloading. A canal boat was moored with her hatches off, ready to take on cargo. The name plate was so tarnished and blackened by dirt that I could only just read it: *The Peary*.

I had lived on the canal for five years and thought I knew the character of the people. But this was different. On the North Leicester Wharf, I was one of a community. But here, accompanying the ice farmers, I found myself an outsider. Or worse. Searching the faces on the boat, I found only suspicion.

A price must already have been agreed because the wagon was immediately manoeuvred under the crane and the loading began. All that seemed to matter was the number and quality of the blocks. The ice farmers and the boat captain kept count.

"Can't have that one," said the captain, kicking the toe of his boot into a block that had been swung across and was dangling above the hold.

I could see what he meant. The bottom corners had broken off. It was three quarters of a block rather than a full one. The ice farmers didn't like it but there was no other customer to sell it to so their bargaining position was weak.

"Call it half a block," said the captain.

They argued it back and forth. It took five minutes before ice was being loaded again. The delay would be no good for either side. I had little idea how big or small the difference would be – a fraction of a penny perhaps.

The ice farmers heaved the empty wagon back to the base of the slope and made it secure to the rope once more. They waved goodbye to us and climbed on. There was a pause. Then the wagon jolted up the slope and away. A loaded wagon passed it half way and presently a fresh group of ice farmers were working the crane, swinging ice blocks over to the hold of *The Peary*.

"She's a narrowboat, isn't she?" I asked one of the crew.

He looked at me suspiciously. "She is," he said.

"What locks do you have between here and Derby?"

"Why'd you want to know?"

"I'd have thought you'd use a barge for a cargo like this. Unless the locks haven't been widened."

He nodded, slowly, as if assessing me anew. "There's a long flight. All narrow."

"Must take time to get through them all," I said.

"It is what we're paid for." Then, after a pause he added: "What do you know of boats?"

The more of my life I revealed to him, the more information he'd be able to give to any bounty hunter who might be following. But if he believed that I belonged to the canal, he would be less likely to gossip to outsiders. So I said: "My home's on the North Leicester Wharf. The boat I live on was built narrow for speed. But it's not a real narrowboat. She wouldn't pass the locks you have to get through. My neighbours are real boat people. Not like me."

Ironically, it was that last part that convinced him – my understanding of the difference between a person who merely lived on a boat and one who worked them. By putting myself further away I had halved the distance between us. Seeing the change in his face, I asked: "May I come aboard?"

He offered a hand, which I took, though I didn't need any help to step across from the bank. The captain shot him an angry look.

"She knows her boats," said my new ally.

I could see the captain wasn't convinced, but he was busy keeping watch on the ice blocks and couldn't leave his post. I had no doubt the ice farmers would sneak through more substandard blocks if he turned his back. He was keeping no written tally that I could see.

The Peary was unlike any working narrowboat I'd seen before. Instead of a canvas tent covering an open cargo hold, it was arranged more like an oceangoing steamer. The hold was accessed via rectangular openings in the flat metal deck. Into this void, the crane lowered the blocks. I could hear voices below.

I stepped to the edge and looked down but it was so dark inside I couldn't make out any detail.

"It's not like a coal boat," I said.

"Coal don't melt," said the boatman.

"How do you know how much ice you're carrying?"

"Once we're full, we're full."

I considered this. The captain might not need to keep a record if all the blocks were the same size. He would know how many it took to fill the hold to capacity. But with the ice farmers illiterate and the boat captain not counting the blocks, it was no wonder that suspicion had grown up between the two groups.

"How do you get down there?" I asked, gesturing into the hold.

"You can jump. Or ride the rope." He pointed to the ice block swinging across from the wagon.

"I'd like to try. Could I?"

He seemed less sure of this. Rather than wait for his answer, I grabbed the rope as it swung near and stepped onto the block of ice. I had not thought to warn the ice farmers that they were about to take my weight, so found myself lurching down into the black. I came to rest with a jarring bump.

I couldn't see anything, but I could feel the presence of the ice.

A man's voice greeted me. "Hello? What's this?"

He stepped into the pool of light below the hatch and I saw that he wore a long greatcoat and gauntlets that stretched up to his elbows.

"Hello," I said, flashing what I hoped was a winning smile.

I started to extend my hand by way of greeting, but seeing the palms of his gauntlets I pulled it back again. They were studded with short metal spikes, as were the forearms. It was a similar design to the gloves we had found at the ice farmers' cottage.

"Morning, ma'am," he said.

He seemed young. A teenager.

"Morning," I said. "Is it good work?"

"Not bad."

"They feed you well?"

He grinned. Fine white teeth shining in the darkness. Something about him reminded me of Tinker.

"Do they buy the clothes for you? And pay you too?"

"Yes, ma'am."

"How did you get the job?"

"My dad asked the captain. Why d'you want to know?"

"No reason," I said, though I was thinking of Tinker again, wondering if such work would suit him.

My eyes were adjusting and I started to be able to see the cargo, which had been stacked evenly across the boat, some forward some aft. The hold was metal-lined. Two hatchways above. No room for secret compartments. No way for the ice to leave except by the way it came in. Or through a drain hole ready to be pumped out if it melted.

I shivered. The cold was working inwards.

Looking up to the hatchway, I could see the depth of the deck above. There had to be layers of insulation to make it so thick.

"Is it only ice you carry?"

"Yeah. Ice. And cold stuff."

"What do you mean? Cold stuff?"

"Fish. And cheeses. Sometimes. They pay good for us to carry cold stuff with the ice."

I was about to question him further, but a shadow fell from the hatchway. The captain was peering down at us.

"She's stopping the loading. Get her out."

No sooner was I back on land than Julia wanted to know what I'd discovered. But there was nowhere to talk without being overheard so she had to contain her curiosity. But presently the loading was done. Peter sat down for a smoke with the remaining ice farmers, The Peary steamed away and we were alone.

"What did you find in the boat?" Julia whispered.

"Only ice."

"I mean, did you make discoveries?"

I related what I'd been told about the boats carrying other things.

"Perhaps boxes of food are taking space that ice should have filled," said Julia. "Could that be what's happening?"

"Perhaps," I said, though the idea did not ring true.

I had learned more of the captain's character from the way he treated his youngest crew-member than I ever might by questioning him directly. A man who would steal cargo worth pennies wouldn't have clothed or fed the child half as well. The ice farmers and the boat people were too much alike to trust each other. But too much alike also for either side to get away with dishonesty on a significant scale.

"Let's hold judgement," I said. "We'll know more once we've followed the ice to the end of its journey."

At last Gideon arrived with the ponies. His way had been longer than ours and with a gentler descent. I watched him drink deeply from a water flask. He seemed tired.

"This is as far as I go," he said, wiping his brow. "Tha'll be safe enough with the youngster."

Peter nodded. "I'll guide from here."

I caught his eye as he said it and he flinched as if stung. The others didn't seem to notice, but at that moment my vague fears started to crystallise; this had been his plan from the start, to be alone with us as we entered Derby, to claim the reward without anyone else knowing. I forced a smile, pretending to listen as Julia and Gideon chatted about what weather the evening might bring. But my mind was churning. I'd spent almost three days in Peter's company but still had no sense of who he really was. If I just waited, I would surely learn what he was capable of – but at a time and place of his choosing. That, I could not afford.

"We'll need to sort your luggage," said Gideon, who'd been talking all the while.

He and Julia strolled off towards where the horses were tethered.

"Thanks for your help." I blurted the words before

Peter could follow them.

He hesitated, eyes still on my feet. I held out my hand, hoping he wouldn't see it tremble, for my heart was racing. Reluctantly he took it.

Then, my breath coming short, I said: "When did you first recognise me?"

He did not answer but his face went slack with surprise.

"When was it?"

He could have denied knowledge. I might yet have believed him. Instead he turned his head away. Still gripping his hand, I sidestepped bringing myself back into his eye line.

"Why didn't you tell Gideon?"

He wrenched himself free but I grabbed his wrist.

"You wanted to keep the reward for yourself."

"No!"

"Ashamed then? Ashamed to hurt a woman who came to help your people?"

"Hurt? I wouldn't–"

"Do you have a daughter?"

He shook his head.

"A sister then?" I saw from his eyes that he did.

He tried to pull free again, but with less strength than before.

"You know what'll happen to me if I'm sent back?"

"But you're a criminal..."

"Who told you that?"

"In the pub – there was a poster – they said you were on the run."

"That's right. I am on the run. An old man – very rich – paid bribes so the court would make me his property. How old is your sister?"

He tried to get away from my gaze but I moved again, forcing him to look at me.

"To him, I'm just runaway property. You know what he'll do to me?"

"I... I didn't know. They read it for me. I can't–"

"What were you going to do? Wait till we were settled in our lodgings then find the nearest police house?"

"I won't tell! I'm sorry. I promise I won't tell."

I released him. For a heartbeat he stared directly back at me. Then he was scurrying away towards the others and busying himself with the saddlebags. I watched, rooted to the towpath, trying to catch the meaning of his final glance, not knowing if I'd witnessed sincerity in his expression or if it had been fear.

CHAPTER 25

*In this gilded age, perfection shall predominate over
the wild horses of innovation and science.*

FROM REVOLUTION

There were three of us riding along the towpath back
towards Derby. Then, when we had gone a mile or so,
I pulled my horse to a stop.

"We can find our way from here," I said.

Peter opened his mouth as if to speak but then
closed it again. He turned his horse in the path and set
off back the way we had come. Julia didn't question
me about it and I chose not to explain.

Three empty narrowboats passed us one after the
other, climbing through the locks as we descended. I
reminded myself that any one of the captains could
have been responsible for the theft. We waved to
each. The crews waved back, more friendly than the
master of The Peary had been. But then, we weren't
in the company of the ice farmers. Arguments over the
missing cargo must surely have soured the relationship.

"I've been thinking about the code," said Julia after
a long period of silence. "Or, I should say I've been

thinking of the code *book*. I might have been wrong about it being made rather than bought. There's another way to do it. The key could be an ordinary printed book."

"Like a novel?" I asked.

"Certainly. Any would do."

"*Pride and Prejudice?*"

"Don't tease," she said, her cheeks colouring. "A banned book would be no use. The coder and decoder both need to be able to access it. Each triplet in the code would direct the user to a particular word from the text."

There was an elegance to the idea. If it were a common enough text, the spy wouldn't even need to carry it with him.

"It's still no good though," Julia said. "We don't know what books he had in his room."

"We know of one," I said. "It lies in the bedside drawer of every guesthouse and hotel in the land."

"*From Revolution*," said Julia.

She said no more on the matter, but I could see the excitement that had kindled in her eyes.

She urged her pony on faster after that, eager to reach Derby and find a lodging place. But every mile south brought us closer to the border and increased the danger of my being discovered. With the outskirts of the city just ahead, I stopped to put on the mousy brown wig, which I'd not worn during our time in the mountains.

We found a coaching inn outside the city on Duffield Road. The stable master expressed surprise that two women should be riding unaccompanied. I smiled, though silently berating myself that I'd not foreseen the danger. I imagined the stable master relating the story of two strange women riding without escort. A jar of ale and it would be everywhere. We'd not be able to stay there long.

Julia was too well brought up to take the stairs at a run, but she climbed so fast that I was out of breath by the time we reached the room. She was at the bedside table in two strides and had *From Revolution* open before I could bolt the door behind us.

"The code," she said, flapping her hand in my direction.

I pulled the papers from my case and handed them to her. She was immediately leafing through the pages of the book. "If the letter represents the essay and the numbers are line and word, it gives us... Charter... The... And..." She frowned.

"That makes no sense," I said.

"Then we try them the other way. The first number defines the essay. Then the letter can be the line number..."

I watched her leafing through the book, licking the tip of her finger the better to turn the pages.

"If... And... Almighty... That's no better."

The puzzle of the code kept Julia working late into the night. It was the small hours of the morning when she finally admitted defeat and turned down the lamp. Her breathing slowed as she dropped into sleep. For a long time after, I listened to those small sounds that every building makes, searching in them for signs of danger, hoping that Peter's shame would not be overcome by greed.

•••

We had been to the metal troughs where the ice was formed in the mountains and to the disused mines in which it was stored. We'd ridden the ice carts down the mountain to the boats, which we had then seen loaded. And we had followed the path of the boats back to the city of Derby. Now we approached the final stage – Derby's famous ice factory. Here the ice was processed before it was distributed to the great cities of the south.

Having bought our tickets, we slipped in with the other tourists and picked our way down a flight of damp stone stairs, into a well of cool air at the bottom. But when our guide opened the double doors and we followed him through into a lamp-lit antechamber, the gentle chill turned to harsh cold. The walls were milky with accreted frost. Sharp corners were rounded. Melting and refreezing had caused ice stalagmites to form on the ground below brass lamp fittings projecting from the walls.

Our guide, the least warmly dressed of the party, had a bristling black beard and a constant grin. He clapped his hands and the chatter of conversation stopped. "It's here you put on the spikes," he said. "Tight as you can. We don't want feet slopping around. There's two miles of tunnel ahead. It'll feel like four if you don't get the buckles right."

Julia had been out of sorts all morning. She hadn't mentioned the code, but I could see it weighing on her mind. She had convinced herself that *From Revolution* would be the key. I believe her mood was kept low by a sense of failure. And so preoccupied was I by the risk of capture that I could find no enthusiasm to offer her.

Since returning to Derby, I'd not looked at the face of a stranger without asking myself if he or she might know my identity. I surveyed the others in our tour party, all busily buckling iron spikes to their footwear. None looked like a spy. But paradoxically, no spy does.

Clockwise around the room there was a pair of elderly ladies, a genteel husband-and-wife, a small party of students and a young couple who clung together even more tightly than the cold and slippery surfaces required. Honeymooners, I thought. A suitable wedding gift, this visit to an industrial facility.

I had never understood the Republican fascination with factories, warehouses and building projects. Wherever working men sweated to shift earth or to grease machines, there would be the middle classes looking on and feeling good about themselves – as if through some vicarious process they were absorbing the virtue that came with toil.

They did things differently in the Kingdom. The closest most Royalists wanted to be to sweat was in a steam bath. And the only workers that made them feel good were waiters and shop attendants.

Julia parked herself on a pile of hay bundles by the wall. She examined the spiked irons, turning them until they matched her boots. I sat next to her and did the same with mine.

"Forget the code," I whispered.

"I *had* forgotten!" she hissed, shooting me an angry look. "I wanted to enjoy this. I've never been to an ice factory before. Now code books will be filling my mind all morning!"

"The way to solve a problem is to think about something else."

"Then please stop raising it!"

She stood and took a tentative step, holding her hands out to either side. I tightened the leather straps over my own boots and followed. Others were getting to their feet. The young couple clung together tighter than ever. Perhaps in their case I could understand the enthusiasm. A week travelling the factories of the Midlands would be a week spent away from the eyes and ears of his family. The elderly ladies looked on and tutted.

"It might feel shaky out here," said our guide. "But once we're on the thick ice the spikes'll sink in. Be glad of 'em."

He looked around the party, satisfying himself that all was in order. While we had been busy he had lit two storm lanterns. One he held on a pole above his head. The other he passed to the leader of the student group. "You stay at the back. Don't let anyone lag behind."

Then he pushed open a set of double doors and we followed him into the dark beyond. Though the tunnel must have originally been cut square, the accumulation of ice had rounded its corners. The air was so cold that it felt painful to inhale. After a few paces, I realised that we were descending a gentle slope. A layer of mist clung to the floor, deepening as we progressed. At first it covered only our boots but by the time we were fifty paces in, I was wading through it waist deep.

Up ahead I could see our guide's lamp dipping

under the surface. One of the elderly ladies in front of me wore long black feathers in her hat. Soon these were the only part of her projecting above the mist. I found myself ducking involuntarily to take my head below the surface.

"These tunnels were built during the construction," our guide announced. "That was one hundred and twenty years ago. Now we use them only for the tours and as part of the ventilation system. They're cleaned through once a year. Else they'd be iced up in no time."

We had passed three side-tunnels already, narrower than this one. One was so heavily iced that it had grown oval in cross section. It seemed that not all the tunnels were cleaned so often.

Our guide had stopped at a crossroads where the tunnel was wider. He gathered us in a loose circle, waiting for the leader of the student group to arrive before he began to speak again.

"All still present? Very good. Wouldn't do to lose anyone. Though we've two miles to walk, there's more than ten miles of tunnels, if you add them all together. And that's the ones we know. Every few years the cleaners find something to add to the map. Last year it was a room where the navvies used to sleep. The doorway was full of ice. But once we broke through, it was like Tutankhamen's tomb. No gold or ebony though. There was plates, cups, bedding. Even the food on the table – just as they left it. A loaf of bread and a hunk of cheese.

"And fifteen years ago – I worked in the factory proper back then – they found the body of a little girl. All iced in. Curled up in a corner of one of the side rooms just like she'd gone to sleep. We called the constables. Got relatives of missing girls to come look. None of them knew her. Then someone sees her shoes and says them buckles went out a hundred years ago. And they bring in museum people then. They look over her clothes and say it's true. The girl's been lying there for a century. Turns out she was the daughter of one of the factory foremen. Went missing in 1905.

"Ice preserves. Stops things living. Whether it's rot or animal or man. That's the beauty of it. And that's the peril too. So don't go wandering off or they might be finding you curled up in a corner in one hundred years' time."

He grinned, looking around the party for anyone to share his joke. A few of the students laughed, though the smiles were not quite as easy as before. The reaction seemed to satisfy him, though. He clapped his hands again and started leading us down the side passage to the left. After a few yards he glanced back, checking the rear marker was still following.

We had been walking for some minutes when I noticed a slowly repeating boom. It was so quiet and low that at first it seemed to be a tremor rather than a sound. But as we progressed through the ice tunnel it grew, and I recognised it as the rhythm of some large beam engine. I was about to mention it to Julia but stopped myself. Her expression could have been a sulk or focussed concentration. Either way, I decided it safer not to disturb her.

It was a curious quality of the tunnels to play tricks with sound, sometimes muffling, sometimes amplifying. Turning into yet another passage, the engine noise became suddenly louder. The young couple whispered to each other. The lady in front turned her head as if trying to determine the direction it came from. Hat feathers twitched above her.

Our guide stopped in front of another set of doors, did a quick head-count, then without introduction led us through into a vast underground chamber. Lamps in the wall and ceiling, regularly spaced, receded into the mist. Before us stood towering racks of shelving, on which lay blocks of ice, each perhaps two foot thick and six foot along the sides.

"Don't touch the metal," shouted our guide.

Three of the students who had been edging towards the nearest ice block, pulled up mid-step. Frozen, so to speak.

"Down here it's twenty below. Touch the racks and you'd freeze to the metal. Don't want you leaving your skin behind."

It seemed strange that he hadn't warned us before. But it came to me that this apparently genial man took pleasure in shocking his audience.

The rhythmic boom echoed in the cavernous hall. I could now make out other rhythms, quieter than the first. Strips of cloth fluttered from a metal grille in the wall. I put my hand next to it and felt the frigid breeze.

"We've seven Rawlings and Buckley heat exchanging engines," our guide announced. "Four of them are in use at any one time. The others can be maintained or fixed if they're broken. That's what keeps it so cold in here. Takes a ton of coal an hour to feed them. But if we had to freeze the water to make these blocks we'd need ten times that. And it would take too long. That's why we bring ice in from the mountains."

One of the students put up his hand. "Why don't you stack the blocks on top of each other? Why the shelving?"

"That's how they tried it at first," said our guide. "Like stacking blocks of stone. And it worked. Three or four blocks, straw scattered between. Worked fine. But you try making a stack as high as this room. That's when ice flows. More like tallow than brick. Then the piles fall over and you're in all kinds of mess.

"The racks were built in 1897. Over a hundred years old and no one's found a better way. You can't improve on perfection. The blocks get pushed along by shunting pistons. They start at the top of the hall, then work their way down by stages. The ice comes here at maybe two degrees below. We form it into these blocks, send it on its journey. By the time it reaches floor level, we've taken it to minus twenty and it's ready to go out."

Our party set off at a brisk walk along the edge of the room. I was glad of the movement because I had started to shiver and was having to clench my jaw to stop my teeth chattering against each other. I saw now that the racks sloped like a child's marble run. I imagined the life of a block of ice, sliding down from near the roof all the way to the floor.

A loud crash made us jerk our heads around. Ice was sliding along the rack. Another loud crash – the sound of a block reaching the end of the room and dropping to the shelf below.

"Why are the blocks that size?" asked the leader of the students.

"It was the largest the boats could carry back in 1897. That was before the canals were widened. There are hoists at the very end of the line to lift the blocks up to where the barges are waiting. From there, they're away to keep the best ice houses stocked. We send two hundred blocks a year to the king himself in London town."

The elderly ladies gasped audibly, displaying a virtuous distaste for the monarchy. I wondered how many times our guide had used that line and enjoyed a shocked response.

I put my hand up. "How do you keep track?"

"Keep track?"

"If this were a wool warehouse, you'd have a system to account for it all. You'd know which farmer had given how much. Otherwise how would you know what to pay them?"

He scratched at his beard. "All the ice is weighed as it comes in. We keep records just like any warehouse."

"But wool doesn't melt," I said.

"You think our ice melts? Must be a warm coat you're wearing."

"Wasn't there a dispute. In the newspaper it said–"

"Don't believe what you read!" he snapped. Then just as suddenly as it had gone, the jovial tone returned. "Ice farmers, eh? Sleeping all summer. Not what you'd call the deserving poor."

Others in the group laughed, though not as easily as before.

"I read someone had been stealing their ice," I said.

"Stealing off each other most likely. Just because you read it, don't make it true. If someone had been stealing their ice, then it's further up the chain. We keep account of it all. We've shown the books to the lawyers."

"They think it's being taken from this factory."

"They're wrong. And that's an end to it!"

So saying, the man who enjoyed shocking his visitors wheeled and marched away. It was all the elderly ladies could do to keep up.

The way back out of the ice factory proved considerably less interesting. Once we'd left the giant warehouse the tunnel ran on for half a mile before we came to an elevator cage. Our guide ushered in the student with the lamp. The other students followed as did the elderly ladies and the newlyweds. Julia stepped in after them and I was poised to follow when our guide held out his arm to stop me.

"She's full," he said. Then he slid the metal door closed with a crash. "The topside foreman will be there to help you out," he called. Then he pulled a lever on the wall. A bell chimed and the cage juddered upwards. Within a second it was out of view and we were alone.

He stepped closer. I wanted to keep my distance but the tunnel wall was directly behind me.

"Don't know what your game is," he said. "But you'll do no good messing with men's business–"

"Are you threatening me?"

The words just blurted out. As soon as I heard them

I regretted it. His fists clenched and unclenched. The hum of the winches stopped. Far up the shaft I heard the door clang as it was slid open.

"We don't threaten," he said. "Not in the ice factory. Got to stick together down here. There's too many accidents waiting with all the machines and the ice. It's Mrs Raike isn't it?"

The winches hummed to life again. I could hear the cage rattling down the shaft towards us. He bent closer.

"Answer me, girl!" he growled. "Was it Mrs Raike sent you?"

"No."

He stared. I stared back, as no Republican woman should ever do. The moment stretched. The rattling grew loud. Then he looked away.

"Women!" He fairly spat the word.

The door slid open. Inside the elevator cage stood Julia, her expression alive and intense. She held out her hand as if to grab me. I jumped in beside her, expecting him to follow. But he remained in the tunnel.

I slid the door closed. The bell chimed and we lurched upwards. Only then did I release the breath I had been holding. "Thank you," I gasped. "Thank you! Thank you!"

"For what?"

"For coming back to rescue me."

She looked puzzled. "I came back because I couldn't wait to share the news. I know how to break the code!"

CHAPTER 26

*That man is rare who will feel enriched on learning
the workings of a trick.*

THE BULLET-CATCHER'S HANDBOOK

"What's the first sequence?" Julia asked.

I read from the coded message: "C 7 3"

She was kneeling on the floor next to me with the
two pages from the Nottingham Post spread out in
front of her. "I'm going to try column C, line seven,
word three."

I watched her trace the page with her first finger,
repeating with the other page. "That gives us 'Was' or
'January'. Write them down."

I did as instructed. "The next sequence is D 1 9."

"That's 'Which' or 'Bad'."

"Doesn't sound right," I said. "No sentence starts
'Was which'."

"So we eliminate that."

But the words from the other page gave us an
equally unlikely opening: January, bad, the, and. Julia
sat back on her heels. She bit her lower lip. Then her
frown dropped away and she turned the pages over.

"Try again," she said.

"Write down 'The' and 'Returned'." Her finger traced the pages again. "Now write 'What' and 'Nottingham'."

"That's it," I said. "The second side of the second page." I read out the sequences one after the other. She called the words: "Returned. Nottingham. Late. Your. Message. Waiting."

"It's actually working!" I said, grinning with the unexpected victory. Her eyes were wide and seemed brighter than I had seen them before. "It was in front of us all the while," she said.

"How did you work it out?"

"I just thought about something else. Like you told me. It popped into my mind. Now read the rest of the numbers. I want to know what it says!"

> Returned Nottingham late. Your message waiting three days. Will send this reply first post. Name you gave for target A previously unknown. Sudden increase security Mrs Raike Charitable Foundation makes membership records inaccessible. Pursue new target B. All expenses will be met.
>
> Addendum. Have this morning learned of possible identity target A living North Leicester. Dispatched intelligence gatherer with description from your message. Fox.

After I finished adding punctuation as best I could, we read it through again. Alarm had replaced our excitement.

"Am I target A?" asked Julia.

I nodded. "It's most likely. And I'm target B."

"My parents..."

"... Are in no danger. Intelligence gatherers work quietly. He probably just went to the pub and bought a drink or two for the local gossips."

"And Fox?"

"A name perhaps?"

The word had come from an article describing a meeting of the South Nottinghamshire Hunt. It seemed unlikely that the writer would add a name to a coded message since the recipient would know already who had sent it.

"Let's do the next one," said Julia.

Knowing the system, it took little time to unlock the second message. Using the other newspaper page as key, we transcribed the words:

> *Confirmation. North Leicester intelligence gatherer reports target A signed up Mrs Raike three weeks ago. Will send message indicating disapproval.*
>
> *Your description woman target B too vague. Determine identity. Highest priority. May require intervention as before. Usual bonus. Half payment on collection. Half on autopsy.*

After Julia had read the mess out loud, we took turns at reading it silently. There was no name at the end of this one. But I could find no article containing the word fox on the second page.

I'd just been handed the transcription for a third time when I was jolted from my focus by a heavy knock on the door. Julia clasped a hand to her chest.

The knock came again and a boy's voice called from outside. "Message for Miss Swain."

Neither of us answered. There was a pause before he called through the door again: "He said to put it in y'r hand."

The floorboards creaked as Julia stepped across the room. I positioned myself next to the wall so I would be out of sight. But when she pulled back the bolt and opened up, I found I could see through the crack of the door jamb.

"You Miss Swain?" asked the boy.

"Yes."

"He said you're to have this."

She accepted a small parcel.

"He? Who?"

"Dunno."

"Tall? Short?"

"Tall," said the boy, illustrating by stretching a hand above his head.

"Bearded? Shaved? What kind of hat?"

"Shaved, miss. And it were a bowler."

He scampered away.

I held the package while Julia re-bolted the door. It was cold to touch, the brown paper damp with condensation. Julia cut the string and opened it up to reveal a grey metal box. I prised off the lid. A quantity of crushed ice lay within. And resting in the middle of it, a woman's severed finger.

CHAPTER 27

*Allow the audience time to anticipate what they are
going to see. The longer the moment of uncertainty, the
greater will be their applause.*

THE BULLET-CATCHER'S HANDBOOK

I understood what it was on first glance. But
realisation grew more slowly for Julia. The horror of
the object seemed to stop her mind from grasping its
reality. Seeing her face whiten, I tried to take the box
from her but she wouldn't release her grip. I peeled
back her fingers one after the other and set it down
on the small table.

She drew in a sudden breath and, with both hands
clutching her heart, stepped backwards until she half
fell into a chair. I walked directly to the window and
looked out.

"Is that...?" she managed.

"A finger," I said. "Yes."

I could see no one watching on the street, so
returned to the table. There was water in the base of
the box. Not much though. The ice could not have
been in it for long else more would have melted. I

guessed the time at between ten minutes and half an hour.

Tipping the box, I spilled the water, ice and the finger onto the table.

"What are you doing?" Julia cried.

"Looking for clues."

I turned the box searching for markings or writing but found none.

"The thing itself is the message," I said.

"Does he mean to do the same to us?"

"If you want to cut someone's fingers off, you don't tell them first. It's a warning. Worse will happen unless..."

"Unless what?"

"We're supposed to know the answer."

Clenching my jaw against revulsion, I picked up the finger and dropped it back in its box. Then I marched to the washstand and scrubbed my hands until they were sore. Even then they felt unclean. Julia got back to her feet and approached the box. As I dried my hands, I saw her peering into it. "Whose finger is it?"

"I fear we're supposed to know that as well. Unless we do as they wish, more fingers will follow. They have this poor woman a prisoner. They assume we know it already. And they believe we care deeply. This was meant to shock."

We both stared at the finger. It had belonged to a delicate hand, unscarred and without calluses. The owner had lived free from physical labour. The nail was long enough to project beyond the finger tip – another indication that she did not work. Though manicured in the past, the end was chipped in one place. I brought my head down low to examine the wound where the finger had been cut from the hand. It had been removed at the middle joint. The end of the finger bone peeked from the surrounding flesh, unmarked, as if it had been cut free with the delicacy of a scalpel rather than the brute force of a cleaver.

"They know where we are," Julia said, the obvious truth hitting her at last. "They know!"

"The question is how. We've been in the mountains for days. I can only think it was Peter. No one else knew where or when we'd return."

Julia's hand went to her mouth.

"What is it?"

"I sent a letter," she said. "A report. Those were my instructions – to keep Mrs Raike informed. You don't suppose..."

"You gave an address?"

"I'm not such a fool!"

"We've not been near a postal office. How did you send it?"

"Downstairs. At the reception. I paid the desk clerk."

Understanding rushed at me and I felt sick. "He franked the envelope for you?"

"Yes. I didn't have a stamp."

"The franking machine will print the name of the inn. Anyone looking at the envelope would know where we are."

"But the only person to read the letter would be Mrs Raike."

I had no means of explaining my mistrust of the woman. It would lead to an argument just when there was no time to talk.

"Pack," I said. "Do it now. Somehow we have to get out of here without being followed."

But before either of us could move, the door rattled under the impact of another heavy knock. I grabbed a towel and threw it over the metal box and the pool of melting ice. Then I took up my position, flattened to the wall.

Julia stood trembling. "Who is it?" she called.

The knock sounded again, louder this time.

"Who is it?"

"Open the door, girl!" A woman's voice.

Julia fumbled with the bolts. In strode the unmistakable, bombazine-clad figure of Mrs Raike, followed a step behind by the housemistress who swiftly closed the door.

Julia flustered, moving first one way and then the other until she had the room's two chairs arranged for the guests. I sat next to her on the bed.

Immediately Julia stood again. "Would you like tea?"

"Sit, girl!" said Mrs Raike, in that crackly voice that I knew to be part of her disguise.

Julia obeyed.

"What have you to say for yourself?"

"I... That is, we..." Julia's eyes darted to the table, on which the severed finger lay concealed.

"Well?" demanded Mrs Raike.

"What is it you want to know?" I asked.

"Why did you announce yourselves as working for me?"

"We didn't," I said. "Why would you think otherwise?"

"Don't speak in that tone!" said the housemistress.

I caught Mrs Raike's eye. The shared look was a mere flicker of a glance, but enough to remind us of each other's vulnerabilities. She gestured for the housemistress to back down.

"We received a complaint," she said, her voice more measured. "The Ice Factory state that you visited. You were there?"

"What did the complaint say, exactly?" I asked.

"That two women working for the Foundation used deception to gain access to the factory. Staff were questioned. Aggressively so. Other visitors in the party were distressed."

"Just that?"

"It would have been sufficient on its own. But then you announced your connection to the Foundation. You brought us into disrepute!"

"We didn't!" Julia's protest came out as a squeak.

"You were there, girl?"

"Yes, but–"

"Did you make an appointment?"

"We went as tourists, but–"

"And you asked questions?"

"We... I mean Elizabeth–"

"Were questions asked, girl?"

"Yes."

I didn't intervene. The decoded message was echoing in my mind. *Target A signed up Mrs Raike three weeks ago. Will send message indicating disapproval.* I had always known that petty ice theft did not merit the urgency given to the case. Picturing the neatly severed finger, I understood.

I had drifted into my own thoughts, losing track

of the conversation. Now I became aware of it again. Julia was still being interrogated.

"I... it wasn't like that," she said.

"Then explain!"

"He asked for questions. We just–"

I stood. Everyone looked at me.

"We've received a complaint about *your* conduct," I said, stepping to the table.

"How dare you..." the housemistress began, but then faltered as I held my hand above the table.

I waited until both women were watching. Then I whipped the towel away. They leaned forwards trying to see into the box, but were seated too low. I picked it up and, with a showman's flourish, placed it in Mrs Raike's hand.

"This is the message we received."

At first Mrs Raike seemed to be having a convulsion. She threw the box onto the floor, spilling its contents. She staggered from her chair. Her reaction was quicker than Julia's had been and so much more powerful.

"You expected this," I said. "You were waiting for it."

Mastering my own revulsion, I picked up the finger. "You see the cut? Look closely. See how fine the work?"

Mrs Raike had backed away as I advanced. But now she had reached the wall. "It came packaged in ice. To keep it fresh, it seemed. But everything was part of the message. The finger, the ice, and the way it was severed. Look." I held it close to her face. She was crying.

My wrist was grabbed from behind. The

housemistress pulled me sharply. I dropped the finger.

"Stop!" she cried. "Stop it! Stop it! Can't you see what you're doing?" She knelt and picked up the finger, holding it in both her hands as if it were a wounded bird.

Julia was on her feet, her mouth opening and closing as if she couldn't cope with the rapidity of unfolding events. "What's happening?"

"The message wasn't meant for us," I said. "And it was never about ice, though ice was part of it. It's about death and bodies. And kidnapping."

Mrs Raike stepped back to the chair as if in a dream. The act of walking like an old woman had been forgotten, though Julia was too beset by other revelations to notice the slip in her disguise.

"Her name's Antonia," said the housemistress. "Sweet natured and quick. When the ice farmers asked for help, she was the perfect choice. She didn't go to the mountains as you did. She watched the boats as they came to the ice factory. For weeks she kept tally, counting the blocks being unloaded. Each day she sent a letter to say the number. At the end of the month, if the factory made short payment we were ready to present the evidence. The ice farmers would have their redress. But then..."

Here the housemistress faltered. For a moment there was silence. Then Mrs Raike spoke.

"The letters stopped."

"Didn't you contact the police?" I asked.

"We had decided to," said Mrs Raike. "Three days had passed. Then a letter did arrive. This one unsigned. The writer said he had taken Antonia and was holding her safe but if we told anyone she would be harmed."

"He?"

"No woman would do such a thing."

Her assertion of female virtue seemed ill-founded but I let it pass.

"Why didn't you say before?" I asked. "In the name of all that's sacred, why?"

Mrs Raike and the housemistress shared a look, as if this was a question they had wrestled with. I hoped she was sweating under the layers of makeup. Flush with anger, I hoped she was suffering.

"You've risked Julia's life! Did you not think she might be taken also?"

"She wasn't to admit a connection to me," said Mrs Raike.

"And that would help, how?"

"She was instructed to be discreet to the utmost."

"It's true," said Julia.

"No!" I gripped Julia's shoulders and looked into her eyes. "They knew the danger. They wanted my brother to help. And me. They'd read reports of our activities last year. We'd be easy to control. That's what they thought. In case we found anything inconvenient."

Mrs Raike looked away.

"We refused to help," I said. "But it was my brother and me they wanted. So they took you – my dear friend – and sent you out, expecting you to be taken. And once you were, I would have no choice. They knew I'd travel through hell to find you. And in doing so, I'd find the lost Antonia."

Julia was shaking her head. "They wouldn't."

But Mrs Raike would not contradict my story.

"Why didn't you ask directly? If not us then some other intelligence gatherer. It isn't as if the Gas-Lit Empire's poorly provided with spies!"

"We did ask," said the housemistress. "We asked five. Three said no. One said he would do it, but asked an amount of money we couldn't access. And one agreed – the youngest of them all. A man we later discovered had no experience. He ran away with the money."

"Disappeared or ran?"

"What's the difference?"

"What's the difference? Do you really not understand? And then you sent my friend into danger!"

"There's no need to raise your voice."

"I'm angry! You sent a woman to investigate and she's been taken. Then you sent a man, who's now most likely buried in a shallow grave. And then you send Julia in the expectation that she'd be taken too – so that my brother and I would descend into the same pit of snakes! Why does this Antonia's life play on your conscience more than ours?"

Mrs Raike was crying silently, tears running over the makeup, which had begun to smear. For a moment she seemed paralysed. Then she ran to the door. Only after she was gone did the housemistress answer.

"Antonia is Mrs Raike's daughter," she said.

The housemistress got to her feet and brushed down her skirts. "I'm sorry for your trouble," she said. "But you're safe now. And I trust you're not out of pocket."

She held out her hand to Julia. "Shall we?"

"Shall we what?"

"If you wish, you can go back to North Leicester. I'd understand. But before that you have to walk out of this inn in plain view and return to Upper Wharf Street with us. You have to be seen. *They* have to see. Whoever they are."

She was right. Even through my anger, I knew it. The spy had been following Julia. She was known to be working for Mrs Raike.

Julia was on her feet. "I won't go!"

"You must," I said. "However badly we've been treated, there's a woman's life at stake."

"Then you'll come too."

"I'm a fugitive, remember. I can't retrace my steps." Then, turning to the housemistress, I said: "Mrs Raike made a bargain with me – do you know what it was?"

Her eyes flicked to Julia then back to me. She nodded.

"If I track down these people, would she honour her promise?"

"I've known her since we were children. I've never seen her break a promise. Bring back her daughter and she'd give you the world, if that was in her power."

"What promise?" asked Julia.

"To help me stay in the Kingdom. It's that or I travel north and try to lose myself in Scotland or beyond. I'm furious that she risked your life. Unspeakably furious. But I've got to give it a try."

"How can you find them? You don't know anything about them."

"I wouldn't say that." I took the metal box from the

housemistress and turned it to show the cut where the finger had been separated from the hand. "The coded message said: *Half payment on collection. Half on autopsy.* This is hardly a butcher's work. More a surgeon's, don't you think? And then, what did it say: *returned Nottingham late*? So a surgeon based in Nottingham, who needs quantities of ice but can't be seen to be buying it. Someone who'll go to any lengths to keep his activity secret."

If it were possible, the housemistress became paler still. "You don't mean body snatchers?"

That was exactly what I meant. "Please tell Mrs Raike that our agreement stands. Nothing has changed. I'll keep to my side of the bargain. She must keep to hers."

With the housemistress waiting outside, I said goodbye to Julia, charging her to see that the horses were returned to Ashbourne. She gave vent to her distress. I held mine back. But when the door was closed between us, I sank to the floor and wept.

CHAPTER 28

Art has aforetime been the plaything of kings. We shall recommission it to the service of the common man. He shall it uplift and educate.

FROM REVOLUTION

Autopsy – the word glowered at me from the decoded message. *North Leicester Intelligence Gatherer reports Target A signed up Mrs Raike three weeks ago.* Target A was surely Julia. *Will send message indicating disapproval.* We had received the message – Antonia's severed finger – and passed it on to its intended recipient. *Your description woman target B too vague.* That had to be me. I took comfort that the description had been insubstantial. *Determine identity. Highest priority.* It would be disastrous if they did discover my identity. But again, comfort could be taken from the fact that they had not done so yet. *May require intervention as before.* Intervention could mean anything. But a young intelligence gatherer had gone missing. Mrs Raike might assume he had run off with the advance payment, but I feared worse. *Usual bonus.* It had happened before. That supported my theory about the missing intelligence gatherer. *Half payment on collection*. The man was a hired hand. *Half on autopsy*. The skin on the back of my neck tightened as I re-read the transcription.

Then the final word on the first message: *Fox*.

The recipient must have known the identity of the sender. Perhaps the name was some deeper code. Even so, it felt like cold vanity to include it. To make free with any badge of identity in such a conspiratorial message is to believe yourself beyond harm.

From Derby to Nottingham is a journey of just fifteen miles. There was no time for better precaution so I travelled by coach with no disguise but the wig and a small beauty spot. I found a respectable boarding house just south of Castle Rock and secured a twin room on the ground floor with the story that my aunt would be joining me in a couple of days and that her arthritis made climbing stairs quite impossible.

I heaved the sash window up and open, then leant out to survey the small back garden. Cucumbers grew under glass in a line of cold frames against the side wall. A brick path ran between a potting shed and a greenhouse. The thought came unbidden that there would be places for Tinker to hide should he find me again. Irritated with myself for the sentiment, I shoved my case under the bed and set about my tasks.

My first call was to the postal office. I scanned the notice board behind the counter and was relieved to find no picture of myself. Emboldened, I asked the clerk for the city directories. He pointed me to a stack of volumes further down the counter, the biggest of which was devoted to medical businesses.

Every town was famous for something. With North Leicester it was trade and smuggling. With Derby it was ice and heavy industry. But with Nottingham it was medicine. Any doctor who hoped to rise through the ranks of his profession would surely study there. A year spent in one of its hospitals was as good as a certificate on the consulting room wall.

I leafed through the heavy volume to the list of principal medical establishments. The Women's Hospital on Peel Street, the Borough of Nottingham Lunatic Asylum and the Forest House Children's Hospital could all be discounted. None of them had operating theatres. The City Hospital did carry out surgical procedures. But it was to the General Hospital that bodies were transported for autopsy. The list of surgeons who worked there took up nine pages.

Having thanked the clerk for his help I purchased, for one penny, a sheet of notepaper and an envelope. Then, making sure that no one overlooked me, I wrote:

Dear Mr Farthing,
    You told me once that I should contact you in the event that I needed anything. I am doing so with this letter, which is my request to meet you at noon today in the art gallery in Nottingham Castle. You will understand why I cannot come to your office in person.

When he visited me in the prison camp, John Farthing had told me that he could be contacted via premises situated on High Pavement. The street was easy to find, though I could not at first locate the building. Looking for something of grand scale, I walked clear past it. But on retracing my steps, noticed the brass name plaque next to the door. It seemed too ordinary a property to be occupied by an agency of world-encircling power.

I offered a boy tuppence to put the letter in Farthing's hand, but he was too afraid to approach an agent. Tenpence restored his courage and he scampered into the building. I climbed a short flight of steps on the opposite side of the road to the grounds of a library that must once have been a church. From this vantage point, I could look down on the street, whilst pretending to study old gravestones.

I did not have long to wait. John Farthing emerged at a great rush, followed closely by the boy. I slipped into the library before either had a chance to look up and see me.

Nottingham Castle is built on top of a rocky crag in the centre of the city. Little more than a gatehouse remains from the original fortifications. Instead of a drawbridge and portcullis there stands a ticket window and turnstile. I paid my money and entered. Immediately before me were manicured lawns and borders of roses. Paths led to a large building of pale stone at the top. It was towards this I climbed. Instead of entering, I chose a bench overlooking the gatehouse and sat to wait.

I was still unsure of Farthing's reaction to my escape. He had seen my preparation – the folding of my stocking to thicken the ankle. I felt myself blushing as I remembered. He had stared at my reflection in the dark glass of the window and seen what a man should not see. I believed it was shame that stopped him reporting me. Or perhaps it was simply beyond the narrow focus of his loyalty. Though Patent Law transcends all borders within the Gas-Lit Empire, it is of limited scope.

Even if he had planned to make a report, one of the prisoners in the hut had got there first. The image of Tulip swam in my mind, the woman who saw me leave. She'd told me that she was a bad person. I had not believed her.

Now, at last, one question from that episode would be resolved. If Farthing came accompanied by the constabulary, I would know the nature of his loyalty. I had already planned my escape route.

The town clock struck twelve with no sign of him. Feeling a pang of disappointment, I decided that ten more minutes could do no harm. But it was not until the fading of the half hour chime that he at last came hurrying through the gatehouse turnstile. Even at a distance he was unmistakable. Some men seem to lurch or tumble as they run. John Farthing had balance.

I kept watching the turnstile. The next person through was a nurse leading two toddlers. There were no constables.

He did not notice me. I counted to ten before getting up and following him inside the building. I took my time climbing the stairs to the art gallery on the first floor. He took off his hat as I stepped towards him and I saw that he was perspiring.

He ran a hand back through his hair. "I thought I'd missed you."

"And I thought you might be fetching the constables."

A look of pain crossed his face and I immediately regretted my words. He turned, as if to examine the paintings on the wall – a triptych of Ned Ludd smashing the stocking frames.

"Forgive me," I said. "You came as I asked."

"I couldn't have not come, Elizabeth."

"Thank you."

"I was surprised by your letter. Getting away was... difficult. Discreetly, I mean." He faced me again. "Why did you call me here?"

We found a pair of back to back benches and sat one on each, heads close together but facing in opposite directions. To an observer it would have seemed we studied the paintings on different walls. In a low voice I related my adventure – in edited form. I did not give away the real identity of Mrs Raike. Nor her relationship to the kidnapped Antonia. And I was especially careful to steer away from any hint of my method of disguise. That was one card I was glad to keep up my sleeve – one power I still had to use against John Farthing if the need came.

When I told him about the perfectly severed finger and the evidence that pointed to Nottingham, he stood and began pacing. I followed him. When I caught up he said:

"I don't approve."

"Of severed fingers?"

"Of your investigation."

"I should have conducted it some other way?"

"I have a duty to protect," he said. "And this is too dangerous."

"Think of poor Antonia. Kidnapped by bodysnatchers. Is she owed no duty?"

His mouth opened and closed again, caught between speaking and silence.

A party of teenage girls with satchels entered the gallery, shepherded by two women who might have been governesses.

"Your brother should be doing this," Farthing muttered. "Not you."

Then he strode away, as if he had merely been passing the place where I stood. On the other side of the room, the governesses gave instructions and the girls began getting out pencils and sketch pads. I caught up with Farthing in the next gallery along.

"Even if your deductions are correct," he said, "what can you possibly achieve?"

"I can follow clues."

"You intend to visit every hospital? Question every physician?"

"Remember the name from the message? Fox. There are only two medical men with that surname. A dentist and a chiropodist. Not promising. But there's also a Dr Foxley. Erasmus Foxley. He does public autopsies. What odds would you have put on that?"

Farthing checked and wound his pocket watch. I walked away and stood in front of a huge canvas depicting the battle of Stanhope. Heroic lead miners doing battle with the soldiers of the Prince Bishop. Other visitors were ambling through the gallery. Farthing did not join me until they had moved on.

"Your reasoning could be wrong," he said. "Have you thought of that? Elizabeth Barnabus could have made a mistake?"

"You think me proud?"

"I think you clothe yourself in virtue and call me corrupt whenever I disagree!"

"Then you fault my reasoning?"

"I cannot. That's what I'm afraid of. You're walking into terrible danger."

"Then help me!"

"You know the risk I've taken merely coming here?"

"And why have I asked you? Why am I forced to do these things? Because an agent of the Patent Office took a bribe and–"

"Say the word and I'll raise your complaint. There could yet be an investigation. If an agent is guilty as you claim…"

"The Patent Office investigating its own? I'd win my case, do you suppose? We both know that's not going to happen."

"Then what can I do?"

"You have files on important people. Check to see if anything's written about Erasmus Foxley. That's all I ask. Without information, I'm fighting blind. If there was something, even a suspicion, you could ask questions. Officially, I mean. As an agent."

"There won't be anything," he said.

"But you will look?"

"I don't know why I'm agreeing. But yes. I'll look."

"How soon can we meet?"

"A week?"

"Too long."

"Searching the files, I put myself in danger! I'll need four days, at least."

He began telling me of a tea shop on Bridlesmith Gate where we could meet. I gazed at the canvas on the wall in front of us.

"Elizabeth, did you take in what I said?"

In truth I'd drifted, distracted by the unfamiliar thought that an agent of the International Patent Office could be in danger from his own organisation.

"I was saying that he's a doctor. That leaves slim chance of finding anything in the records."

I gestured to the painting. "Look at those miners. You know the story. What chance did they have against trained soldiers? But all other choice was gone. So they took up arms."

"You're not fighting a war, Elizabeth."

After a moment in which we both stared at the picture, I asked: "Why didn't you report me?"

"I'm sorry?"

"At the prison camp. You knew I was planning to escape."

"I... I didn't mean to look at you. But–"

"A woman prisoner raised the alarm. You refrained."

"She was driven to it. Don't think too badly of her."

I tried to drive the image of Tulip from my mind. I had thought her my friend.

"Neither you nor I have children," said Farthing.

"We can't know the desperation that woman felt. I was there when she raised the alarm. I can tell you she wept."

"Children?"

"Her son and daughter. They were together on the end of the same chain that held you. She informed in the hope it would win their release. It did not."

CHAPTER 29

Misdirection is your trick. All else is polish. A pretty girl dancing will leave an elephant unseen.

THE BULLET-CATCHER'S HANDBOOK

Public autopsies cannot be read about on day-bills. Nor even in exclusive magazines. But the third hospital porter I approached proved susceptible. The more rapidly I fanned myself, the more he seemed encouraged.

"They love to see a body cut open," he said.

"Who could bear to watch such things?"

"Gents as you'd think respectable," he said. "Gents as hold more cash than kindling."

"And have you seen it?" I asked.

"No, miss. But I see the bodies laid out, 'coz it's my job to keep the ice topped up. And I take the bits away, after." He put special emphasis on the word *bits*. "You wouldn't believe the things inside a body. And the colours. Not just red. There's blue and black and white and yellow."

"I think you're brave," I said, fanning myself extra hard for good effect. "I could never look at such things. Who attends?"

"The richer a man, the more he likes it."

"Are the demonstrations advertised?"

"You wasn't thinking of going, was you?" After laughing heartily at his own joke, he added: "Word gets round. Day before a show, there'll be a crowd of servants waiting out the back to buy tickets."

"I've heard of one surgeon," I said. "Erasmus Foxley."

"I like his work," said the porter, nodding like a connoisseur. "Always a clean cut. He's doing one Tuesday. I iced the body this morning. A man from Bristol. They do like to see a Royalist on the slab. Bet he never thought he'd end up in the Republic, eh? When it's an old wrinkly, died in debt, they won't sell all the tickets. But this one's a young'un. The place'll be full. Better still if it was a woman, young and pretty..."

I hadn't been aware of the nausea creeping up on me. Each revelation had been more gruesome and compelling than the last. Unexpectedly I saw Florence May in my mind's eye, standing with the noose around her neck and a casket of ice to the side. I had to turn away and cover my mouth with my hand. My skin felt cold and damp.

"You like that do you?" he said.

Though the porter had misjudged much, his description proved accurate. On Monday morning, I found my way to a rear door of the hospital where a crowd of young servants mingled. They smoked and chatted in the sunshine, giving the impression of a familiar routine. A sign next to the door read: *For Night Deliveries First Call at Lodge.*

My arrival was like a stone being dropped into the middle of a pond. Awareness that something was wrong spread through the group. Conversations stopped.

"Can I help you, miss?" inquired a man not much older than Tinker.

"Is this the place to buy the tickets?" I asked.

"Yes, but…" He looked around the group as if for moral support. "It's not for a lady, miss.

"It's the master wants one," I said, trying to match the pattern of his speech.

But he was shaking his head. "It's not right."

I looked to the others. Arms were folded. Their faces were a stone wall. Had I not been wanted by the law I might have pressed my case.

"I'm sorry," I said. "A mistake." Then hurried away before they started asking questions I could not answer.

The front of the hospital presented a grand aspect with a Georgian range and the round tower of the famous Oak Wing. But the addition of further wards and ancillary buildings had been haphazard and the rear of the hospital sprawled into a maze of disreputable-looking passages.

Once the young men had collected tickets for their masters, most would make their way to the front and disperse via the main road. But I noticed a small alleyway, which might serve as a cut-through for a brave soul wanting to head in the opposite direction. It did not run straight but doglegged between a laundry and the ambulance stables, creating a blind spot a few paces across that could not be seen from either end.

It was here that I positioned myself, prostrate as if fainted, face resting on outstretched arm. Then, thinking of my likely audience, I hitched up my skirts a few inches, bunching the material above my knee so to reveal a gap between boot and hem. I'm not a practiced dipper, but with enough distraction anyone can pick a pocket.

The first footsteps I heard approaching came from the wrong end of the alleyway. I scrambled to my feet with just enough time to brush myself down before a medical orderly hurried into view, carrying the poles of a stretcher on his shoulder. Busy about his work, he passed me without a glance.

Once he was away, I lay back down on the cobbles, repositioning myself as might an artist's model. Two minutes passed before I heard footsteps coming from the other direction. I held my breath. The footsteps scraped to an abrupt stop.

"Hells bells!"

It was a man's voice.

"Miss?"

He patted the back of my hand. Then, when I didn't move, he lifted it and pulled gently. Fearing that he might rush off to get help, I let out a groan as if coming round from a faint.

"Wake up. Please. Miss?"

Through my eyelashes, I could see that his jacket was of poor cut, but likely there were pockets within. I shifted my position and gripped his arm. In moments he was lifting me. I grabbed his jacket lapel, as if for support. There was no pocket on his right side.

He had me on my feet and was about to step back so I let my knees buckle again and he was forced to grab me under the arms.

The unfamiliar contact was distracting enough for me, let alone for him, a man of perhaps nineteen years. My hand darted within the left side of his jacket and dipped into the pocket. I covered the move with a forward lurch. He was obliged to use his body to stop me falling.

"Let me sit," I said.

As he lowered me I contrived to drop the contents of his pocket onto the floor beneath my skirts.

"Are you well?" he asked.

"Water," I gasped. Then added, as an afterthought in case the water proved too near: "And smelling salts."

He seemed grateful for the chance to run away. As soon as the sound of his footsteps had died I got to my feet, grabbed what I had stolen and set off at a brisk pace in the opposite direction.

If you ever find yourself on the run and looking for a place of safety, choose somewhere with an entrance fee. I paid my money and once again pushed through the turnstile into the grounds of Nottingham Castle. Having followed the curving path up the hill, I selected a bench with the security of a wide view over the grounds below. No one gave me a second glance. Once a tourist has paid her money, it is no one's business to ask how she spends the time.

The contents of the man's pocket I now laid out on my lap, seeing them properly for the first time. I felt little guilt. The finer morals are easily forgotten when life itself is under threat. I wondered whether he would be punished. His master might think he had stolen the money. Though, if the gentleman was a regular, he would most likely have an account. The servant would not be trusted with substantial sums.

The first item was a slim tin box that rattled when I shook it. Opening it, I found five greenish pills and a sheet of finely printed paper. To steal the poor man's medicine had not been my intention. But on reading the paper, I relaxed. *Dr Farnham's patented strengthening pills. A tonic for masculine vigour.* The accompanying illustration showed a sailor embracing his sweetheart. I guessed the servant's life would not be threatened by their loss.

I dropped the tin into the flower border behind the bench and disposed of a small purse in the same way, having first extracted four tenpences and three pennies, which I added to my own money. How easily I had become a common criminal.

Next on the pile was a sheet of paper. I unfolded it, flattening out the creases on my knee. It was a daybill advertising the performance of *Artistic Tableau on the Classical Themes*. The illustration included strategically placed fig leaves. I could not believe such shows would be tolerated in Nottingham. Sure enough, the flier gave an address in Cank Street, deep in the Leicester Backs. How like my adopted city. It had been peeled from a wall to judge by the wrinkles and the tear down one side.

Finally, I came to the ticket itself.

For admission to the public autopsy of Mr Jeremiah
Tuesday, convicted murderer, hanged in Bristol. In
life the specimen was a working man of twenty-eight
years. The body shows finely developed musculature.
Since execution it has been kept in ice. Autopsy to be
performed by Doctor Erasmus Foxley.

I turned the paper over and saw the price – fifty
guineas. My skin prickled with perspiration. Men have
hanged for lesser robberies. The rightful owner of the
ticket would surely inform the constables. They might
go to the hospital to search for the thief. Whatever
I could have learned attending the demonstration
would remain undiscovered. The risk was too great.

In spite of the chance I was losing, I felt a wash of
relief.

CHAPTER 30

For good or ill, knowledge has ever threatened the settled order. A keg of gunpowder may make matchwood of a sturdy house. But a book can set the world on fire.

FROM REVOLUTION

Though fruitful, I now realised that my library visit in Leicester had been ill judged. It was not solely my sex that had made the librarian regard me as unsuitable. I had seemed insufficiently studious. I decided to remedy this before attempting a similar visit in Nottingham.

From a used goods store near the law courts, I purchased a pair of spectacles. They made everything blurry and on wearing them for more than a few minutes, I could feel a headache starting to throb. But I fancied they made me look the part. A well-worn document case under my arm completed the illusion. Thus arrayed, I made my way to North Circus Street and strode into the hallowed halls of the famous medical library.

"I'm writing a biography," I whispered to the

librarian at the information desk.

He inclined his head to indicate respectful understanding. "And how may I be of help?"

"My subject is an eminent surgeon. Perhaps you might have some of his writings?"

"The name?"

"Foxley."

"Erasmus Foxley? His text book of oncology is well regarded. But the bulk of his work will be in medical journals."

"That would be perfect. Thank you."

"Without medical training... that is to say the language will be technical."

"Nevertheless – I trust I'll glean something."

A frown wrinkled his brow. "The articles may be very numerous."

"Then could I suggest a trolley?"

I placed the empty document case on my allotted table and settled down to wait. Removing the spectacles, I was able to read the clock on the far wall. It was three in the afternoon. Most of the other library patrons were young men. Medical students, I judged them to be. The scratching of their pens and the occasional cough were the only sounds to penetrate the sanctuary of the Reading Hall. I looked from face to face. Most were pale from hours of indoor study. A few were passably handsome. One particularly so. I allowed myself to watch him work. But after a quarter of an hour he lost his appeal. My eye moved on to the high ceiling, the flagstone floor and even the cracks in the whitewashed wall plaster.

At half past three a book fell to the floor somewhere

in the library. The sound reverberated among the stone columns and Norman arches. The scratching of pens stopped. The students craned their necks to look. But nothing happened. One by one they returned to their studies.

At last, the squeaking of wheels alerted me to the approach of the librarian manoeuvring a trolley between the tables. He parked it next to me and hovered for a moment as I cast my eye down the wobbling stack of scientific journals. I could not hope to read a tenth of them. He had been trying to tell me as much. But I had so expected him to block me that I had not listened. Perhaps he caught the look of understanding on my face because I saw a flicker of a smile on his before he bowed and left.

I took the first journal, leafed through it and quickly found Foxley's name listed alongside several other authors of an article on the use of bacterial toxins in nerve paralysis experiments. I understood perhaps half the words in the first paragraph but little of the meaning. A diagram filled one page, but most of the explanatory key was written in Latin. I worked my way through three similar articles in different journals. None of them made sense to me. I could not even find a pattern in the subjects of his research.

By the time I had scanned five more journals, the wall clock showed it to be an hour before closing time. I retraced my steps to the information desk, where the same librarian stood.

"Finished already?" he asked. Republican servility prevented him from saying *I told you so* but his acerbic tone was eloquent.

"We were speaking about Erasmus Foxley," I said.

"Indeed."

"I've glanced at some of the articles. But time is limited. I was wondering if there is somewhere a summary of his work."

"A summary?"

"A biography of sorts?"

"I thought that's what you were writing."

"These are early days," I said.

"Previously you wanted writings *by* Dr Erasmus Foxley. Now you want writings *about* him?"

"I realise I may have given you a lot of work – collecting all those journals. I'm sorry. I forgot to say thank you."

His expression softened. "It's good of you to say so." He pointed back into the Reading Hall. "You'll find a copy of Who's Who on the first shelf to the left of the entrance. That might be a good place to start." He wrote *920.073* on a slip of paper and handed it to me.

"I should have asked for your advice from the start," I said. "Thank you."

I was turning to leave when his polite cough stopped me.

"One more thing. A delicate matter. One of the students... he enquired about you."

"Which student?"

"He's since left. But I thought you should know."

I pondered this news as I retraced my steps to the Reading Hall. I was probably the only woman in the building. It was not overly surprising that someone had made inquiries. But the way the librarian had spoken made it seem as if there might be more to it than simple curiosity. A *delicate matter* suggested the kind of interest a man may have in a woman he finds attractive.

These thoughts were quickly forgotten when I found the shelf containing Who's Who. The classification code matched the number the librarian had written for me. Each volume had a date printed on the spine, running from 1913 at the top of the shelf. I took the most recent volume, 2008, from near the bottom. Leafing through it, I quickly found Foxley.

The article was three pages long. It gave his birth year as 1962. From his home in Stoke-on-Trent he had travelled to Edinburgh to study medicine. An able student, he had graduated top of his class. It seemed he was ambitious also. He accepted menial jobs in order to work with the most famous surgeons of the day, never staying in any place for long. After ten years he had accumulated enough knowledge to set up his own practice in Nottingham.

Prior to this, his reputation had been confined to a small circle. But now he began to promote himself with public lectures and demonstrations, including autopsies. He gathered around himself a team of researchers and set them up in a laboratory within the General Hospital. His detractors referred to it as *the factory*, implying that those junior doctors who worked for him were little better than the labourers tending industrial machines. Nevertheless, an impressive quantity and quality of new developments in medicine were ascribed to his research.

The article did not mention wealth. To be so brash

would have been unthinkable. But the implication was clear. Money flowed from his work. He sponsored annual expeditions to the rainforests of Africa and South America. Thousands of animal and plant species were thus made known to science. Through good fortune or judgement, many of these species were found to contain medically active ingredients. He was said to be *fastidious in the protection of intellectual property*. I took this to mean that he pursued legal claims against anyone who used his medicines without licence. The article also mentioned that he was unmarried.

His main achievements had been in the fields of oncology, gigantism and cryogenics. I had to consult a medical dictionary to understand the three terms. His interests lay in the fields of cancer, deformities of abnormal growth and the freezing of bodies. I sat staring at the book for a long time.

The wall clock chimed. The students began folding away their work. Footsteps echoed from walls and pillars, breaking me from my thoughts. Somehow it was closing time already. Feeling a pang of hunger, I realised I'd missed lunch. I gathered up my things and left. As I passed the information desk, the librarian favoured me with the hint of a smile. I smiled back. It seemed we had achieved some kind of understanding.

Walking towards the exit, I remembered the *delicate matter* about which he'd spoken. Talking in the Reading Hall was forbidden. The interested student could not have come over to introduce himself. Perhaps his reason for leaving early had been to wait for me outside. There was no place in my life for such matters, but the thought came to me that it could have been the man I had earlier admired. I pushed the thought away as my cheeks began to flush.

Nevertheless, I paused in the shadowed porch just outside the door and took a moment to survey the plaza and the street beyond. The handsome student was nowhere to be seen. But something had made my pulse quicken. At first I couldn't pin it down. Then I remembered my previous library visit and the black Maria that had been waiting outside.

If I'd believed that lightning would never strike twice, I might have walked out into the late afternoon sunshine. But I hesitated. And as I did, a new thought came into my mind – another explanation for the student to have inquired after me. Perhaps he had recognised my face from a poster.

The final students jostled with each other as they headed into the sunshine, their books tied in bundles. I watched them go. So did a man who was standing on the far side of the road. He held a newspaper open but was not reading it. After that it was easy to spot other watchers. I counted three, though there could have been more beyond my view. They had not enough subtlety to be intelligence gatherers. More likely they were constables in plain clothes. And they would see me the moment I stepped out of the shadow.

The doors behind me creaked. I glanced back and saw that they were being closed by a porter. I was set to dive back inside, but the rattle of an approaching vehicle made me turn again. It was a double-decked omnibus, accelerating along the street. It would pass the library in a few seconds. I took deep breaths until my head began to spin. The horse team was level, blocking the view of the watchers on the other side of the road.

I ran, my pounding footfalls covered by the clatter of horseshoes. I'd crossed the plaza and was next to the omnibus when a man's voice shouted from behind me. I snatched a glance over my shoulder and saw another plainclothes man sprinting out from the shadow of the library wall.

The omnibus had almost passed. I grabbed for the pole on the alighting platform. My arm and shoulder jolted as I caught it. Acceleration swung me around and in, so that my shoulder crashed against the base of the stairs.

The policemen were giving chase on foot, shouting for the driver to stop. I hauled myself to my feet. There was a commotion among the passengers. One woman screamed. But if the driver did hear the shouts, he took no heed. I felt the omnibus pick up speed as he flicked his whip over the horses' backs. One by one the constables gave up the chase, gasping for breath in the middle of the road. I closed my eyes and let out a sigh. When I opened them again, I saw that everyone in the omnibus was staring at me.

"Ruffians!" I said. "The city's full of them!"

CHAPTER 31

Beware the bullet-catcher in your audience. He is
there for no good. All of them are thieves and liars and
tricksters, with the exception of yourself.

THE BULLET-CATCHER'S HANDBOOK

The constables would be back at their station within
the hour. It might take another hour for news to reach
Nottingham's central police house. Wheels would
be set in motion. Freshly printed fugitive posters
would be despatched bearing an updated picture and
description. The wig had lost what little power it had
to protect me. The Duke of Northampton's promised
reward would stir up the city. Such news travels
fast among the working classes. The danger would
increase with every hour. Taking care, I might hope to
last three days. Beyond that, I would have to choose
between moving on and facing discovery. The risk of
inaction had grown, tipping the scales of my decision
the other way.

The dinner gong sounded in the guesthouse hallway
outside my room. It was Tuesday evening. The

autopsy would take place in a few hours. I listened to the footsteps of the other guests coming down from their rooms. There was a smell of beef and onions in the air.

I folded the corset into my case and began wrapping the binding cloth over my chemise. By the time I had fully transformed, the garden was dark enough to risk. Having made up the bed in the usual way, I turned off the gas lights, opened the window and climbed out into the garden, mouthing a silent thank you to my non-existent aunt's arthritis.

I had intended to leave directly. Instead I found myself standing to listen for small sounds in the gathering night. Tinker had come unbidden to my mind. The boy had followed me so tenaciously that his absence seemed strange. But Ashbourne had been an easy proposition. He would not be able to find me in the sprawling city of Nottingham. From here on, I would be free of him.

Irrationally, I found myself whispering his name: "Tinker?"

There was no response.

Though it was evening, there were enough people on the street to leave me inconspicuous. I headed north towards the castle, perched on its rocky outcrop. Around its base, houses and pubs had been built into natural caves. Gas light shone from windows in the sandstone cliff. I could hear music and singing from Ye Oldie Trip to Jerusalem. Climbing Castle Road, I passed the statue of Robin the Revolutionary, his bronze bow pulled taut. Flowers had been heaped around the base of the plinth.

There is something about the act of walking that helps to compose the mind. The simple repetition of movement began to relax me and I found myself thinking about the statue. The great things Robin achieved were done after he had been driven from his home. The very fact of his stepping beyond the law enabled him to take such action. Desperation had been his strength. So might it be mine.

By the time I reached the hospital my hope and determination had returned. The sky was quite dark. I made my way through narrow alleyways to the rear entrance I had approached the day before. Crouching behind a cluster of evil-smelling dustbins, I kept watch. All remained quiet until just before nine o'clock, when the door was opened from within and private carriages began to arrive. The gentlemen who got out of them slipped inside without delay, hat brims pulled low. My disguise would not be out of place among them, though a sharp observer might see too many years of wear in my shoes.

But even as I watched the door, I had yet to make up my mind about attending the macabre demonstration. On realising the price of the ticket, I'd decided against it. But my time in the city was now limited and there were no other threads to follow. The rightful owner might come looking for me. But the ticket was not numbered and thus could not be picked out from any other. In the half hour I'd been watching, there had been no sign of a constable or an intelligence gatherer.

The coach that had disgorged the last arrival began

rolling away. The next one was rounding the corner a hundred paces distant. There were a few seconds in which I might emerge from my hiding place unseen. As I stood, I still was not certain of my decision. But I found myself marching to the door nonetheless and once inside there was no easy way back.

Having presented my ticket and kept hold of my coat, despite the offer to have it hung up, I followed the last arrival along a wide corridor and then down a flight of tiled stairs to the basement level. We began to catch up with three other men, who whispered together as they walked. All seemed to know where they were going. I was not the only one to be wearing a coat. My reason had been to retain one more layer of disguise. But as we entered the operating theatre I felt the chilled air and understood their motivation.

The room was unlike any I'd seen before. A horseshoe of steeply tiered stands looked down on the central space. It felt more like a dog pit than a place of science. Men stood waiting at different levels. Ebony hand rails prevented anyone falling forwards. The standing positions were not numbered. I climbed to the rear-most level, which was the least illuminated, and positioned myself close to the exit.

Most of the light shone down on the central space, which I could only think of as a stage. There was an entrance to one side, leading off into the wings, as it were. Though the stands were made of wood, the stage floor was polished stone. I noticed a small channel cut into it, leading to a drain hole. Feeling a vertiginous lurch in my stomach I gripped the rail harder.

The stalls were filling up. I was aware of someone taking the position next to me. His bare hand rested on the rail near my gloved one. His skin was smooth and he wore a wedding ring.

"First time for you then?" he whispered.

I nodded.

"They always start at the back. Look at them." He pointed to the front row. "They've been coming for years. What must they have spent?"

I risked a glance and saw his profile for a moment – a fine chin and aquiline nose. "Why do they do it?" I asked.

"Why do you? Curiosity perhaps? That comes first. Ask me again at the end of the show. By then you'll either get it or you won't. Some men gamble. Some climb mountains. We all reach for the infinite as our talents allow."

A man edged past us, taking up the final place on the rearmost stand. I attempted a head count but was confused by the trickle of late arrivals. There had to be more than fifty. Whispered conversations sounded like the indistinct buzzing of flies.

A man in brown overalls stepped in from the wings. He crouched to adjust the lights around the rim of the stage, bringing them up so that the empty space was brilliantly illuminated. Then he turned and left. The whispered conversations had stopped.

Then in strode Dr Erasmus Foxley. Though he wore no hat and an apron had been tied to protect his clothes, I recognised the stance of a ringmaster. He turned slowly, his steel gaze cutting across the ranks of his audience. He paused to build our anticipation.

"Councillors, gentlemen – I wish to thank you for gathering here to witness another step in our exploration of the vast unknown. Our journey today is not to follow the winding course of the Congo River into the interior of its dark continent. Yet it is a journey as marvellous, connecting the vast and unnamed tributaries of the capillary system through the vascular system all the way to the heart itself."

He snapped his fingers and two more apron-clad men manoeuvred a wheeled table in from the wings. The form of a body lay on top, covered by a white sheet. They positioned it centre stage then took up positions behind, one to each side of Foxley. The arrangement brought to mind an altar, complete with priests and human sacrifice.

A fourth man carrying a camera entered. He set up his tripod behind the surgeons, angling the lens down at the shrouded body.

"Our subject today is one Jeremiah Tuesday, dead two weeks but immediately preserved in salted ice. The cadaver has been thawed naturally over forty-eight hours but kept all the time below four degrees celsius."

He took hold of the sheet's hem. There was a creaking of wood as every man leaned forward on the hand rails. Then with a neat flourish he revealed the face and chest of the dead man.

I had seen the dead before, laid out for a community to pay its last respects. But this was different. Jeremiah Tuesday lay naked, an ugly purple line conspicuous around his neck. But the shock I felt was not from these things. It came from the unholy mixing of performance and death.

"The arteries and veins of the circulatory system have been named and classified. But no one can count the vast network of the capillary system. Each channel is connected to every other. Insert a needle into the skin at any point on the body and you will have punctured the self-same system. But where shall we begin this journey?"

Again he gripped the sheet. With another crisp movement he pulled it clear so that it fell to the floor behind the altar. Again the audience leaned forwards. Though my first reaction had been to pull away, I confess that I found myself following their movement.

"Mr Tuesday belonged to the criminal classes. You will have noted the strong brow ridge, indicating reduced intelligence. And the abundance of dark hair covering the body. Note also the excellent definition still visible in the muscle groups of the arm, stomach and thighs. And the tumescence of the male member."

I knew I should not look, but still I did.

The surgeons stood aside whilst the photographer removed the lens cap. I counted three beats of my heart before he replaced it. Dr Foxley had strapped on a set of surgeon's eyeglasses. As he returned to his place by the body, he swivelled something that looked like a microscope down in front of his left eye. I saw a flash of steel as he received a scalpel from the man on his right.

"And so we begin," he said.

With a single, swift movement of the blade he cut the first incision around the ankle of the dead man. A second cut travelled up the leg. There was no blood. That surprised me. But then he peeled back the skin revealing a pattern of blue veins and red flesh.

I turned away. Several of the men along the row next to me were peering through opera glasses. I looked around the audience. At first it seemed I was the only one to have averted my eyes. Then I caught a movement by my shoulder and saw that the man with the aquiline nose had been looking directly at me. It was a small thing – little more than a flash of the eyes. I might hardly have noticed.

I forced myself to look back to the performance. The entire right leg of Jeremiah Tuesday now looked like an illustration from a medical textbook. Dr Foxley was working to expose a great artery in the thigh.

"Though the brain of a murderer is an organ perverted from its natural purpose, yet the geography of his circulatory system is much the same as any of us here. Indeed, we would find little difference in the arteries of a gorilla or a chimpanzee."

I had shifted back from the rail, out of the eye line of those around me. Now I sidestepped to the walkway and silently moved to the exit.

As I ran back along the corridor, the door to the operating theatre closed on its springs with a dull thud. My footfalls echoed off the bare walls.

Then the theatre door creaked open again. I had reached the stairs but there was no time for thought. More on instinct than through logic I continued three more paces and jinked through a side door, mercifully unlocked. Inching it closed behind me, I stood gulping air in the near darkness, trying to hear beyond the pulse booming in my ears.

The crisp click of hard leather soles on stone approached along the corridor at a brisk walk. The door was still open a crack, for I had not dared risk the sound of the latch. Every muscle in my body tensed. Then the footsteps switched rhythm as my pursuer began climbing the stairs. The sound grew fainter until I could hear it no more.

Time in the basement room passed slowly. The man who had followed me did not return but I dared not leave.

It was not his sidelong glance at me that had given him away. Rather it was the fact that he had tried to hide it afterwards. In retrospect, my suspicions should have been raised by the way he had positioned himself next to me when the whole row had been empty. Also by the way he had engaged me in conversation, probing my level of experience, apparently giving me more information than he received but revealing nothing of himself.

The man was an intelligence gatherer and no doubt could there be about it. I didn't think he could know my real identity. Thus he wasn't after the reward from the Duke of Northampton. Most likely he had been commissioned by the gentleman I had robbed of his ticket. But it was also possible that he was the man who had kept such skilful watch on Julia in Ashbourne.

I had seen enough to understand that fortunes were being made. There had been at least fifty men in the room. Each had paid fifty guineas. This was one of many such demonstrations. The body of Mr Tuesday had been procured by legal means. I wondered if there might be private shows for select clients using bodies otherwise obtained.

Two hours after I had fled, I heard the door to the operating theatre creak open and the audience begin to leave. On arrival they had spoken to each other in whispers. Now the only sound was their footfalls. I slipped in behind them, quickening my pace so that by the time we spilled out onto the pavement, I was hidden in the middle of the crowd.

The sky was quite dark. Several carriages were already waiting and I saw that others were queued down the road. Men touched their hats and nodded their farewells before climbing in and riding away. I scanned the road for a public carriage, but all were privately owned. At fifty guineas a ticket it could not have been otherwise.

The queue of carriages continued to roll forwards, picking up the wealthy men one by one. The crowd thinned. Anything I did would draw attention – walking away, asking for a ride with one of the others, remaining where I was until they had all departed. If my pursuer was watching, he would have me.

Making a snap decision I strode out of the crowd, passing four of the queuing carriages and opening the door of the fifth. I climbed up and in.

"Sir?" the coachman called. "You've made a mistake."

"My apologies," I said, then opened the opposite door and climbed out again. The line of carriages now hid me from the crowd and the hospital doors. I strode away, listening for anyone following. But the chinking of harness and the clack of horseshoes on stone was too loud. I glanced over my shoulder. A figure in a top hat stepped between two of the carriages. He was silhouetted against the lights from the hospital immediately behind him. For a second we both stood immobile. Then he started towards me at a run. I was off, sprinting away from him.

Cursing myself for not mapping a getaway route, I grabbed the end of the railings and sling-shotted myself around a corner into the same narrow passageway in which I'd picked the pocket of the servant.

I heard my pursuer pounding around the corner just before I reached the dogleg. I might pretend to run like a man, but I didn't have a man's speed. He was out of the dogleg well before I reached the end of the passage. I turned again, down a road too narrow for pavements. Overhead walkways linked factories on either side.

I counted my footfalls until I heard him loud again. The gap was fifty yards and closing. The lifts in my boots made me taller, but didn't help me to run. He would have me before the end of the street. So I jagged right into a courtyard, hoping for a doorway, finding only a metal fire escape. My feet clanged on the cast-iron, making it ring as I zigzagged towards the roof. He was just two flights below me. I could hear his breath rasping.

At the top, I found a pitched roof flanked by a narrow walkway and low balustrade. I couldn't outpace him along the flat, so began to scramble up the slates towards the apex. I'd escaped across rooftops before.

A slate slid and crashed behind me. The man swore and I felt the first flutter of hope. I'd reached the ridge tiles and was standing with one foot on either side. The man was only a few paces behind and below me. But he was struggling. As I watched, his foot slid from under him and his knee dropped, cracking another slate.

I began walking, arms stretched out for balance. My breath felt ragged in my throat but the distance between us had begun to grow. I'd found my first advantage. There was a chimney-breast ahead of me. I heard him sliding down the slates. Then he was running along the flat fringe of the roof, keeping pace with me.

Steadying myself with a hand on the chimney bricks, I turned to face him.

"There's nowhere to run," he shouted. "You can't stay up there all night."

"Follow me if you can," I said, then stepped down the far side of the roof from him. Once out of sight I crabbed across to hide behind the brickwork of the chimney. Immediately he was clambering up the slates. I should have brought my pistol. But I'd been afraid of being searched on entering the hospital. I pulled out my fountain pen and unclipped the lid.

Another slate crashed just beyond the ridge. I flattened myself to the bricks. I could hear his exertion as he hauled himself up over the top. Instead of standing where balance would have been easy, he hunkered low.

I gripped the pen like a dagger and launched myself at his back. The impact knocked him off balance and we both began to slide. I wrapped my arm around his neck. We were picking up speed. He struggled, digging his heels into the roof. A slate cracked and his foot went half through bringing us to a sudden stop just short of the edge. He threw his shoulders forwards and I felt myself being lifted, almost thrown over him towards the balustrade. I held on tighter. Then his head lashed backwards and I slammed into the roof and lost grip of his neck. As he began to twist, I lunged, jabbing the pen into his spine.

He froze.

I looped my arm around his neck again and whispered. "I'll stab you to the heart."

"You don't have the balls," he said.

"Then try me!"

"You couldn't watch a dead man being cut. You won't do it."

I pushed the pen nib hard enough to put ink under his skin. He would feel the prick of it. And the mark would stay with him till he died. "Unbuckle your belt," I said.

With him face down on the slates, I looped the belt around his wrists and pulled it tight, tying the loose end so it couldn't work free. For good measure I slid his trousers down his legs so they bunched around his ankles. He'd be hobbled if he got to his feet. Pushing against his shoulder, I slid him off the slope of the roof so he fell face down in the narrow gap next to the balustrade.

"Who do you work for?" I asked.

"You don't know already?"

I pressed my knee between his shoulder blades and leant all my weight on it. He groaned.

"Who?" I released the pressure so he could speak. At first I thought he was gasping for air. Then I realised he was laughing.

"Idiot!" he said. "You pull a stunt like this and you don't even know who you've crossed."

I pressed down again, knowing it would hurt. "Who?"

"You – won't – kill – me." The words escaped from his mouth as the air was forced from him.

He was right. Killing was not in my nature. Reaching under his neck, I fumbled the cravat free. It was fine silk. The light was too low to be sure of its colour. I threaded it around underneath his head as a blindfold and tied it tight. Then I heaved him onto his back and knelt on his chest.

"That hurts," he said.

I unbuttoned his coat and pulled a heavy flick knife from the pocket. I'd never seen one so large. I pressed the catch and felt it judder in my hand as it snapped open. The blade was long and keen, designed to kill. I turned it in my hand but could find no patent mark. That made it a dangerous weapon to own. But for the time being it would serve better than my pretend dagger. I put away my pen.

"You really are lost," he said.

"Then tell me who you work for."

"You know I can't."

I frisked his jacket one handed and came away with a wallet and some small papers.

"Then perhaps your pockets will talk."

I opened the wallet to find three Republic pound notes. They were crisp, as if freshly issued. I folded them into my pocket and tossed the wallet to the side. I was earning more freely through robbery than I ever had as an intelligence gatherer.

"Why did you follow me?" I asked.

"You stole a valuable ticket. You think that goes unreported?"

"You don't work for the police."

His laugh had no warmth. I tried to ignore it as I began leafing through the papers from his pocket. Most were receipts. A couple were from restaurant meals. Three were cab fares. Two kinds of people keep such ephemera – the obsessive and those who wish to claim back money from an employer. Then I found a used coach ticket.

Angling it to catch the light of the moon, which was almost full, I read: *First Class. Ashbourne to Derby*. The date stamp matched my departure from the Green Man and Black's Head. The man under my knee was the spy who had been keeping watch on us.

"You work for Dr Foxley," I said.

"Bravo."

I pulled the cravat from his eyes, making sure the knife blade was the first thing he saw. Though he had watched me go about as a woman, I didn't think he would see through my disguise in the dark with the moon behind me. But I needed to be able to recognise him if our paths crossed again.

I examined the lines and angles of his face.

"I know who you are," he said.

"You've never seen me before."

"But now I do. I suppose you've been told this before – but you're very like your sister. You are Edwin Barnabus, I presume?"

"And you're W Keppler," I said, fanning out the visiting cards I had taken from his pocket."

"How careless of me," he said. At which point I realised the cards must be false.

"The name will do for now."

"I have a message for your sister," he said. "It's about her friend."

I reacted without thinking, shifting the knife closer to his cheek. He flinched but when it didn't touch him, the flicker of alarm was replaced by a slow smile.

"Killers don't wear gloves," he said. "You've got to want to feel it going into their flesh. And the blood – it ruins leather."

I touched the flat of the blade to his neck. "What did you mean about my sister's friend?"

"I mean, I'm going to tell you something. We've been trying to reach her. You'll be the perfect messenger boy. Her friend's going to be taken to Derby tomorrow night. Interesting things will happen there. Painful things. If your sister wants to stop them, she'd better be at the gates of the Ice Factory at nine o'clock."

"Her friend's long gone!" I hissed the words between my teeth.

"Oh, I'm afraid you're wrong. Her friend's securely tied."

"No," I said. Though I'd not heard from Julia since she left with Mrs Raike. "She's out of your reach!"

"She?" he laughed again. The sound made the hairs stand on the back of my neck. "Not *that* friend. Not the girl. It's the urchin boy. She seems fond of him. You know how women are."

CHAPTER 32

*If man is possessed of free will, the future cannot be
set. Thus the history of an empire may stand balanced,
waiting for a breath of air to choose the direction of
its fall.*

FROM REVOLUTION

Keppler did not thrash around or try to escape as
I walked. He wouldn't have wanted to give me
that satisfaction. Nor would I have given him the
satisfaction of knowing how desperate I was to get
away. But I accelerated as soon as I was around the
corner of the roof and out of his view. The thought of
him following made me feel sick. I hurried back down
the fire escape then ran from the building, pausing
only to drop his knife down a drain.

I arrived back at the guest house, desperate with
fatigue. Seeing the downstairs windows dark, I risked
the front entrance. No one saw me as I slipped through
the hallway to my room.

I closed the door behind me and heaved the chest
of drawers in front of it. Then I stripped off my male
disguise, unwound the binding and removed my

chemise, which was damp with perspiration. I stood naked in the unlit room.

The binding cloth and a corset had been familiar to me since I turned thirteen and my body began to change. With each I presented a different aspect to the world. And depending on that aspect, the world treated me differently. Neither role seemed more strange to me.

Standing alone and unclothed, I was gripped by a hollow feeling in the pit of my stomach. At first I could not give it a name.

I remembered the naked corpse and found myself wondering what had become of the dissected parts. They would be burned, I supposed, rather than buried. Either way, they would end up as dust. Given time, so would I and all the grand gentlemen who had watched the autopsy.

In death, laid out and inert, they had named Jeremiah Tuesday as a member of the criminal classes. It had seemed strange to me at the time. But now I understood. They'd needed to make such show of classifying him precisely because he was naked – un-uniformed so to speak. Else, in death he would be level with them all.

There I stood alone in a guesthouse room, un-uniformed also. I, who committed the taboo of mutability. I stepped between roles. I eluded class by being a traveller yet educated, a foreigner in exile. A chameleon. What would they say of me if I had not escaped across the rooftop, if my pursuer had clicked his knife and slipped it between my ribs? How would I have been defined in death?

Here is a woman from the criminal class. A liar, trickster, conjuror, impersonator, a breaker of every social code. A gypsy. An anarchist. A cancer. An underminer of the foundations of the world.

I had lost count of the rules I'd broken since fleeing from the Kingdom. Theft, robbery, breaking and entering, making threats to life, using forged documents.

I looked down at my body, ran a hand from my breast over my waist to my hip. The outline was too curved for me to be mistaken for a man, yet not curved enough to fit the ideal of womanhood. The faint lines of muscle on my arms and stomach suggested a labourer, yet my hands were as smooth as a lawyer's.

I pulled back the bedcovers and lay down. Those few who knew of my adventures thought them a facet of my character. As if hiding came naturally and living as an imposter had no cost. Perhaps they fancied I would always be able to reach a little further or perform some magic trick to escape. They couldn't see the narrowness of the tightrope I walked.

The hollow feeling gripped me again. This time I knew its name was loneliness.

CHAPTER 33

There are but a few with the capacity and education to understand a system as complex as revolution with its many principles, actors and workings. To the rest is given the capacity to believe.

From Revolution

The day of my meeting with John Farthing had arrived. According to our agreement, he would have searched the archive for mention of Dr Erasmus Foxley. I made my way to Bridlesmith Gate. But instead of entering the tea shop he had nominated, I selected a similar establishment on the opposite side of the road.

I told myself this contrary act was a precaution. From my table, I would have a good view of the street. If Farthing had had a change of heart and brought the constables, I would be able to watch as he led them into the wrong building. His chosen tea shop was austere, even by Republican standards. This one had tiered cake platters in the window display. I knew he would hate it.

I had never asked where in America he came from. He had an expansive stride that suggested wide open spaces. It was so unlike the clipped movements of English gentlemen that I spotted him approaching from the end of the street. It seemed wrong to me that a man who walked without restraint could hold the law in such close affection.

He had halved the distance to the tea shop when I realised he was not alone. Another man strode beside him, hurrying to keep up. He wore a longer coat than Farthing's and a top hat instead of a Homburg, yet there was something about the two men that was indefinably alike.

I stood, making my chair legs scrape on the floorboards.

The waiter hurried over. "May I help?"

Farthing and the other man were standing just outside the window. There was tension between them. They exchanged words. Then the other man was marching back the way they had come. Farthing waited, checked over his shoulder and then disappeared inside the teashop opposite.

"Miss?"

I was surprised to see the waiter still standing next to me. He arched his eyebrows.

"I'm sorry, did you ask something?"

"I said, are you ready to order?"

"Not quite. But do you have a boy who could run a message?"

I took a new table at the back of the shop, far from the window. From there I observed as Farthing was led inside. Fresh from the sunlight, he would not be able to see me. I took the chance to look at him straight

on. He had come to help me, but I still felt angry.
My chest constricted and my pulse began to speed.
Somehow he always had that effect on me.

He took off his hat and dismissed the boy with a coin
from his pocket. Then he saw me and I lowered my gaze.

"May I join you?"

"Please do," I said. "Though the waiter will have all
manner of bad thoughts about us." I held out my left
hand to remind him of the absence of a wedding ring.

"But we're–"

"You're an agent of the Patent Office. It doesn't matter
what he thinks. You can meet whoever you want."

"No," he said. "I can't."

At which point, the waiter stepped to our table,
notepad and pencil poised. After a moment during
which neither of us had spoken, he made an effete
cough.

"A pot of tea," I said. Then, as an afterthought,
because I imagined the indulgence would annoy
Farthing, I added: "And a platter of cakes."

"That's not necessary," he said, after the waiter had
gone.

"But they look delicious."

"Why change the meeting place?" he asked.

"Who was the man who came with you?"

"A colleague."

"An agent?"

"It was hard to get rid of him."

"So I *was* wise to wait here and not there."

"I found an excuse," Farthing said. "You should
have trusted me."

"What excuse?"

He opened his mouth to respond but the waiter had returned carrying a silver stand, each layer of which supported a plate of cakes. I gestured to the lowest layer, the most abundantly piled. The waiter removed the plate from the stand and positioned it on the table. Farthing seemed appalled. When small plates had been placed before us, I chose a cream pastry for myself and a custard slice for John Farthing.

Two waitresses brought the tea things. I watched as teapot, saucers, cups, spoons, sugar and tongs were arranged on the table. It was like a dance, each person coordinated with the movements of the others. Once they were done, the waiter made a final adjustment to the angle of the tongs in the sugar bowl and retreated to his place by the counter.

"Shall I be mother?" I said, pouring the tea.

"What's the meaning of this charade, Elizabeth?"

"What charade?"

"Excess disguised as civility."

"Did you check the files?" I asked.

He pushed the plate of cakes to one side, leaned closer and whispered: "I don't think you know to what danger I put myself. Every time we consult the archive they make a record of the fact. We have to give a reference. I created a spurious case number. If they were to investigate me..."

"You're an agent. They won't."

"They might!"

"But you checked?"

Farthing sat straight, taking a moment to compose himself. He picked up his fork and scooped the corner of the custard slice. I watched as he savoured it.

"It's really good," he said. "Thank you."

"The files?" I prompted.

"The files. Yes. But before that, I thought perhaps you could help me. A trade of sorts. There's still a loose end to tie from the Florence May case." He looked up from the custard slice.

"They hanged her," I said.

"I'm sorry to remind you of it."

"Her legs kicked after she dropped."

He squirmed in his chair. "She... that is to say, the prison guards... they told us she sent a package from her cell. We now know it was addressed to you."

"And?"

"I need to know what it contained."

"Why is the Patent Office concerned?"

"You know I can't answer that, Elizabeth."

"Is it something particular you're looking for?"

"Indeed, yes."

"Something of value?"

"In a manner of speaking."

I remembered returning from the hanging – throwing Florence's copy of the *Bullet-Catcher's Handbook* into the fire. I did not know why I'd taken it out again.

"Did you receive it?" he asked.

I looked into his eyes and said: "No."

"I'm afraid that's hard to believe." He blushed. "It may seem merely an artefact of your childhood profession. But there're things about it you don't understand. It's very much our business."

"You speak in riddles."

"I'm of necessity constrained."

Now it was my turn to pick up my fork and eat. The sweetness and cream spread through my mouth. I'd not tasted such rich food in weeks. The sugar made my heart kick. I took a sip of tea as I waited for it to slow. Farthing watched me.

"Now tell me about the files," I said.

After a moment of apparent indecision he produced a slim notebook and started leafing through its pages. "Foxley has seventy-three registered inventions and discoveries. They're stamped 'medical research'. Every one of them. Which makes his work exempt from inspection. We can't interfere. And because his personal file has the same designation, I couldn't approach him without approval – even if this was a sanctioned investigation – which it isn't."

"That was the information you were trading?"

"There's nothing more I can do."

"But Foxley's a criminal."

"Then Republican law should put him in prison."

"There isn't proof."

"Ah... so he *might* be a criminal?"

The waiter returned. "Is everything satisfactory?" he asked.

"Quite," said Farthing. "Thank you."

"The cakes?"

"Delicious, yes."

"The tea?"

"Thank you. All is fine."

The intervention was fortunate because my anger had been gathering. By the time the waiter stepped away I had counted to twelve and was able to speak in a level whisper. I leaned forwards again.

"There's been another kidnapping. A boy this time. They're holding him as bait."

"Bait?"

"To trap me."

"So the boy means something to you?"

"He's an unfortunate. An orphan."

"How does a threat to him put pressure on you? If he is just an orphan–"

"*Just* an orphan?"

"Forgive me. I forget your history. And I've seen your kindness. I shouldn't doubt that you'd want to help any child. But why did *they* believe kidnapping him would bring pressure on you?"

"The boy, Tinker, he's got no one else. Somehow – I don't know why – but he's attached to me. And I... I won't rest until I've seen him safe."

Farthing nodded, as if this made perfect sense. But my words had been a revelation to my own ears. The resentment I'd felt towards the boy, my rejection of the unasked-for responsibility – in that moment I knew it had gone.

I'd been leaning forwards as I spoke but suddenly felt exhausted and had to rest back in my chair. With so much misfortune in the world, I didn't know why my pity had settled on that child. I was not aware of having made a choice.

"Tomorrow evening I must go to meet them," I said. "At the Ice Factory in Derby. They'll try to kill me. And then Tinker."

Farthing was staring at his hands. "I beg you not to go."

"Look at me!" I said.

But he spoke without meeting my gaze. "If you go there, I won't be able to help."

"What if Foxley is killing for his research? Would the Patent Office still not help? He's published research on the freezing of live animals. Can't you think what he might be doing with the people he takes?"

"Don't you understand? Medical research is *never* unseemly."

"It is the most unseemly science of all!"

"Not legally. As an agent, if I set foot in his laboratory there'd be uproar. It'd be like a constable from London going to Carlisle to arrest the Council of Guardians! Elizabeth, I know you hate the Patent Office, but we're holding back the chaos. There are people who'd do anything to bring us low. If I were to help you, they'd use it to attack us."

"They're hurting Tinker…"

"If the Patent Office falls, millions die."

"That's not true."

"It's what I believe!"

"Well I believe my father died because of it!"

"Must you say that? You still blame me after all I've done! You can't bring yourself to think that a man from the Patent Office – me – that I could do any good, without it being an attack on your dignity. Elizabeth, will you not just this once think better of me! Must your history and mine always stand between us? From the first time I saw you, I admired your intellect. I've wanted nothing but good for you. It's circumstance that stands between us. If my wishes had agency, the wrong you've suffered would already have been undone!"

It was not the words themselves that shocked me – not at first. It was the intensity of emotion etched into his face. One of his hands gripped the edge of the table. The distance between us seemed to have shrunk. I could smell the vanilla on his breath.

I tried to speak. But a feeling that I could not understand or name had taken hold of my chest. I was suddenly aware of my heart, the pressure of my clothes on my skin, the heat of my breath as I exhaled.

"Elizabeth?"

I stood and my chair fell. The waiter jumped. Everyone in the tea shop was watching.

"I need to use the ladies room," I said. "Please forgive me."

The waiter snapped his fingers. One of the waitresses hurried over and took my arm. She led me past the counter to a passageway and through a door. As soon as it had closed behind us I whispered: "I need to get away from that man."

"You do?" Her eyes were wide with imagined scandal.

"Is there a back way?"

She showed me through another door to a kitchen and then through that to a pantry and finally to a rear yard. I found myself wishing that John Farthing would not have the money to pay the bill. And I hated myself for thinking it.

CHAPTER 34

The magician's assistant must be long gone before the wand is flourished to make her disappear.

THE BULLET-CATCHER'S HANDBOOK

The ticket office for the tour around Derby's magnificent ice factory was an unassuming building of red brick. It acted as a gateway, the entrance being on the street and the exit within the perimeter railings.

I advanced into the bare foyer in the manner of a man and I paid my money at the office window. The machine chattered, spewing out my ticket. A clock hand displaying the number of visitors ratcheted one place forward. From my previous visit, I knew that every visitor would be counted out again with the same machine at the end. If the numbers did not tally, a search party would doubtless be dispatched. It was this system I needed to subvert.

Stepping through the building, I went to join the other visitors who were assembling out at the back. The guide with the bristling black beard was there to check my ticket. As we waited for the party to be complete, I meandered back until I was next to the ticket office once more. When the foyer was empty and the guide was looking in the other direction, I disappeared inside.

"I've changed my mind," I said to the man behind the ticket window. I loosened my collar as if in need of air. "I've come over poorly."

"Can't give refunds," he said, gesturing with his thumb towards a list of terms and conditions on the wall. "Sorry."

"So be it."

I watched as he pressed a key on the ticket machine. It made a double click and the clock hand ratcheted back to remove one from the number of visitors. I stepped away as if leaving. Then, having checked that no one observed, I ducked below his window and re-entered the site.

In that way, I disappeared.

Wearing extra clothes concealed underneath my male outer garments, I was sweating by the time I followed the group down the steps into the well of cold at the entrance to the ice tunnels. The problem had been to pack so much clothing and equipment without appearing to be burdened. My skirt, petticoat and blouse I had wrapped around my waist. My precious flintlock was strapped vertically against my back. When I wore a binding cloth alone, I had a handsome figure. These additions gave me a more rounded outline. They altered my gait also and I found myself swaying like a duck as I stepped inside.

I sat on a pile of hay bundles, as I had done before, and buckled the iron spikes to my boots. The guide was lightly dressed just as he had been on my first visit. My fellow tourists were a mix of earnest Republicans, all keen to learn about the perfections of the age.

"Tight as you can," said the guide, his beard bristling as he spoke. "We don't want feet slopping around. There's two miles of tunnels ahead. It'll feel like four if you don't get the buckles right."

He used the same patter, so far as I could remember. That was good. My plan relied on his routine being unchanged. I watched his eyes flicking around the room – doing his first count of the number of people in the party, which was now different by one from the number on the ticket machine.

He lit the pole lanterns and passed one to a middle-aged man on whose arm clung an expensively-dressed young woman. I remembered to hold my arms out for balance as I stood, as if the spikes were unfamiliar to me. Indeed, the experience was new, for I had never walked in them as a man.

Setting off into the first tunnel, I realised that the spikes were more suited to a male gait. It was easier to walk planting my heels than it had been carrying my weight on my toes. As we descended into the layer of mist, I let myself drift back through the group until I was just in front of the rear marker.

"Isn't this exciting?" I said.

"We've wanted to see it for years," responded the man with the lantern.

I wondered how many years they had been together. She seemed too young for it to have been long.

"What is your line of business?" he asked.

"Dairy produce," I said, relieved when his expression betrayed indifference. "What's yours?"

"Carpets," he said. "Wholesale, naturally."

We had arrived at the first stopping place. The party were gathering in a semi-circle. I positioned myself just behind the shoulder of the carpet man and watched as our guide went through the expected headcount.

Having heard his talk before, I was able to observe more closely. This time I caught the flick of his eyes around the group as he delivered the line about the frozen child. A woman raised a hand to her face, failing to mask her horror. A momentary smile curled the mouth of the guide – the same unwholesome pleasure I had observed in him before.

Speech delivered, he led us on. I noted again how the tunnels played tricks, deadening some sounds and amplifying others. I could hear the deep boom of the engines long before we reached the entrance to the giant ice warehouse.

I watched the front lamp dip under the lintel of the doorway. We followed in single file. When it came to my turn, I made a point of holding the door open for the carpet man's wife. He followed through after her. As the door swung closed, I slipped back through it into the corridor.

If the guide followed the same routine, he wouldn't count heads again. The visitors would be returned to the surface via the elevator cage. They would be escorted back out through the little red-brick building. The ticket man would press the button on the machine for each head that passed. When all were through, the clock would register nought. To the system, I no longer existed.

When the noise of voices had receded from the other side of the door, I fumbled in my pockets for matches and candle. Soon I had light again, though not as bright as the lanterns had shed.

I checked my watch. It was five o'clock in the afternoon. Four hours remained before they would expect me to arrive and bargain for Tinker's life.

Cupping the candle in my hand, I retraced my steps through the tunnels. The door to the anteroom was locked, but not sturdy enough to resist my shoulder. I broke through without too much noise and positioned myself on a pile of hay bundles to wait. Discovering that two of my fingers had gone numb, I got up again and began to pace, squeezing my hands into fists and releasing them again and again, trying to get the blood to circulate.

The cold continued to work its way in. By half past seven, I was shivering intermittently. Running on the spot warmed me, but my throat and lungs became raw from dragging in the icy air.

At eight o'clock, with one hour remaining, I set off back along the passageway at a brisk walk, counting side tunnels and memorising as much of the place as I could. I found a small chamber in which to change. It could not have been any warmer than the passage outside, but the sense of enclosure made me feel less exposed.

All the cold I had felt before was merely prelude to this. I stripped off the male disguise, unbound myself and hurried to dress again. Then I made a pile of the discarded clothing. At first my hands were trembling too violently to strike a match. When at last one caught, I held the tiny bead of flame to the false beard hair, which caught quickly. The rubber adhesive flared, giving off acrid smoke. Then the trousers were burning and the binding cloth.

The warmth was a sudden and blissful relief. I had brought with me a small can of oil – the tool of a burglar who wants to move silently in a house of creaky doors. As the fire started to subside, I dripped it into the embers, making new flames dance. At the end it was little more than a lantern flame but the heat had been enough to bring feeling back to my hands and feet. The shivering had stopped, though my cheeks smarted as if I had scoured my face with salt water.

I had not endured all this merely to gain access to the ice tunnels. My enemy had set the parameters of our meeting. In doing so, he had surely intended my fatal disadvantage. My task was to overturn his plans and trip up his expectations. He would look for me to arrive from one direction. I would announce myself from the other.

This place of unmapped tunnels and hidden rooms – I had come to believe it more than a supplier of ice. Indeed, if I had thought more clearly, I might have realised this sooner. The ice farmers loaded the boats. The boat captains brought the cargo to the factory. Antonia had recorded the comings and goings. The ice was somehow disappearing. I had assumed there was some secret tunnel via which it was being taken out. Then I learned of the doctor's experiments in the freezing of bodies and it came to me that the ice would not need to leave the factory if it was consumed there.

Erasmus Foxley was making a fortune through his work. The public autopsy had an aura of illicit mystery and the wealthy gentlemen who attended felt like a secret society. But all of it was legal. As a medical researcher he was immune from the Patent Office. And as an expert in the field of cryonics, he could have ordered as much ice as he wanted to be delivered to the hospital in full view. There was no need for petty theft.

Warmed by the fire, my shivering had subsided. I set off back towards the anteroom where I placed my ear to the outer door. There was nothing to hear but the indistinct hum of the city. I put my eye to the crack but could see no lights outside.

My plan, such as it was, relied on the doctor entering the tunnels to chase after me. Therefore, I struck a match and lit the pole lanterns, which were propped against the wall. Then I went back to the door.

The first sign that my vigil had reached its conclusion was the sound of approaching horses. Then, much closer, I heard the footsteps of perhaps three men. They spoke to each other in hushed voices so that until they drew closer, I could only make out a few words.

"...what you agreed."

"...so it is."

"You wait..."

They had reached the flight of steps just beyond the door.

"She's due in ten minutes. There'll be a gentleman here. He'll lead her over."

"What gentleman?"

"Doesn't matter."

"You didn't say anything about a gentleman."

"Forget the gentleman! You'll see him just this once and you'll forget him real quick. He goes. You take the girl. That's it."

"We're not sharing the reward. No one said anything about a gentleman."

"That's still the deal. You take her tonight. Get her across the border. Make sure she speaks to no one. You get all the Duke's reward."

"All right then. I was just saying."

"Are we square?"

"We're square."

One man walked away. The other two would be within arm's reach had the door been open. They would be bounty hunters or constables working on private commission. Not workers in the ice factory. Even if they turned to look, they might not understand the significance of lamplight glowing through the cracks of the door.

Then I heard another sound – horses and carriage wheels. There were more voices in the distance. I expected to hear the doctor. Instead there were heavy boot falls – men labouring under a weight. And then swearing followed by a scuffle.

"Get him!"

Running feet. A clatter. The cry of a boy in pain. It was Tinker.

"Tie his legs!"

"And what's this other one?"

"Caught him snooping."

"God's teeth!"

"Where're the bounty hunters?"

"By the door."

After that the voices dropped.

Perhaps I should have felt flattered that so many men were there to wait for me. My watch showed a minute short of nine o'clock. There was no reason to wait longer.

I dragged hay bundles from around the wall and stacked them against the door. Then I unscrewed the filler cap from one of the lanterns and sprinkled oil over the pile. At first I thought the oil had soaked away, but when I smashed the lamp down, the flame rippled out so fast that I had to jump back to save my skirts from catching fire. The room was suddenly bright, milky walls reflecting orange flame.

The men outside had heard the noise. One of them was calling for help. Flames licked the inside of the door.

The heat of it was extraordinary. I backed away but still my face felt as if it was burning. Smoke ran out across the ceiling. Where it met the walls it cascaded down. The chamber began to fill with it. I grabbed the other lantern and backed away into the tunnel. There was shouting outside now. The door rattled under a heavy impact. I retreated into cleaner, colder air.

Then the door burst open. There were men outside. One shouted for water. It would take minutes to get the fire under control. What happened after that would tell me if my reasoning had been true. If something of value was hidden in the tunnels – the thing that had been consuming ice – they would fear I'd located it and would chase me. But if my reasoning had been false, if there was nothing to be found, they would simply lock the doors and leave me to freeze to death.

CHAPTER 35

All war is lunacy. Therefore, raising an army is not sufficient. The enemy must believe you are insane enough to use it.

FROM REVOLUTION

I tried to run but the iron spikes threw me off-balance. So I returned to walking but with my stride lengthened to an ungainly degree. The shouts of men battling the fire receded behind me, becoming distorted by the shape of the tunnel until their voices blended into an indistinct hum.

I was well beyond the light from the fire when something changed. I stopped to listen. The silence was absolute. It took me a moment to understand what had happened. Then the animal excitement that had been driving me curdled into a queasy fear. My heart, which had been pumping regular as a piston now seemed to sprint and slow. I closed the lantern cover, reducing its light to almost nothing.

I heard and saw them in the same instant – the distant crunch of spiked boots on ice and the glow of lanterns reflected from the milky tunnel walls. The light was so faint that I might have missed it. But it moved. They were through the fire and heading towards me at speed.

I set off away from them. I'd passed side passages already. I could have dodged down any one of them. My pursuers would not be able to check them all. But if I could hear their spikes in the ice, so too would they hear mine. I had to disappear completely.

I didn't bother removing the spikes from my boots. Rather, I pulled off boots, spikes and all. The cold didn't shock my stockinged feet at first. The feeling started mild. But within twenty paces, I was gritting my teeth against the pain. I tried to run, but my feet slipped underneath me. Only when I accelerated slowly was I able to pick up speed. At last, I was moving swiftly. And I was silent.

The side passages that I had passed so far had been broad and rectangular in cross-section, as if frequently used and maintained. But now I came to the narrow tunnel I'd noted on my previous visit. Its corners had been filled in by the accretion of frost, shrinking it to an oval. I slowed as best I could without falling, then ducked into the claustrophobic entrance. Having retreated far enough to be out of view, I doused my light.

The first thing I noticed was how close the crunch of footsteps had become. They had gained on me even though I'd been running. My feet were growing numb, so I sat on the ground and kneaded first one and then the other. Despite the noise they would make, I had no choice but to put my boots back on. My pursuers were travelling at speed. If I was lucky, my footfalls would be lost in theirs.

Whatever it was they had hidden in the ice tunnels, they would fear that I'd discovered it. It was for a reason that I'd chosen to reveal myself with fire. They needed to believe I was capable of wanton destruction. There were ten miles of tunnels, the guide had said. Since they couldn't search them all, they would run to protect the thing they thought most precious. And I would follow them.

Noticing a faint light, I thought the lanterns of my pursuers must be close. But the main passageway along which they approached was still dark. I turned around and stared deeper into the oval tunnel. The light was coming from further in. I had chosen this place to hide because it seemed unmaintained. It seemed others had chosen it for the self-same reason.

I had left it too late to run back to the main passageway, so I set off away from it. From ahead came a new sound – the gurgle and hiss of gas lights. As the passage curved around to the left, I saw a lamp mounted on the wall. The heat of it must have stopped ice accreting there, for the tunnel widened at that point. There were more lamps beyond it, regularly spaced. And now I saw openings to the left and right. I took the first one and found myself entering a small chamber, quite dark. I backed into it, stumbling on a low step and almost falling. But my flailing arms found purchase on what I took to be a block of ice dangling from the ceiling.

Crouching, I was able to keep watch on the lit tunnel. Two men hurried past in quick succession. Then came another two, hauling a ragged sack between them. Then the sack kicked out and I realised it was Tinker. Next were two men carrying the poles of a laden stretcher. And finally the bearded guide.

I was ready to follow, but first took a backward glance into the chamber. I could now make out the shape of the dangling ice block. It was one of many, hanging in rows. I blinked, trying to understand what I was seeing. The room had the appearance of a butcher's cold store. Except that the dangling objects were not sides of meat. Rather, they were people.

The bodies were hanging upside down, legs bound together at the ankles, wrists tied in place over the stomach. They were men and women. Children too. Each wore an identical garment – a loose fitting gown held in place by drawstrings. Onto the chest of each was pinned a sheaf of papers.

I grabbed the papers from the nearest body, ripped them free and hurried back out into the oval corridor, ready to give chase. My spikes were crunching the ice, so I began to place my feet with care. The men had slowed now. Perhaps the burdens they carried were tiring them. Or perhaps they were approaching their destination.

"Everyone quiet!"

The instruction stopped me mid-step. It had been spoken by one of the party up ahead. And though it was more of a hiss than a shout, it had come to me as crisply as if it had been whispered into my ear. The passageway ahead veered sharply right. They were not far beyond the bend.

I waited. The cloud of my breath made a halo around the wall lamp. There was no sound except the hiss of gas. For the first time I looked at the papers clutched in my hand.

Name: David Clarke Davidson
Place of birth:Unknown
Date of birth:Unknown
Age: Approximately 30
Weight:79.4 kg
Height:177 cm
Date of freezing:28th of September
Cause of death:Not applicable

The pages that followed were thick with technical language. Though I didn't understand the words, they seemed to be descriptions of a medical treatment – chemical names, dosages and dates. Alongside them were notes of body function and temperature. These had been written in a different hand. The first date mentioned was the 22nd of September at which point the temperature had been 38°C. The final date was a week later. The temperature had dropped to ten degrees below freezing. I looked back to the cover sheet and re-read the words: *Cause of death not applicable*. A shudder ran through my body.

"Told you. She's not here."

"You underestimate her."

I recognised the first voice as the guide. The second voice was Erasmus Foxley.

"She'll be lost," said the guide. "We'll find her frozen solid in a day or two."

"Nevertheless…"

"Or maybe in ten years."

"Nevertheless, we search."

"For what? What could she do?"

"It would be a waste to let her die don't you think? Unused."

Not waiting to hear the answer, I started back along the oval tunnel. I would not abandon Tinker. But letting myself be captured could not help him. I chose the third of the side passages I came to. It proved short, opening quickly into a dark chamber. I dared not light a match in case the smell of phosphorus drew them to me. So I stepped deeper into the room with my arms stretched out, feeling blind, fearing more bodies might be hanging there.

There were none.

Four paces in, I bumped into a table with a top that seemed to be made of metal. The base was a solid pedestal. I felt my way around it to the side furthest from the entrance and crouched low.

I folded the papers and stuffed them into a pocket of my coat. By way of exchange, I removed my father's pistol and cocked the hammer. The energy of flight had warmed my limbs, but as I waited, the cold began to creep back into me again. I was confident of my grip, but my trigger finger felt numb and unresponsive. I applied pressure to the trigger guard, trying to reassure myself that I would be able to shoot if it came to that.

I could hear nothing beyond my own breathing. Some quality of the chamber and its entranceway was deadening external sounds.

Minutes passed. Then the faint glow from the entrance dimmed and spiked boots were crunching the ice. Lamplight flooded in. The table grew a shadow which swung left and right. I could see my surroundings properly for the first time. A line of barrels rested against one wall. Above them, shelves had been stacked with laboratory glassware. The shadow of the table shifted as the lamp progressed around the room. There was a dead drumbeat as something knocked on the barrels, one after the other. He was checking that no one hid inside. Then he was around the edge and I could see him. It was the guide – a lamp in one hand, a short handled axe in the other. I started to lift my gun, using both hands to steady it. He must have heard the breath of my coat shifting, for I made no other sound. The axe head had been reaching out to tap the next barrel in line. Then it was swinging towards me. Even if I pulled the trigger, his momentum was going to carry it to my head. I threw myself to the right and the heavy blade whispered through the air inches from my ear. I scrambled in the other direction. There was a crash of steel splitting ice as a blow landed on the floor just behind me. I rolled into a crouch and raised the gun. His axe hand came to a stop at the top of its arc. Then he threw the lantern at my head. I deflected it with my arm, losing aim as I did so. It smashed and the light went out.

I sidestepped in the dark. At the same moment I heard a grunt of effort. There was a sudden tug on my coat and the sound of the axe striking the floor next to me. I sidestepped again. Fragments of the lamp mantle broke with a crackle under my boot. He took a step towards me, silhouetting himself against the faint glow from the entrance passage. I would be invisible to him. I raised my gun, holding it in both hands. Then as he stepped towards me, I jumped left and jabbed the muzzle hard into his side. There was a fraction of a second when he might have swung at me. But then I was behind him.

"You're not getting out of here," he said.

"Where's the boy?"

"Out there. Fifty yards."

He made to turn. I stepped around keeping myself behind him until he was facing the entrance.

"You're not getting out," he said again. "You've got one gun against... you don't even know how many." He began walking towards the entrance. I matched him step for step, increasing the pressure of the gun barrel against his back.

"I just want the boy. Then I'll go."

"After what you've seen? Do a deal, that's my advice. Give up. In exchange we'll kill you."

"What sort of deal's that?"

"You don't know, do you?"

"Don't know what?"

"I thought you were brave coming here. But you don't know nothing."

We'd reached the oval tunnel. He turned left. I followed.

"What does it mean on the papers – 'Date of death not applicable'?"

"Now that's a stupid question," he said.

"But they're dead!" "You want that to be true."

"Then can they be woken?"

"You might say. And then you might not."

"What does that mean?"

When he didn't answer, I jabbed him hard with the gun.

"We'd have given you to the duke," he said. "That was the plan. Just to get rid of you. But we can't let you go. Not now you've been in here."

"Where's the boy?"

"Not far."

The passage curved sharply to the right, so I didn't see the end until I reached it. Ahead lay a large, brightly-lit chamber. Keppler and Foxley stood looking at us. Tinker thrashed on the floor between them, bound hand and foot. Next to him was the stretcher I'd seen carried. A man's body lay inert on top of it, face down.

The guide stepped into the room and turned to face me. "You should see yourself," he said. "Your face is white already. White as ice."

I was staring past him. At the back of the room was a large machine. I'd not seen its like before, though I could recognise some of the parts – crank handle, wheels and geared belts. In the middle was a metal trough, wide and deep. A great mound of crushed ice had been heaped into it. On either side of the trough was a flat surface, like the draining board of a sink.

"Miss Barnabus, I presume," said Dr Foxley.

"What's that?" I asked.

"A freezer. Would you like a closer look?"

I shifted my focus to aim at the doctor. "Untie the boy!"

"You have but one bullet, my dear."

"But I can choose where to spend it."

Keppler began circling to the left, the guide moved to the right. I switched my aim back and forward between them.

"You've made our job easier," Foxley said. "By coming here. And this way you'll contribute to my research."

"One of you unties the boy. One of the others, I shoot."

There was a hesitation, then a nod between them. The guide stepped towards Tinker. I aimed the gun at Keppler, touched my finger to the trigger. And then, without warning, a sack was pulled down hard over my head. Strong hands were holding me. I whipped my hand down, pointed the gun behind me and pulled the trigger. I saw the muzzle flash through the sacking. Though half deaf from the shot, I could hear the man behind me screaming in pain. But other hands had grabbed me. I lost grip of the gun as they wrestled me to the floor.

CHAPTER 36

Beware the gin soaked audience. You see them as they really are.

THE BULLET-CATCHER'S HANDBOOK

When I became conscious again, I was lying on my back on a smooth, hard floor. The sack was still over my head. The air inside it stank – a chemical smell like strong spirit mixed with something sickly sweet. I could remember struggling and a foul smelling rag clamped over my mouth and nose. I remembered falling but not hitting the ground.

The thought of sitting up made the floor tip and sway like a small boat in rough water. There were voices around me, drifting in and out of focus. At first they seemed to come from near the ground. Then the owners of the voices were walking around me and I understood that I was lying on an elevated surface. A table perhaps. It was cold – though no colder than my own skin.

I lifted my arm. It felt distant, as if not part of me. The memory of a dream came rushing back. I was on the autopsy table in the operating theatre. My arms and legs had been replaced by automaton limbs, driven by belts and gears.

"She's waking already."

"Strap her down."

The voices of the guide and the doctor swam in the air. I felt a pressure across my chest and heard the clink of a buckle. I kicked my feet into the air.

"Get her legs!" ordered the doctor, his voice near my head.

Strong hands grabbed my ankles and wrestled them down. The doctor pulled the strap tight over my chest. I inhaled, filling my lungs beyond comfort. At the same time, I tensed my muscles, making them flex. The buckle clicked home. My arms were pinned just above the elbow.

I kicked again, catching something with my foot. The guide swore. But now the doctor was there to help him. As they secured my legs in place, I let out the breath I'd been holding and felt the strap over my chest grow looser. I lay still, resisting the temptation to move my arms and test how much wriggle room I'd won myself.

"She's a wild one," said the guide.

"What did you expect?" said Foxley. "She's unnatural."

He was holding my right arm. There was a ripping of cotton and I felt the lower part of my sleeve being pulled away. He prodded the inside of my elbow. Then I felt a sharp prick as if I had been pierced with the tip of a knife. The sensation that followed was like nothing I'd felt before. Fire began at the elbow, creeping up my arm and down towards my fingers. It was cold and hot at the same time. It was liquid pain spreading through a limb that now definitely belonged to me. The sudden intensity of feeling made me cry out.

"Excellent veins," said the doctor. "The boy was a nightmare." Then footsteps were departing.

Tinker – the chloroform had driven him from my mind. But now the urgency of his rescue slammed back into my consciousness.

The guide's voice whispered very close. "I'm going to enjoy this."

The sack was ripped away from the front of my eyes. His face was inches from mine.

"I like to talk to them when they're going under," he said. "How does that arm feel?"

The heat-cold-pain had reached my fingertips and was creeping up towards my shoulder. "It hurts."

He made an appreciative sound. "Mm. Wait till it reaches your heart."

"What's happening?"

"You're getting super-human strength."

He straightened and I saw for the first time that an apparatus stood behind him. A metal stand supported a large glass flask. With the lamp behind it, the liquid in the flask seemed to glow pale blue. A rubber tube ran down from it towards me. I craned my neck and saw that it was connected to a metal spike the size of a knitting needle, which had been embedded in my skin. My head felt woozy.

"They all died when we started," the guide said. "Their bodies looked perfect frozen. But needles of ice grew inside them. It corrupted the flesh. Then we discovered this."

He patted the side of the flask. "It'll keep you alive when we freeze you."

The ice-fire was creeping over my shoulder and

beginning to spread across my chest. It was hard to think clearly. Not just from the pain. Tendrils of smog were reaching between my thoughts.

"The bodies..." I had to force the words out of my mouth. "...hanging in that room..."

"You saw them?" He grinned again. "Good. For most, I have to describe it. We call it the dormitory. It's a kind of joke."

A wave of panic and revulsion rose in me. I tried to keep my voice level. "Are they alive?"

"Now there's a question. Some just die when they're warmed and woken. Like they forgot how to breathe. But others – the heart pumps. They move. They stuff food in their mouths. But what's human in them doesn't come back."

"You're lying!"

"That's going to be you," he whispered. "Dribbling and snarling like a mad dog. When we thaw you out in a year or two or three. Some get dissected. Others we turn out onto the street. That's one of the doctor's experiments. He wants to know how long they'll live. Maybe they'll start to learn. Your Mrs Raike – she feeds them. Now that's rich."

He chuckled.

The agony was burning and freezing in my stomach and shoulders. I tried to focus but my mind wouldn't sharpen. "Why?" I gasped, hardly able to form the words through my pain.

He seemed puzzled by the question. "This is science. You don't need a reason. Look at me – I've had the treatment. I don't feel cold. I don't get frostbite. I get a small dose every week. Only a fraction of what you're getting. But I could walk across Antarctica in shirtsleeves. Imagine if we could freeze a man solid and wake him up after a hundred years with no ill done? Or a thousand years. Imagine that!"

I wanted to speak but the pain left no room for thought.

"You want to know where the ice was being taken?" he asked. "You'll like this - it never went anywhere. We crush it. Add chemicals to make it melt. That sucks out the heat. You'll see. Once you're filled up, I'll be taking you to the freezer to join your friends."

The pain was converging on my heart. I cried out. He examined me, head tilted to one side in fascination. Then the spasm passed and I breathed again. There was something I had to remember about the strap that held me down.

"This liquid's got alcohol in it," he said. "You might be feeling that. Once you're out I'll strip you and put you in a sleeping gown. Then I truss you like a chicken."

His face hovered over me, as if waiting for my revulsion to show. I stared up at the ceiling, which was yellowish in the lamp light. I had to think. But not about the horror he was feeding me. There was something else. Something that needed doing.

I dug my thumbnail into the skin of my first finger. That was real pain. It was different from the other feeling, which was working its way through my body. I pressed harder with my nail, sharpening the sensation. I was lying on a table in a room in the ice tunnels. It was the room of barrels and medical glassware. I'd hidden in it before. How long ago had that been? The ceiling above me was darker in patches where rock showed through the ice. I stared at it.

The guide's face relaxed into an expression of boredom. He turned away. Only then did I look at him again. One of the barrels was resting on a work bench. He hefted it down to the floor and began rolling it back into its position by the wall.

There was something I'd meant to do when he wasn't looking. I observed the glass flask on its stand. I followed the rubber tube down to the needle in my skin. I stared at the strap across my body. Then I remembered.

I breathed out, expelling all the air from my lungs. The strap went slack. I started wriggling my left arm. I felt my skin scraping as it slipped under the leather. Then it was free. I felt blind, for the buckle. My fingertip touched it but I couldn't reach far enough to grip it. The guide turned and saw me. He was across the room in two, long strides. I pulled the needle free of my arm and held it away from his reach. Blue liquid dripped from the hollow tip. He lunged over me, trying to grab it. Instead of pulling it further away, I thrust it up into him. I felt it make contact. He recoiled and it pulled from my hand. The rubber tube went taut and the metal stand toppled towards him. I was struggling my other arm free when the glass hit the ground. The flask shattered. With both arms out from under the strap, I had more movement and could reach the buckle.

I saw the guide extracting the needle from his throat. Then he was coming towards me again, one hand clamped to his neck to slow the bleeding. I found myself sitting up, fumbling with the strap over my ankles.

He stooped to pick something from the floor. Then he was at the table, scything the air with a shard of broken glass. I threw myself to the side and it hissed past my face. I must have got the other buckle open because I found myself falling from the table. I landed on the far side from him.

He was clambering over the top. But I'd already rolled away. I was woozy from the drug, but panic was driving the smog from my mind. He jumped down from the table. The spilled liquid dripping from his clothes and pooling on the floor.

I scrambled to my feet. He advanced, still sweeping the jagged glass left and right like a knife fighter. My right arm dripped. I blinked, trying to focus. Blood welled from between the fingers of the hand he had clamped to his neck. I backed into a bench, felt behind me for something to use as a weapon, seized on the handle of an oil lamp. I swung it in front of me, trying to knock the glass from his hand. I missed. He lunged and I had to jump to the side to avoid it.

If I didn't find a way to pass him, he would back me into the corner of the room. I shifted left and right as he advanced, but he matched my every move.

"You're going to suffer," he hissed, swinging his arm. The glass cut the air between us. "I'll dissect you whilst you're still alive!"

I'd reached the corner. He took a sudden step forwards. I flung the lamp at his face. He batted it away with the hand that had been covering his wound. It shattered on the floor. Blood started pouring from his neck but he had his hand quickly back over it, staunching the flow.

He seemed about to say something. But a sound like a cloth flapping brought him up short. The pool of spilled liquid had caught the fire from the smashed lantern. A wall of blue flame leapt from the ruined flask. In a heartbeat it was over the table, following the path the guide had taken. There was a fraction of a second in which realisation showed on his face. Then he was ablaze. I ducked under his swinging arm, jumped the edge of the burning pool and ran. At the entrance to the tunnel, I turned. Consumed in flame, he had dropped to his knees. The man who could not feel cold cried out in agony.

Only as I stepped into the oval tunnel did I wonder why no one had come running to help him. The seconds seemed weirdly stretched. Perhaps too little time had passed. Or perhaps it was the strange attenuation of sound in the tunnels that had stopped anyone hearing the fight.

I stood for a moment, listening. The extreme focus that comes with danger had started to ebb. I put a hand to the ice wall to steady myself. It stuck. I panicked and yanked it back. It pulled free, leaving a bloody hand print. Seeing it, I remembered the guide's words from long ago. *Don't want you to leave your skin behind*. I looked at my hand, still gloved. The leather was soaked in blood from the wound where the needle had gone into my arm.

Acrid smoke was flowing along the ceiling. In the tunnel it drifted left, caught by the ventilation current. Sound might not have travelled, but the smell would.

I noticed again the bloody hand print I'd left on the

ice. I had no sense of time flowing or how long I'd
been standing there. I slapped my face. Then I slapped
it harder. My cheek smarted.

Tinker. I had to rescue Tinker. I slapped again and
again, feeling my mind sharpen with each blow.

The boy was a nightmare. Those were Foxley's words,
comparing my veins to Tinker's. They'd worked
on him before starting on me. I brushed down my
pockets, searching for my watch. It had been taken.
I could have been hours under the chloroform. Days
even.

Memories swam. Something about a dormitory. A
freezer.

I watched the smoke flowing along the ceiling
then lurched off following it as if on borrowed legs.
There was no sleeve on my left arm. A large blue-
black bruise marked the inside of my elbow. I stared
at it, not remembering being beaten. I squeezed my
gloved hand into a fist and felt the blood squelch.
Blood ruins leather. Someone had spoken those words
to me.

The passage curved sharply right. There was a
bloodstain on the floor. I could hear a noise around
me – the soft clacking rhythm of a machine in motion.
I stumbled into a large room, brightly lit. I blinked,
trying to remember when I had been there before.
A memory of Tinker struggling made me look down,
but he was not on the floor.

When I looked up again, I saw the machine. I
remembered the sack pulled over my head. I had shot
someone.

The machine sounded like a huge clockwork

device. A regulator spun. A belt turned a wheel. The trough at the centre of it was no longer heaped high with crushed ice. Now a mist hung over it, flowing out over the rim and spreading across the floor. With the ice gone, I could see a metal drum, half-submerged in the middle of the trough. Its purpose seemed to be guiding a set of chains down into the depths and then up out on the other side.

Foxley had called it a freezer.

I watched the wheels turning. The chains were being dragged over a flat surface. I remembered thinking it looked like a draining board. Two packages were being dragged over the surface. I stared at them, dumbly. The contraption was like a clock – the regular clicking of the mechanism, the inching forwards of the packages towards that well of cold.

I stumbled into the chamber, unsure if it was a clock that had a freezer attached to it or a freezer that had a clock. The packages were being pulled by the chains. In time they'd fall over the lip of the trough and be forced by the drum deep into it. The chain continued out on the other side. The packages would be hauled through to the opposite draining board. The clock would keep them submerged for a set time.

How cleverly designed it was. But the word *them* had snagged in my mind. I started to circle the machine, staring at the packages. From the side I could see they were people. A small one further back and a larger one approaching the freezing trough.

They were Tinker and John Farthing.

The panic slapped me harder than my hands had done. My breath came in short gasps. Farthing was inches from being pulled over the lip. I dashed to the side of the machine. He was trussed up with ropes but only a pair of straps held him to the chains. My hands fumbled with the strap nearest me. My glove was slippery with blood. But on my second try the buckle came undone.

The strap around his feet was still dragging him. I scrambled around to the other side of the machine. His bare feet had already descended into the mist. Dipping my hands into it, I took hold of the loose end of the strap. My glove stiffened as the blood-soaked leather began to freeze. I tried to thread the end back through the buckle, but one of my hands was no longer able to grip. His bound feet slid deeper. In a few seconds, his whole body would be pulled over the edge. I grabbed the strap with my right hand and leaned back with all my weight.

There was a crack like a breaking twig. I fell back, still gripping the strap. The metal link that held it to the chain had shattered. In falling I'd dragged Farthing's legs out of the ice bath and half off the edge of the draining board. I hauled again and again until gravity took over and the rest of his body followed. He thudded, inert, onto the floor next to my feet.

I tried to pull the glove off my left hand but it was still rigid with ice so I turned my attention to the strap that held Tinker's feet. I managed to thread the leather back through the buckle. But as I was about to pull it free, I caught a movement on the rim of my vision.

I jerked around to see Keppler lunging towards me, arm first. He seemed to thump me on the shoulder and I staggered back. I had been so fixated on the rescue that I'd not seen him enter the room. His bare hand glistened red. I saw a wink of silver – the blade of a knife. All this, I took in at a flash. Then he lunged again, but this time tripped on Farthing's prone body and lurched forward off-balance.

I jumped back around the corner of the machine, not understanding where the blood on his hand had come from.

The regulator continued to spin. A link of chain clinked as it tipped over the lip of the trough. I scrambled back around another corner putting the body of the machine between us. Keppler advanced, his face expressionless. I backed up until I was next to Tinker's head, which was closer to the edge than I remembered. I reached out to undo the buckle and for the first time saw the gash at the top of my arm where Keppler's knife must have opened my flesh.

He rushed at me. I turned and ran, circling the machine. He was slower than me on the corners, but faster on the straight. I reached Tinker's feet and hauled the last of the belt free. Then I had to dive back to avoid another lunge of the blade. I jumped Farthing's body and was away.

Another chain link clinked as it tipped over the lip of the trough. Keppler seemed to notice it for the first time. He stopped and looked at the slowly turning wheels, at the chain being forced down into the mist. Then he walked back around in the other direction. I matched him, keeping myself on the opposite side. When he stopped, we were facing each other over Tinker's body. The feet were next to me. Now free of the chain, they'd already lagged behind the rest of him. Keppler had taken up position next to the boy's head, which was still being dragged.

I watched as Keppler shifted the knife from one hand to the other.

"Your brother might have stopped this," he said. "But he couldn't do it. He isn't a killer. Except by not doing it, he's killed you. And your friends."

The winding drum turned. The chain clinked. I watched Tinker's body judder forwards another inch. The only way to stop it was to undo the strap around his shoulders. Keppler was waiting for me to come to him.

It would mean death to walk around the machine, so I chose instead to clamber up onto it. On hands and knees, I started crawling across the draining board over which Tinker was being dragged.

Keppler smiled and matched my movement, climbing up from the other side. With one hand he gripped the knife, with the other he steadied himself on the chain.

Mist from the freezer was flowing over the side of Tinker's head. White frost was growing on his hair and eyelashes. The knife darted at me. I ducked and slipped. My chin thudded down making lights dance. Keppler launched himself at me. The chain lashed and his leap fell short. He shouted in pain. His knife hand was next to me. I swung my elbow down onto his wrist and the knife skittered away.

He thrashed his hand and the chain danced, as if he could not let go. It took me a second to understand. His bare skin, wet with my blood, had frozen to the metal.

With my gloved hands, I fumbled the strap through the buckle and released Tinker's shoulders. Keppler was stretching his free hand towards the knife. He got a finger to it but only knocked it further from his reach.

I hauled Tinker's lifeless body away from him.

Another link of the chain clicked over the lip of the trough, pulling Keppler's hand an inch closer to the freezer. The cold mist was flowing over it already, his hairs whitening with frost. He hit it again and again with his other hand, as if trying to crack the ice. I was off the machine and pulling Tinker after me. I lifted him, feeling pain from the wound on my upper arm.

Clenching my teeth, I carried him out from behind the machine. He was cold, but not yet frozen. I had to get him out of the tunnels. There was a trolley that looked like a stretcher on wheels parked next to the wall. I laid Tinker on top of it then went back for Farthing.

Another link of chain clinked over the lip. Keppler's hand was deeper in the mist. He was stretching with his other hand, trying to grab the belt that drove the wheels.

"Help me," he said. "I'll do a deal."

I took hold of Farthing's feet and heaved. My spikes bit into the ice and he started sliding. At the side of the trolley, I tried to lift him, but he was far heavier than Tinker and I fell to my knees.

"You won't get them out on your own," Keppler shouted, panic in his voice. "I'll help you if you just free me!"

The chain clicked forward. He was forearm-deep in the trough.

I slapped Farthing's face. "Wake up!" I slapped again, harder, making his head roll to the side. "John Farthing, don't you die on me!"

I hauled on the ropes with which he was trussed, forcing the body into a sitting position. Then I crouched, wrapped my arms around him and heaved, lifting him from the floor. I couldn't get him fully upright. When he started to fall back, I threw all my weight to the side so that his upper body came to rest on top of Tinker.

The chain clinked.

"I'll kill Foxley for you!" Keppler shouted. "Just let me out!"

I lifted Farthing's legs and hauled them around. Somehow I'd managed to get him onto the trolley, half on top of Tinker.

I pushed, leaning my weight into it. At first the trolley wouldn't budge. Then the wheels started turning and it trundled forwards over the uneven ground. As I entered the tunnel, I took a final look over my shoulder. Keppler was shoulder deep in the trough, straining to keep his mouth above the freezing mist. There was wild panic in his eyes.

He screamed. "You don't want to leave me! You're not a killer."

"You did it to yourself," I said.

Then I turned away, not wanting to see the moment his head was pulled under.

CHAPTER 37

Humility is the birthright of the common man, whereas the king knows himself all-powerful. Thus he sees not the dagger that strikes him down.

FROM REVOLUTION

Pushing the trolley into the oval tunnel, I felt the wheels drop into grooves in the ice. I'd not noticed them before. Suddenly it was easier to push and I was away around the curve. I wondered how many times they had moved bodies between the freezer and the dormitory to wear such a track.

As I worked I began to sweat. The burning sensation that had passed through me was now all but gone. Tinker and Farthing had been given the full dose of the drug and perhaps other drugs to follow. I feared what would happen when I got them outside and their bodies started to warm.

It grew darker towards the end of the oval tunnel. I tried to remember which direction I'd turned to enter it. The fog was starting to clear from my mind. I decided to try left. Within a few paces I was walking in blackness. I patted down my clothes, only to remember that my possessions had been taken. There would be no candle or matches to light the way and I had lost my father's pistol.

My encounters with the guide and Keppler could only have taken a few minutes. If Foxley and the other men were still in the tunnels, they would soon discover my escape. I leant my weight into the trolley and pushed harder. There were no more wheel tracks to run along and I was pushing blind. I drifted into the left hand wall and then into the right, each time jarring my weary muscles.

My eyes were stretched wide open, as if that would help me to see. And then, when I did start to see, hallucinations began leaping in front of me. I saw writhing snakes with the faces of people. And then they weren't hallucinations anymore, but my own shadow cast over the ceiling of the tunnel. At first I thought daylight must be reaching me from outside. But the shadow was ahead, which meant the light was coming towards me from behind.

"How far did you think you were going to get?"

The voice belonged to Erasmus Foxley.

I turned and had to shield my eyes from the approaching lamp. I sensed several people behind it, but couldn't see to count. Panicked, I tried to push on faster. But the light grew as they closed the distance. At last I stopped and turned to face them.

"Take her," said Foxley.

The lantern shifted to one side and a man emerged. He stepped around behind me and took a grip on my arm.

"Where are you taking me?" I asked.

"Back to the Kingdom," he said.

"No," said Foxley. "There's been a change of plan."

"But the reward..."

"You'll be compensated."

"We were promised four hundred."

"Bring her," Foxley ordered. "And you... bring that."

A second man emerged from behind the light and started manoeuvring the trolley.

I felt a shove in my back but resisted. "Do they know what you've done?"

"Just bring her!"

"Do they know the trouble they're in?"

Another shove between my shoulders, stronger this time. I stumbled to my knees. The doctor started walking back the way we'd come.

"What does she mean?" the man behind me asked. "What trouble?"

"Didn't you see the bodies?" I asked.

"She means the morgue," said Foxley.

"Did you see them hanging there?"

"Hanging?"

"From meat hooks in the ceiling."

"Shut her up," Foxley snapped. "She's just trying to unnerve you."

I felt my hand pulled up behind my back.

"Do you know who–"

But my arm was pulled higher and I could not speak for pain.

"Shut up!"

"What does she mean?" This was the other one speaking – the one pushing the trolley.

"You're in trouble," I managed to say before my arm was yanked upwards again.

"I want to know what she means!"

Foxley wheeled to face us. "You want your money? That's what you'll get. And a bonus. I'll pay another hundred guineas on top to each of you. Now, put your hand over her mouth."

The man did as he was told. His palm pressed down on my face. I bit him. Hard. He yelled and released me.

"He's killing people," I gasped.

The bounty hunter lunged at me. I jinked away from him and leapt towards the one pushing the trolley, who grabbed me by the shoulders.

"What people?" he demanded.

"The niece of the Minister of Patents."

"She's lying!" shouted Foxley. "The Minister of Patents doesn't have a niece."

"She'll be hanging from a meat hook. They cut off her finger to send to her parents."

The other bounty hunter grabbed my arm and pulled me off my feet. I hit the ground hard enough to knock the breath from me. Then he was kneeling by my head, trying to stuff a rag into my mouth.

"It's all lies," said Foxley.

"You can check!" I managed to say before my mouth was full of cloth.

"Can we do that?" asked the other one. "Can we check?"

When the doctor answered, his words were measured. "There is someone with a missing finger. But she's someone else. This story is concocted. She's trying to unnerve you. Be a man!"

"I want to hear what she has to say."

There was a scuffle and the pressure was suddenly released from my mouth. I spat out the cloth.

"The man on the trolley – d'you know who he is?"

"It's one of her friends," said Foxley. "We caught him hiding outside."

"He's an agent of the Patent Office."

One of the bounty hunters swore.

"No," said the doctor. "That's impossible!"

But there was a tremor of uncertainty in his voice. The other men must have picked it up too. I felt a shifting of their postures away from me, away from the trolley on which Farthing's body lay.

"She's lying!"

"Then let's check," said the one who'd been pushing the trolley. "If he's one of them, he'll have the mark on his skin."

"That's a myth," said Foxley.

The man gripped Farthing's gown and ripped the cloth away. I scrambled to my feet. There was no mark on his chest.

"You see," said Foxley. "Nothing!"

Then the man heaved Farthing over onto his side and pulled the gown away from his back. On the bare shoulder, a symbol had been tattooed. The letters "O" and "I" superimposed.

He released Farthing, who slumped back down onto the trolley.

"Is he dead?"

"Not dead yet," I said. "But we need to get him out."

The man turned to Foxley. "You can keep your money."

I believe the bounty hunters would have left at that moment. Perhaps they would never have spoken about it again. But the doctor, seeing the risk, dipped into the deep pocket of his coat and produced a pistol.

Immediately they stepped away from each other then moved towards him, one on either side of the passage. The final dash was so quick I couldn't clearly see what happened. They were on him. There was a struggle. The gun fired. The doctor fell.

I was on my feet with the sound of the shot still ringing in my ears. "Help me get the trolley out and I'll never say what you did."

They didn't even need to look at each other to agree. I picked up the lantern then noticed the pistol on the floor next to Foxley's body. A leaping hare was inlaid on the stock in turquoise. It was my father's gun.

There was a windowless carriage waiting outside the ice factory. Doubtless they'd intended to use it to transport me back to the border. But all thought of the reward had now gone. When they looked at me it was with pleading eyes, hoping I would fulfil my part of the bargain.

I knelt on the floor of the carriage, rubbing Tinker's

arms and legs, trying to re-kindle warmth and circulation, not knowing if he would wake. Not knowing if there would be anything human left in him. Next to him on the floor lay Farthing. And on the seat, within my reach, rested the gun, loaded with borrowed powder and shot. If either of them woke as a drooling monster, the right thing would be to end their half-death. If I could. Keppler had said I was not a killer. I hoped I'd not have to find out whether he was right.

The boy's arm twitched. I put my head to his chest and listened again. The flutter I had heard before was now a heartbeat. I rubbed his skin more vigorously.

"Wake-up! Come back. Please."

There was a groan, but not from Tinker. Farthing's hand was clawing at the thin gown. I grabbed the gun and pulled back the flint.

He coughed and retched. There was spit running from the corner of his mouth. He turned onto his side, one arm flailing.

"Say something!"

Tinker shifted. I scrambled backwards onto the seat, taking aim at Farthing's chest.

"Speak damn it!"

Tinker sat up abruptly. He lurched towards me, groaning, his hands clutching at my coat. I pointed the gun at him. He opened his eyes. They were yellowed, un-seeing.

"I'm sorry," I said, putting my finger on the trigger.

Then Farthing gasped. "Elizabeth…"

I snatched the gun away, my hand shaking.

"Say something more!"

Farthing held his hands in front of him and turned them, examining each side. "Where am I?"

Tinker blinked rapidly, as if trying to clear his vision. "I'm hungry," he said.

All else that followed seemed grey and distant. The bounty hunters had found clothes for Tinker and Farthing. I didn't ask where they had got them. Soon the boy and the man were able to sit on the carriage seats. We set off in the direction of Upper Wharf Street. Farthing was overtaken by a bout of shivering so powerful that I feared it was a seizure. But it soon passed. Their minds cleared fast after that.

The coach pulled up beside the warehouse and I remembered those other poor creatures I had encountered on my first visit – their minds corrupted by the experiments of Erasmus Foxley.

The carriage door was opened by one of the bounty hunters. The housemistress stood behind him, a lamp in her hand. She peered in anxiously, her eyes flicking from person to person.

"Get the boy inside," I said. "I'll explain later."

They helped Tinker out, supporting him on both sides.

"Elizabeth…" Farthing reached a hand towards me.

I batted it away. "What were you doing? You said the Patent Office couldn't be involved!"

"These things… I can't explain."

"And do you know what happened in those ice tunnels? Living people used for experiments as if they were dead bodies! Yet the Patent Office can't be involved because it's medical research!"

"Elizabeth..." he tried again to touch me.

"You know I hate the Patent Office! And with all my being!"

There was a second in which we held each other's eyes. I do not know what happened, but something passed between us. The same feeling gripped my chest that I'd felt in the tea shop. "Why? Why did you put yourself in such danger?" The words welled from deep within me. They were a cry of pain.

He seemed about to answer, but another shivering fit seized him. He crossed his arms tightly in front of his chest, as if trying to control the tremors. He keeled over onto his side. I felt the sudden impulse to hold him. The feeling was so strong that to stop myself I had to brace against the corner of the carriage. Gradually the shivering passed and he was able to right himself.

"I... saved you once," he said, catching his breath. "You remember? Now you've saved me. We're even. I'll close your case at the Patent Office. You never have to see me or think of me again."

I felt as if an icicle had been plunged into my heart.

I did not turn to watch the carriage go but I heard the clatter of its wheels. The sound repeated in my mind long after it was gone. I could still hear it as I lay that night in bed, trying to let sleep swallow me.

CHAPTER 38

War and science have ever been the bullwhips of change. But with the drafting of this Great Accord we have abolished both. Thus may we at last set sail into the Long Quiet, which is the end of history.

FROM REVOLUTION

Having fulfilled my part of the bargain, I sat in the secret room behind the bookcase and delivered my report. The woman I had known as Mrs Raike sat opposite. Devoid of her disguise, she wore no wedding ring. Foxley believed the Minister of Patents had no niece. It had not made sense to me at the time. But now I understood she was unmarried. Her greatest secret had been her daughter. Her tragedy would be to grieve in secret also.

Antonia had been in deep freeze for over a month. Like all the other victims in the ice dormitory, she might be woken but her mind would be gone. It was news worse than death. Yet, whenever I tried to soften my account, Antonia's mother saw through the evasion and challenged me to be faithful. Thus I revealed the full horror of Erasmus Foxley's lair.

Certain episodes I was made to repeat in greater detail. Through all this she sat still and upright, as if made of porcelain.

"I don't think the owners of the ice factory were part of the plot," I said. "But some of the workers may have been. You'll need to call the constabulary." I handed her the papers I'd taken from the frozen body. "This is evidence. You'll need to move quickly, before they clean the place up."

When I'd finished my report, she thanked me. But a touch might have broken her.

"What'll you do?" I asked, meaning what would she do about Antonia.

Instead of answering my intended question, she said: "I will talk to my brother – about the extradition treaty. He'll do what he can."

I was taken by carriage to a magnificent house set in parkland beyond the sprawl of the city. The usual rules of Republican architecture did not apply, a footman told me, because it dated from before the Revolutionary War.

I was led through a series of halls and state rooms to a study big enough to contain the wharf keeper's cottage in its entirety and still have space to walk around the outside. A huge oil painting of Ned Ludd hung above the marble fireplace. The glass fronts on the book cabinets were closed and the only object on the desk was a carriage clock.

Ten minutes ticked past before the Minister of Patents, Councillor Wallace Jones, entered the room. He looked so much like his sister that I found myself blinking to clear my vision. My eyes flicked involuntarily to his neck.

"We meet at last," he said. As he spoke, his Adam's apple shuttled up and down.

He gestured for me to sit.

"Thank you."

"You'll be anxious to know the results of our efforts. I wish there was a simpler explanation to give. Please bear with me.

"There are factions within the Council. Any proposed change in legislation, however innocuous, is pounced upon by one group or another. Each faction will try to add unrelated amendments to their own benefit. If you've never been in politics it's hard to understand."

"I was brought up in a travelling show," I said. "We called it horse trading."

"Quite so," he said. "I shouldn't have assumed. Then in your terms – one side would wish to buy your horse and the other side wouldn't. Some enjoy giving the Kingdom a poke in the eye. They are champing to sign your amendment. Others moan about trade implications and would block it."

"You're coming around to telling me you haven't been able to help," I said.

"Not quite. The long and the short of it is, they wouldn't take the amendment. Not in the same bill. But a law banning the retrospective application of the extradition treaty will be waved through exactly one week later. It means you'll need to remain in hiding for that week. Then – with the second law passed – you'll be free to remain in the Republic for as long as you wish."

I remembered what his sister had implied about a lack of ability. "This was your idea?"

"It was indeed mine. Or rather, my private secretary's."

"The second law is certain?"

"I have assurances cast in iron."

I stared into the fireplace. The legal manoeuvring he described was ingenious. It was a lawyer's trick. By timing things just so, all the interned Kingdom exiles would be sent back across the border as soon as the first law was signed. By the time the amendment was passed a week later it would be too late for any of them to appeal. The Republic would be rid of them and the Kingdom would have reclaimed its criminals. All but one. How neat it was, I thought. How face-saving.

I thought back to the internment camp. I flexed my ankle, remembering how the iron had cut into my flesh.

"I have a friend among the exiles," I said.

"A friend?"

"Her name is Tulip Slater. I'd like her saved also."

"This friend – what did she run from? What was her crime?"

"I don't know."

"Yet you wish her saved?"

"By whatever means."

In the days that followed, my time was divided between the study, a bedroom with a huge four-poster and the formal gardens, which I took to walking in whenever the house grew oppressive.

Servants brought food and every morning I found the newspapers had been laid out on the desk. In these I read about the end of Erasmus Foxley's empire. Three doctors were arrested and charged with bodysnatching, as were five workers from the ice factory.

The report of Foxley's death did not emerge until the third day. He had been murdered like all the others, the papers said. At first, I wondered why they were suppressing the truth. But some shadows are not seemly to dispel. There could be no way back for those piteous ones frozen in the ice dormitory. Murder is an offence against the law and against the world. Yet I found myself hoping that someone would end the lives of those poor souls for mercy's sake.

On the sixth day, an entire page was devoted to funeral notices for the victims and I knew that it had been done. I began reading but couldn't finish. Instead, I turned my gaze to the windows and watched the rain falling gently on the gardens. The rhododendron bushes were in full flower, branches bowed low under the weight of blossom.

At half past three in the afternoon with the chimes of the clock still ringing, the door opened and I turned, as ever hoping to see the Minister or his footman carrying news. But in walked the unmistakable figure of Yan Romero, solicitor, resplendent in green corduroy, with a waistcoat so purple that it put the flowers to shame. He lifted his top hat, placed his other hand on his rounded stomach and bowed.

"I am at your service," he said.

"You!"

"No other."

"Why are you here?"

"Your benefactor – aren't you moving in lofty circles these days – he was searching for help in saving a woman, Tulip Slater, from imminent extradition. Thus, I am here. And humbly at your service."

I'd seen two faces of this lawyer – mercurial salesman and brutal opponent. Here was a third to add to the collection.

"Humbly?" I asked.

"Indubitably," he said.

"You're being paid then?"

"Handsomely."

"The newspapers haven't mentioned the treaty. When is it due?"

"Tomorrow."

"Then you should be at the internment camp!"

"It's not so easy. Yet it may be achieved. The principle is this – we lodge some spurious appeal against her extradition. It cannot win. But neither can it be ignored. Thus, they must hold a hearing. But in that time the second law will have been signed – with your friend still on this side of the border."

"Then do it!" I cried.

"But our appeal – it must have grounds. Enough to force a judge to take consideration. We cannot say she was born in the Republic – there's a birth certificate to prove otherwise. Thus we must claim some failure of process. If she was perhaps arrested without proper caution…"

"I wasn't there to see."

"Or if her treatment was degrading."

"We were chained."

"You were prisoners. Chains are part of the uniform, so to speak."

"At first they didn't feed us."

"But they did eventually."

"And they gave us no light. They–"

"No light?" he cut in. "That will do. Indeed that's perfect. With no light one cannot prepare a legal defence. There are precedents. But we need a witness. Could you testify to this effect?"

"I can't go to the camp," I said. "They'd send me across the border with the rest of them."

"No, no, no," he said with a trill. "For the same appeal can be lodged both ways. You each testify for the other."

I examined his face, animated now with anticipation. To win a case against the Republic – he would be the toast of the London lawyers for years to come.

"What guarantee do I have?"

"You have the law, Miss Barnabus. The law shall be your guarantee. Even the governments of our nations must bow down before it."

I had never before travelled by private airship. We took off from a mooring pole at the back of the mansion. The pilot shook our hands as we climbed aboard. Romero and I were the only passengers. The carriage was small, there being but four seats behind the pilot. The envelope above us was narrow. And though there was but one propeller, we accelerated more rapidly than I would have thought possible. Within minutes we had reached our flying altitude and the landscape was slipping past beneath us.

Romero leaned back with his hands behind his head. He was in his element – riding high at the expense of the Republic, flying in luxury to take on a different arm of the same government. He had been commissioned to save Tulip. I trusted him that far and no further.

I watched him exploring the walnut cabinets in front of his seat. One contained cut-glass decanters. He poured himself a brandy. His nostrils flared as he swirled the glass.

"Republicans, eh? Behind closed doors they're no different from us." Then he threw back his drink in one, his eyes fixed on mine as he swallowed. "You're most loyal to your friend," he said.

"I'm in her debt."

"Honour among thieves?"

"We're not thieves."

"True," he said. "You're merely an absconder and she... do you even know her story?" He must have seen that I didn't. "Ah – you should choose your friends with care, Elizabeth. Tulip Slater is notorious. She killed her own father, accusing him after the event of unbearable provocation and sundry abuses. But him not being alive to answer, it was she who would stand trial. Except that she ran. A court case awaits her. She would hang, no doubt, if it was put to the test. The public are hungry for every detail that would emerge."

The airship came down at the Anstey Terminus, drifting to a stop behind the main hangars in an area I'd not seen before. The minister must have sent a pigeon ahead because a steam car was waiting for us, luxurious as the airship had been. The interior walls and ceiling were upholstered in grey velvet.

I was closing the door, but Romero put out a hand to stop me. A cadaverous man whose jacket was too short for his arms had been loitering close by. He ducked low as he climbed into the carriage. Once he had folded himself into his seat, Romero offered an introduction:

"Elizabeth Barnabus. William Carlton."

"Excuse me?" I said.

"I'm to be witness," said the man.

"I thought that was my job."

"It's complicated," said Romero.

With the door closed, the boom and hiss of the engine was suddenly quiet. I watched the countryside slipping past, remembering my escape along the same road. The place where I had lain hidden next to the hedge seemed quite different in daylight. I craned my neck to keep it in view after we passed.

"Don't tell me you've seen something interesting in this god-awful place?" Romero said.

"How much money have you made since crossing the border?" I asked.

"Five hundred and eighteen guineas."

The witness, William Carlton, squirmed with embarrassment. Whatever his role was to be, he was a Republican sure enough.

"Is that sufficient for you?" I asked.

Romero didn't catch the disgust in my voice.

"No amount is enough. But I might yet earn some more. You have to look on the bright side, eh?"

I felt myself tensing as the car turned onto a narrow lane and I caught a first glimpse of green painted huts through the trees. Then we rolled into the clearing, just as I had done in the black Maria a lifetime ago.

"Leave the talking to me," said Romero.

The constables wanted to put me in leg irons but Romero waved them away. Nevertheless they followed closely. The young constable was there – the one who had put the iron on my ankle and thus allowed me to escape. There was such hatred in his eyes that I found I couldn't look at him.

We were escorted to the same hut in which I had met John Farthing. Tulip was waiting there, a constable standing on each side of her. Her expression of bewilderment crumbled to dismay as she saw me.

"It's going to be all right," I said.

Romero reached into his jacket pocket and produced a document. This he unfolded with a flourish. The thick paper crackled.

"I am today lodging this appeal against the detention of Tulip Slater pending deportation on the grounds of ill treatment, namely the deprivation of the means of illumination and thus the means of preparing her legal defence. The full argument is laid out here..." He passed the paper to the senior constable. "In accordance with the relevant statutes, detailed therein, I demand a hearing before a judge. A sworn affidavit by Elizabeth Barnabus is presented as evidence in appendix A. She being here to sign as witness."

He then retrieved the papers and flattened them on the wooden wall of the hut. I took the fountain pen he offered and signed where he'd marked a cross.

The senior constable's face twisted into an expression of impotent fury. "She's to be deported," he said. "Tomorrow."

"Alas, that will be impossible," said Romero, with no attempt at sincerity.

The senior constable clicked his fingers and pointed at me. "We'll have this one then."

"Not so hasty," said Romero, reaching inside his jacket once more and flourishing a second document. He unfolded the thick paper and read. "This is Elizabeth Barnabus, fugitive, scheduled for deportation tomorrow."

I saw his expression change as he spoke the words. He'd been smug before. Now he positively gloated. "I hereby present her into your custody as witnessed by the public notary William Carlton."

I'd feared betrayal but not been able to see how it might come.

He flattened the papers on the wall as before. I watched the cadaverous man sign and date the document.

"We appeal," I said, already knowing it would not work. "There was no light for me either."

"You have case documents?" asked the senior constable, on whose face a smile was now beginning to grow.

"Alas no," said Romero. "That was never part of my commission. As ever, the devil hides in the detail. The Minister of Patents paid me to obtain the release of Tulip Slater. This I've done. He never mentioned your name."

"But you said–"

"You should have commissioned me from the start. I remember your words. A piano has been dropped from an airship and I was to tell you which way to jump. It was really very good. I may use it myself. The piano has now landed. You'll go back where you belong and I'll receive my reward."

He wafted the papers to let the ink dry, then began refolding them.

No one had noticed as I dropped a hand into the pocket of my coat. But they heard the click as I pulled back the hammer. And they saw the pistol as I pressed it into the back of Romero's head. He froze mid-movement.

Three more pistols clicked. The constables took aim in my direction.

"Don't let her shoot me!" Romero cried.

"Put down the gun, Miss Barnabus."

"I *will* shoot," I said.

"If you must," said the senior constable, without regret. I'd chosen the wrong head to aim at.

"No!" shrieked Romero.

I didn't see the moment when Tulip sprang. But I heard the thud as the body of one of the constables fell. Suddenly everyone was moving at once. There was Tulip, kneeling by the felled man, his blood spreading across the floor, a knife protruding from his thigh. She had his gun and was aiming at the senior constable. If someone pulled a trigger, all the guns would fire.

"Run, Elizabeth!" she cried.

For a moment I hesitated. She seemed to read my

thoughts. "I was never going back. The knife was meant for me."

"You can still come with me!"

"No. Let me do this thing. It's what I want."

The last I saw, she was holding the gun in a double-handed grip and her face was serene. Then I'd closed the door and was marching back to the steam-car that had brought us. The driver jumped out when he saw me.

"The others won't be joining us," I said.

"Very good, miss. Where to?"

I did not hear the gunshot, though in my dreams afterwards I imagined it. The newspapers told part of the story only. I was not mentioned, it being too embarrassing to admit that I had escaped a second time. An officer was injured, they said. Tulip had stolen a butter knife and sharpened it on a stone. She stabbed him in the thigh and ran. Bleeding on the ground, he took aim and shot her as she tried to escape. His bullet caught her in the side of the head. It was an instant kill.

But each time I pictured it, I saw Tulip raising the gun to her own head and pulling the trigger.

The remaining prisoners were gone within a day. Taken to the border to be handed over to the men at arms on the other side. Clarence Hobb would be kept busy entertaining the crowds. For fugitives coming back the other way, hard labour was more likely. The Republic did not have the same taste for hanging.

And then the second law was signed.

*This law is an amendment to the Reconciliation
and Extradition Act (2009). Its purpose is to restrict
the retrospective effects of the aforementioned Act.
Henceforth, no person who arrived in the Anglo-
Scottish Republic before the Act was passed shall be
subject to its strictures. This with the exception of the
fugitive known as Elizabeth Barnabus.*

Councillor Wallace Jones had been tricked by his
opponents. In politics, as in law, there is room in
the gaps between words for the Devil to build all his
palaces and pleasure gardens.

I felt no anger or sadness when I read the report of
the law change and saw my name listed as an exception.
Not to say I'd expected it. But I had too much experience
of ending up on losing sides to have believed I'd finally
won. Instead, I felt a strange excitement – a tingling
premonition of the road that lay ahead.

It was the quiet watches of the night when I returned
to the wharf and made my way to the boat house.
The heavy padlock rested in the hasp, so that from a
distance it seemed secure. But the arm of the lock had
not been clicked into place. I lifted it clear, opened the
door a crack and slipped inside.

My heart constricted as I saw Bessie, my beautiful
home. She was not as I had left her. Gone was the
framework of her cabins. The superstructure had
been ripped out – replaced for most of its length
by a cargo hold covered with tarpaulin. The engine
funnel sprouted from a small cabin at the back. The
nameplate now read *Harry*.

I had asked for it to be done, but never dreamed they would achieve so thorough a disguise. Walking the length of her, I brushed my hand against the paddlewheel. She would surely pass unnoticed among the working boats. I wondered how many hours had been spent to effect so complete a transformation. It seemed impossible that Mr Simmonds and Mr Swain could have achieved it on their own.

From the aft deck, I felt my way down three steps to a covered area of engine controls and firebox. A short passageway took me past the engine and into the tiny cabin that was my new home. I ducked as I entered, but still knocked my head against a lamp that hung from the ceiling. A box of Lucifers had been wedged inside its glass, as if waiting for someone to arrive in the night.

I struck a light and put it to the wick. As the flame grew, I saw the statue, the Spirit of Freedom, leaning from the aft wall, her metal now bright. They had left her uncovered. I reached out and stroked her face. Freedom – that is what this boat would give me. I would be able to steam away and lose myself in the waterways of the Republic. Or if I chose, travel south and cross the border to confront my enemy full-on.

Turning to survey the cabin, I saw that it was filled with familiar objects. The lamp itself had been in Mr Swain's workshop. The wall rack was stacked with plates and cups, the patterns of which I knew from other boats on the wharf. The Measham teapot, pride of the coal boatman's cabin, rested on a shelf of its own. I touched it.

"Oh, Mary, you've given me too much."

Now I understood where the workforce must have come from to transform my boat. The people of the wharf had gifted me with their time and effort as well as their possessions. Perhaps my ill-treatment by the constables had changed their opinion of me. Or perhaps Julia had been right about their feelings and I had misjudged them all along.

An envelope addressed in my friend's careful hand rested next to the teapot. *For my dear sister*. I picked it up and slipped it into my sleeve.

A soft breath made me turn, though not with a start. I had been expecting it – hoping for it even. A ragged boy lay curled up at the foot of the cot. Tinker was fast asleep.

I retraced my steps and opened the firebox. Coal, sticks and newspaper lay arranged inside, ready to be lit. At the bottom of the pile was the crude Kingdom flag I had been obliged to paste in my window. Remembering the lesson that Mr Swain had taught, I tapped the water gauge and saw that the tender was full. She had been left ready in anticipation of my return.

Though I had never so keenly felt my love for the community of the wharf, it was time for me to go. I struck another Lucifer, reached into the firebox and set it to the kindling.

SELECTED ENTRIES FROM
A GLOSSARY OF THE GAS-LIT EMPIRE

The Anglo-Scottish Republic
The northernmost nation formed by the partition of Britain following the 1819 armistice. The city of Carlisle is its capital, the seat of its parliament and other agencies of government. It is a democracy, with universal suffrage for all men over the age of twenty-one years.

The Anstey Amendment
An amendment to the armistice signed at the end of the British Revolutionary War. The border had initially been drawn as an east-west line from the Wash, passing just south of Derby. However, when news started to spread that Anstey was to be controlled by the Kingdom, new skirmishes broke out. The Anstey Amendment was therefore drafted, redrawing the border to include a small southerly loop and thereby bring Ned Ludd's birthplace into the Republic.

The border had originally been drawn so that it

would pass through sparsely populated countryside. An unforeseen consequence of the Anstey Amendment was the bisection of the city of Leicester between the two new nations and its subsequent flourishing as a centre of trade and communication.

Barnabus, Elizabeth

A woman regarded by historians as having had a formative role in the fall of the Gas-Lit Empire. Born in a travelling circus, and becoming a fugitive at the age of fourteen, with no inheritance but the secret of a stage illusion, she nevertheless came to stand at the very fulcrum of history.

No individual could be said to have caused the collapse of such a mighty edifice. Rather, it was brought low by the great, the inexorable, tides of history. Yet had it not been for this most unlikely of revolutionaries, the manner of its fall would have been entirely different.

The Battle of Stanhope

A skirmish that took place on January 30th 1816 between the men of the Prince Bishop of County Durham and local lead miners who had taken to grouse poaching because of poverty. Though it was merely a local dispute, the government crackdown that followed precipitated a series of battles of increasing scale and range. By April, the entire country was in flames. Being the spark that lit the powder keg, Stanhope is regarded as the first battle in the British Revolutionary War.

The British Revolutionary War
Also known as the Second English Civil War and as the Luddite Revolution, it ran for exactly three years from January 30th 1816 to January 30th 1819 and resulted in the division of Britain into two nations: the Anglo-Scottish Republic and the Kingdom of England and Southern Wales. The untamed lands of northern Wales cannot be said to be a true nation as they are ruled by no government.

The Circus of Mysteries
One of the many travelling magic shows to tour the Kingdom of England and Southern Wales. Original home of Elizabeth Barnabus. After years of financial difficulty, it was finally closed in the early years of the 21st Century after its owner, Gulliver Barnabus, was declared bankrupt.

The Council of Aristocrats
The highest agency of government in the Kingdom of England and Southern Wales. It meets in London and has authority over the general population as well as the monarchy.

The Council of Guardians
The highest agency of government of the Anglo-Scottish Republic. Sixty per cent of its membership is appointed. Forty per cent is elected by universal suffrage of all men over the age of twenty-one. Its meetings are held in Carlisle.

Cultural Drift

A phrase used to describe the origin of cultural differences between the Kingdom of England and Southern Wales and the Anglo-Scottish Republic.

The cultures of Kingdom and Republic were not dissimilar at partition. But years of priding themselves on their differences, caused them to drift apart. In *A History of the Gas-Lit Empire*, the process is described thus: *How often do we see an unhappy couple changing over time so that each more perfectly manifests the aspect of their character that annoys the other. So it was with the disunited kingdoms of Britain.*

Derby

One of the three principal cities in the South East of the Republic. Derby is famous for engineering and heavy industry. It is home to the largest ice factory in the Anglo-Scottish Republic.

From Revolution

A collection of writings from the founding fathers of the British, French and American Revolutions. As early as 1828, attempts to compile an authoritative volume of approved revolutionary writings were resulting in fierce argument between moderate and absolutist factions. These were not resolved until the Conference of Nice la Belle in 1843, at which the apocryphal texts were finally excluded.

Originally called "From Revolution: Essays of the New Society", the title was shortened to make it more accessible to the common man. In the years that followed, *From Revolution* was translated into all state languages of the Gas-Lit Empire. Social charities distributed it to prisons, hospitals, workhouses and even hotel and guest houses. Detailed knowledge of the text became part of the core curriculum of public education.

The Gas-Lit Empire
A popular though inaccurate phrase coined by the Earl of Liverpool to describe the vast territories watched over by the International Patent Office.

The term gained currency during the period of rapid economic and technical development that followed the signing of the Great Accord. It reflects the literal enlightenment that came with the extension of gas lighting around the civilised world.

Though ubiquitous, the term Gas-Lit Empire is misleading, as no single government ruled over its territories

The Great Accord
A declaration of intent, signed initially by France, America and the Anglo-Scottish Republic in 1821, which established the International Patent Office as arbiter of collective security. Following revolutions in Russia, Germany and Spain the number of signatories rapidly increased until it encompassed the entire civilised world.

The Ice Economy
A phrase used to describe the physical and economic infrastructure of ice supply. In political discourse it has come to represent the dependence of large cities on food from distant locations.

A village can live off the fields that surround it. Herds of animals can be driven into the centres of large towns and kept alive until their time of slaughter. But as cities sprawled outwards, they consumed the farmland that would have supported the population. The bigger they grew, the greater the distance food had to travel and the vaster the population it had to support. Beyond a certain threshold, cities would have become unviable but for the means of keeping food fresh. There was no single moment when this principle was understood. But as cities grew, the price of fresh food grew with them, stimulating the birth of the ice economy.

The five components of the ice economy are as follows: production, transportation, processing, storage and supply.

Production takes place at high altitudes where night time temperatures fall below freezing for four months of the year. It is carried out by small communities of "farmers". Community ice houses are used to store the product until the canals unfreeze at the end of winter. Transportation from the ice houses is by means of specially adapted barges. Processing is carried out at centralised ice factories (see separate article) which are also responsible for storage. Supply is carried out via the canals and a network of local warehouses.

Ice Factory

Not, as the name might imply, a facility for making ice. Rather a facility for the processing and storage of ice harvested elsewhere. The three main functions of an ice house are as follows: compressing the ice into blocks of standard size, storing it until it is required and bringing its temperature down ready for transportation.

The development of the ice factories was driven by the economies of scale and the inherent inefficiency of cooling technologies. Thus by the turn of the 21st Century, only a small number of ice factories survived, but these operated on a huge scale.

The International Patent Office
The agency established in 1821 and charged with overseeing the terms of the Great Accord. Its stated mission and highest goal is to "protect and ensure the wellbeing of the common man". This it does through enforcement of International Patent Law.

Agents of the Patent Office have wide powers to investigate, prosecute and punish patent crime by individuals and organisations. Were the Patent Office to judge any nation guilty, it would issue an edict calling on all other signatory nations to reduce the transgressor to dust.

Though investing them with sweeping powers, the Great Accord and its amendments also subject agents of the Patent Office to certain restrictions of personal freedom.

The Kingdom of England and Southern Wales
The southernmost nation formed by the partition of Britain following the 1819 armistice.

With its capital and agencies of government in London, it would be easy to mistake the Kingdom as merely the rump of the older, larger Britain. However, with the rule of the country passing out of the hands of the monarch and parliament and into the control of the Council of Aristocrats, it must be regarded as a revolutionary nation in its own right.

The Leicester Backs

Although the Anstey Amendment partitioned Leicester with precision, the density of the Cank Street slums lent an ambiguity to the border that made it impossible to police. This sprawl of narrow alleyways and crooked cut-throughs became known as The Backs because it backed onto the border from both sides.

Though an area of poverty at the time of partition, smuggling brought gold and gold brought vice. Gangs fought for influence over the opium dens, bath houses and betting salons. But all knew that complete anarchy would drive the trade away. Thus a balance prevailed in which the gaslights were turned low in those lucrative streets but not blacked out completely.

The Long Quiet

The cessation of open conflict and technological innovation that followed the formation of the Gas-Lit Empire. It was proclaimed by many political philosophers to be the end of history.

With the eye of the International Patent Office watching over them, no nation could attempt to out-develop the others in the technology of killing. The armaments industry had previously been an advocate of war. Now it atrophied. Bound by international treaty, governments could no longer use their armies as a means of enforcing foreign policy.

On the social front, technological innovation had previously been a driver of social change. During the Long Quiet, that too was reduced to almost nothing. The Anglo-Scottish Republic embraced this aspect of the Great Accord more vigorously than others. But even in the Kingdom of England and Southern Wales, the least enthusiastic signatory, innovation came to mean the application of mere cosmetic changes. Between 1900 and the year 2000 there were fewer patents filed in London relating to engines than there were to differing designs of clock face.

The New Apocrypha
A collection of essays excluded from the canon of revolutionary writing at the Conference of Nice la Belle in 1843. Two categories of writings were thus rejected:

Those that did not reflect the true spirit of the revolution.

Those deemed not conducive to the best interests of the common man.

North Leicester
One of the three principal cities in the South-East of the Republic. It is famous for transportation, smuggling and its proximity to Anstey and thus, by association, with Ned Ludd.

Nottingham
One of the three principal cities in the South-East of the Republic. Nottingham is chiefly famous for medical sciences. It is said that there are more hospitals per

head of population there than in any other part of the Gas-Lit Empire. Most of the eminent physicians in the kingdoms of Britain will have spent time there. The concentration of so much knowledge in one place is said to be better for the patients. Thus, an industry sprang up transporting the sick and infirm to the city – and home again in the event that they survived the journey and the treatment.

Its other claims to fame are lace making, and tourism related to Robin the Revolutionary.

Patent Crime
The production, sale or use of any technology judged by the International Patent Office to be "unseemly" or otherwise lacking a patent mark.

Pride and Prejudice
A novel by Jane Austen published in London in 1813. After the British Revolutionary War it came to be seen as a symbol of the differing characteristics and values of the nations of Britain. Rooted in a world of aristocratic privilege and fixated on questions of wealth and display, it was held to be counter to Republican ideals. Its suppression north of the border caused the people of the Kingdom to embrace it with particular fervour. What started as a subtle difference of emphasis was amplified as each nation reacted to the other. Ultimately the printing and sale of the book was banned in the Republic, though its ownership has never been illegal.

Robin the Revolutionary
A political philosopher who pioneered socialist principles in and around Nottingham Forest during the early mediaeval period. He is famed for promoting progressive as opposed to regressive taxation. Much of his activism was related to the redistribution of wealth.

Unseemly Science
All those sciences and technologies judged by the Patent Office to be deleterious to the wellbeing of the common man. Such judgements are difficult, inasmuch as it is impossible to be certain of the future implications of any invention.

Mistakes are minimised through a combination of three factors: a century and a half of case law, the combined wisdom of the patent judges and the application of the precautionary principle. It is axiomatic that the science of medicine is always for the benefit of the common man. Thus its research can never be regarded as unseemly.

ACKNOWLEDGMENTS

I would like to thank the following people for their help and encouragement during the writing and publication of this novel. Each in a different way made it possible: Stephanie, Joseph and Anya. Ed Wilson, Marc Gascoigne, Caroline Lambe, Mike Underwood, Phil Jopurdan. Terri Bradshaw, Rhys Davies, Chris d'Lacey, members of LWC, Sally Rowe, Stephen Ashurst, and the kind staff of Woodgate Computers.

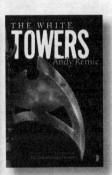
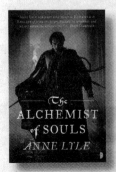

The Fall of the Gas-Lit Empire, volume 1.

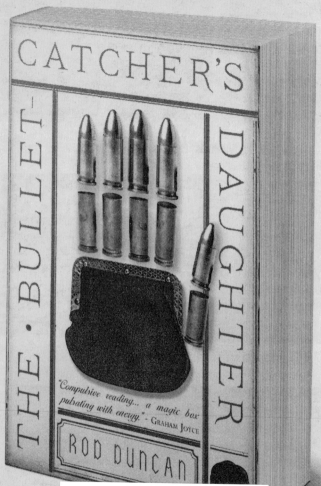

CATCHER'S

DAUGHTER

THE · BULLET-

"Compulsive reading... a magic box pulsating with energy." - GRAHAM JOYCE

ROD DUNCAN

Nominated for the Philip K Dick Award.